The
Ride-Along

a Charlie-316 novel

Frank Zafiro | Colin Conway

The Ride Along: A Charlie-316 Novel

Copyright © 2022 Frank Scalise and Colin Conway

Cover design by Zach McCain

ISBN: 979-8-9859409-2-3

Original Ink Press, an imprint of High Speed Creative, LLC
1521 N. Argonne Road, #C-205
Spokane Valley, WA 99212

Part I: The Ride

"If today, people suddenly truly understood policing, tomorrow there would be twice as many cops on the street, and three times as many people volunteering to help them."

- Spokane Police Chief Robert Baumgartner

"If people truly understood policing today, they would defund the police tomorrow."

- Spokane Mayor Margaret Patterson

Chapter 1

LEE

Officer Lee Salter rapped on the frame of the open office door. "You wanted to see me, Sarge?"

Sergeant Jamie Gelabert leaned back from her computer to look sideways at him. She waved him inside. Her short brown hair was slightly mussed as if she'd just run her fingers through it. "Shut the door."

Lee did as he was told, racking his brain to think why he was getting called into the sergeant's office, or what anyone could possibly be upset with him about. He came up empty, but that didn't mean trouble wasn't still waiting for him. It was the nature of the job these days.

Gelabert seemed to sense his trepidation. "Relax. It's not bad." Then, after a moment, she added, "Well, not exactly."

Lee cocked his head slightly, unsure what to make of that. He waited dutifully for the sergeant to continue.

Gelabert spun in her chair to face him directly. "You've got a rider tonight."

"I had one last week. One of the mayor's executive assistants—some woman named Jean."

"I know. It's not your turn in the rotation yet, but I need you on this one, Lee."

"Why?"

Gelabert rested her elbow on the desk. "You know the chief is trying to open things up, right? With all that's going on, he's trying to make the department more transparent to the public."

All that's going on. What an understated euphemism. The policing world was essentially on fire these days, more so than he'd ever seen in his fourteen-year career. Like always, some of the uproar centered on national incidents that somehow still had local repercussions.

But lately, Spokane had endured its share of controversial

events as well.

"You mean Garrett?" Lee said. "It's like we can't shake that stink."

Even though it happened more than two years ago, the community still reeled from the dark events surrounding the Tyler Garrett scandal. Garrett, a former police officer, was now serving a long prison sentence for murder. Chief Baumgartner had done everything he could to distance the department from him, but those efforts proved futile—the public remembered. It didn't help that, throughout Garrett's career, SPD featured him extensively in a public relations role. He'd literally been the poster child for the department. So when he broke bad, the connection was hard to sever in the public's mind.

Sergeant Gelabert crossed her arms. "I get the feeling the new mayor doesn't want us to be rid of that stink. Not till she's put her stamp on it anyway."

The new mayor, Margaret Patterson, had positioned herself as the one who would "clean up" the agency and "make it ours again." She embraced the ongoing consent decree with the Department of Justice and praised DOJ's efforts to "bring the police department's culture in line with today's values."

Needless to say, the mayor wasn't popular among those who wore the badge—Lee among them.

"It doesn't hurt her brand," Lee said, "or make it harder to bargain with the union, either."

Gelabert puffed out her cheeks. "Best to stay out of politics when you can, Lee."

"I'd be happy to, if politics would stay out of my job."

She smiled thinly. "Fair point. But the chief is on board with this mission of transparency, so we're the ones who get to carry it out."

"I saw something about the transparency thing on the news," he said. "And Mundy had a councilman ride with him a couple of weeks ago, too."

Gelabert frowned. "Monday Mundy," she muttered. "That

wouldn't have been my choice."

Lee didn't have to ask why. The perennially dour officer hadn't seemed like a great candidate to him either.

"Anyway," Gelabert said, "that's where things started. After all the council members and the mayor's executive staff rotate through, it'll open up wide to the public. No matter how you cut it, we're going to see a lot more ride-alongs than we're used to."

Lee reluctantly nodded, then he ventured, "Is there any way you can get someone else for this one?"

"I can't. This is important, Lee. I need you to take this one out, even though it's not your turn."

"Why me?"

"You're a Salter. That name still has some recognition."

"Only to other cops. What's the real reason?"

Gelabert took a deep breath and let it out in a slow exhale. "This one isn't exactly a friendly."

"How so?"

"She's a member of the PRI."

Lee stared at the sergeant, processing the information. The Police Reform Initiative was a citizen organization that had been overly critical of the police department for years. Up until the last few years, Lee had equated their presence to a bothersome mosquito—noticeable and annoying but not life-threatening. More recently, though, events on the national stage rippled into their own community, and local scandals propelled the committee's profile significantly higher. Now the PRI was the leading voice in the call for radical reform of the Spokane Police Department.

After a few moments, Lee found his voice. "Is it what's-his-name? Their chairman?"

Sergeant Gelabert shook her head. "She's a board member. Melody Weaver."

"Know anything about her?"

"No."

"Why is she even here? The PRI hates us."

5

"She's here because she can be. Council President Cody Lofton gave her his slot."

Lee snorted. Lofton was a wolf in sheep's clothing. A couple years back, many on the department thought he backed the blue. But now he was seen as the most anti-police member of the city council. Lee couldn't imagine the arrogant man spending ten minutes in a patrol car, much less a ten-hour shift, so this move didn't surprise him.

"Supposedly," Gelabert continued, "Lofton said he already knew everything he needed to know about the police department. So he sent a representative instead."

"Perfect," Lee muttered.

The sergeant fixed him with a meaningful look. "I probably don't need to tell you that the chief has an eye on this one."

"I bet."

"The mayor, too."

Lee rolled his eyes.

Gelabert leaned forward and rested her elbows on her knees. Her gaze held his. "I need to know I can count on you to do the right thing out there, Lee."

"Of course," he answered automatically.

"Good. And fair warning—she's expecting a female officer."

A spark of hope flared in him. "Then give her one."

Gelabert smiled indulgently. "I would if I could. Between maternity leave, the flu, scheduled vacations, and days off, you're the closest thing I've got."

"To a female officer? What the hell does that mean?"

"Easy, tiger. It means that you can talk to people."

Lee didn't like the answer, so he looked away and studied a Human Resources poster pinned to the wall. Its message was to encourage employees to come forward with reports of hostile work conditions. Lee smirked. His whole job was a hostile environment. "Can't she reschedule?"

"No." Gelabert's firm tone signaled the end of the meeting, so Lee turned slightly and put his hand on the doorknob. He paused and looked back at the sergeant. She was already at work on the paperwork in front of her. "Sarge?"

"Yes?" she answered, without looking up.

"What does that mean, do the right thing? What do you want me to do different? Put on a show or something?"

"Do what you normally do. Show her what patrol is really like."

"That's it?"

The sergeant looked up then. "That's why I picked you for this detail."

"All right."

"Maybe keep her away from any drama, huh?"

"On patrol? That's impossible."

"You know what I mean. Just work your shift." She motioned with her hand. "She's waiting at the west doors."

Lee nodded slowly.

Just work my shift. Sure.

"All right," he said, and turned to go.

"Lee?"

He glanced back toward the sergeant.

"Good luck," she said.

She didn't add that he'd need it, but Lee took her meaning all the same.

Lee stopped at the quartermaster closet to refill his supply of clear plastic bags for prisoner belongings and to get a new pocket notebook along with several cheap Bic pens. Then he slung his patrol bag over his shoulder and headed down to the west doors. As he walked, he first rolled up and then folded over the plastic bags. Once they were ready, he slipped them into the side pocket on his uniform pants and two others into the trauma plate pocket inside his protective vest. He was re-buttoning his shirt when he ran into Officer Matt Thornton on the stairs.

"Hey, Matt," he said in a subdued voice. He and Thornton

had an uneasy alliance, the kind forged when two people who otherwise disliked each other are forced to cooperate to accomplish a greater goal.

"Lee," Thornton said coolly.

Lee started to brush past when Thornton said, "There's a rider waiting for someone outside the west doors."

"I know. It's me."

"Have fun with that. She's a real peach."

Lee slowed, then stopped and turned. Thornton stood smirking down at him, his muscular arms folded across his chest.

"What's that mean?" Lee asked.

Thornton chuckled derisively. "It means everything you say can and will be held against you in a court of law."

"Do you know her or something?"

"I asked her if she needed any help, and she bit my head off." He pointed at Lee. "You're in for a fun night, pal."

Thornton cocked his thumb, then dropped it like a gun hammer while making a clicking sound with his mouth. "Better you than me, though." He laughed before heading back upstairs.

Lee watched him go. Thornton was an asshole, no question. But that didn't make him wrong. He could be in for a long, difficult night.

The early October air bit into him when he exited the west doors.

A woman stood on the sidewalk under the streetlight. Her arms were drawn tight into her, and she blew into her hands. Her purse was tucked under one arm. That, at least, was smart. Standing outside the police department should be one of the safest places in the city, but the reality was something different. Most cops were out in the field except during shift change. After hours, all the detectives and admin were gone, too. About fifty yards to the north, as part of the same city criminal justice campus, sat the jail entrance. Criminals were released from booking at all hours of the day and night. Most wouldn't be foolish enough to commit a crime in the shadow of police headquarters, but that population had its fair share of idiots.

"Are you Ms. Weaver?" Lee asked as he approached.

She was about five-seven with a medium build. Her sandy blond hair was pulled back into a short ponytail. The dark blue Columbia brand jacket hung down mid-thigh.

"I am," she said stiffly.

"I'm Lee Salter." He held out his hand.

She took it briefly and gave it a perfunctory shake. Her fingers were cold.

They stood awkwardly for a moment. Lee adjusted the patrol bag on his shoulder.

"Can we wait inside?" Weaver asked. "It's cold out here."

He pointed north toward the motor pool. "I need to grab my cruiser. You can come with or wait here."

She appeared confused. "Wait. You're who I'm riding with?"

Lee nodded. "I know you were expecting a female officer, but none were available tonight."

She watched his face for a few moments, her expression inscrutable. Finally, she said, "I'll come along."

"Okay." Lee flashed his for-the-public smile.

She didn't smile back.

Lee turned and started walking. She fell in beside him. "Were you waiting long?" he asked, trying to be polite.

"A little while."

"They probably should have arranged to have you wait inside. It is getting cold at night."

"It's not a problem."

He stole a sidelong glance at her. Her expression wasn't entirely neutral—it had the set of minor annoyance to it—but it wasn't the demon's snarl that Thornton's description led him to expect. Still, she didn't look like she was inviting conversation either.

Lee remained quiet for the remainder of the two-minute walk to the motor pool. Weaver strode alongside, also silent. Once inside the fenced area, he quickly located his assigned vehicle for the shift, unit one-nineteen. It wasn't a dog, but it had some hard miles on it. Sergeant Gelabert could have given him one of the newer cars since he had a rider. Best foot forward, that sort of thing. He understood showing off a beater of a patrol car if the rider was a council member they were trying to convince of a budgetary need, but for a civilian?

Then again, maybe she just assigned him what was available. Graveyard always did get the runts of the litter. Power shift gobbled up all the good cars long before he and his cohorts came on duty.

Lee began his pre-flight routine, as he did every shift. First, he unlocked the driver's door and swung it wide. He rested his patrol bag on the edge of the seat. Normally, his patrol bag sat on the passenger seat for easy access to all his gear. That wouldn't work tonight, so he removed a few critical items and dropped them on the seat—flashlight, baton, and ticket book. Then he popped the trunk and hauled his bag to the rear of the car. He nestled it in tight next to the plastic tub already inside. The tub contained first aid supplies, blankets, flares, expandable road cones, safety vests, and a couple of stuffed animals wrapped in plastic. Lee lifted the lid to make sure everything was there before snapping it shut again.

"Can you unlock this door?" Weaver asked.

Lee peered around from behind the open trunk, realizing he'd overlooked including his rider in his routine. Waiting with a frown, she stood with her hand on the door latch.

He cleared his throat. "In a minute. Could you come back here first?"

"Why?"

"I need to show you something."

Weaver let go of the door handle and moved toward him. When she was close enough to look inside, Lee opened the tub again. He detailed through the items inside, listing them quickly. "Just in case we end up on a scene where we need any of this stuff," he explained, and pointed at the safety vest. "Most likely, that's the only thing you'll need to worry about."

She nodded that she understood.

He thought about saying something about how unlikely it was that she'd even need the vest but changed his mind—less conversation seemed better at this moment.

Lee closed the trunk. He moved to the open driver's door and disengaged the passenger's lock for Weaver. While she settled into her seat, he pressed the release for the prisoner door. The knob was located inside the well of the front door, rendering the actual rear handle as nothing more than something to grab onto.

The back seat was covered in thick plastic. Lee lifted the bench-style seat cushion, which was loosely wedged into place. He searched quickly for any left-behind contraband from previous prisoners. It never failed to amaze him how easy it was for officers not only to miss items during a search but how suspects were then able to somehow get to those items while handcuffed and try to secrete them beneath the seat. Once, a prisoner even managed to wedge a knife up behind the seat back that wasn't found until the car was being refitted.

Weaver turned in her seat to watch Lee work. "What are you looking for?" Irritation filled her voice.

Lee simply answered, "Contraband," and continued with his search.

Satisfied that the prisoner compartment was free of discarded items, he pushed the seat cushion back into place and shut the door. He dropped onto the front seat, sitting with one leg in and one leg out of the car. He slid his key into the ignition and started the car. The throaty engine rumbled to life. Almost immediately, heavy metal music blared out of the speakers. A singer that Lee was certain had long hair— and probably a bandana—with a distinct screech lamented about watching some woman walk away from him on the dance floor. "Baby, what's wrong?" he called after her. "Bring that sweet ass back to my song!"

Lee snapped off the radio. "Sorry about that. Last guy must have been a metal head."

Weaver's thin smile seemed forced. "No problem."

"I'm more of a country guy myself."

Weaver didn't reply.

Lee cleared his throat. While the police radio and the mobile data computer (MDC) booted up, he turned his attention to the control panel. He pressed the shotgun release button and pulled the weapon from where it sat upright on the rack between the two front seats. Lee stepped back outside, keeping the shotgun pointed up until he was clear of the car. Then he directed the barrel toward the ground. He checked to make certain the magazine tube was full, then cracked the chamber open to ensure it was empty. It was.

Whenever he had a ride-along, Lee usually explained every step in the process of checking into a vehicle. He thought better of it now. Weaver seemed to not be interested in having an open dialogue, so he would let her sit and stew in silence.

Lee replaced the shotgun on the rack, swinging the metal clasp into place, and tugging on it to be certain the magnetic lock had engaged. He reached across to the glove box and opened it. Weaver pulled back as he did so. Lee stowed his ticket book inside then slammed it shut.

The flashlight holder, complete with charger, was mounted on the passenger side of the car, next to the computer terminal. Lee reached over to snap his mag light into place. Weaver's leg moved away to give him space.

Lastly, before he shut the car door, Lee slid his baton into the foam holder on the car door that held it parallel to his seat.

All his movements were born of habit. His patrol car was his office, and he knew his way around it. Of course, tonight he had a guest in the already crowded space. That threw a wrench into his routine, but he adapted.

Once he shut the car door, Lee rolled down the window

partway. A glance at the MDC told him it was still booting up, but the light chatter of the police radio filled the car. He adjusted the volume down. Turning back to the control panel, he selected a button, activating his overhead lights. The dimly lit motor pool was suddenly awash in red, blue, and white rotators. He switched to wig-wags. The less obtrusive alternating flash of white lights reflected against the wall of the nearby maintenance building.

Weaver's head cocked as she watched the dancing lights on the nearby cars.

Lee quickly cycled through the siren settings, pressing each button in quick succession. A brief yelp, a quick wail, and a short burst from the air horn.

He glanced at his rider who followed his fingers with interest. Lee started to say something, but the MDC signaled it had finished booting up with an insistent beep. He logged in with his call sign and personnel number. While he waited for the login to register, he noticed Officer Colm Murphy outside. His platoon mate traipsed by the front of his car, his own patrol bag slung over his shoulder. Lee turned on the car's headlights, then flashed the high beams, bathing his friend in bright whiteness.

Murphy held up a hand to block the light.

"Sorry, Murph," Lee called out the open window. "Just checking the equipment, you know?"

Murphy turned toward him and grabbed his crotch, thrusting his pelvis forward like a crazed rock star. "Check this!"

Lee quickly shut off the headlights.

Murphy laughed and extended his middle finger before trudging on.

Lee shot a sideways glance at Weaver. The woman sat in her chair, her arms crossed, her face pinched in disapproval.

He cleared his throat. "There's a lot of stuff we gotta do to get ready." He turned his attention to the MDC system where he noted that he had a civilian rider. "Some nights I feel like

I'm getting into a fighter jet, but don't let it intimidate you."

"I'm not intimidated. My husband's a pilot." The condescension in her tone was unmistakable.

"Well, cool." He spun the MDC slightly on its swivel to show her the screen. "This is the mobile data computer. All priority one and two calls are dispatched over the air, but pretty much everything else happens on this computer."

Weaver stared back at him, expressionless.

"Priority one and two are emergency calls in progress where someone is in danger."

"I know."

"Oh." He gestured to the MDC. "Then you probably know that this lets us see all the calls that are holding, check unit status, or run names and vehicle plates. It takes some of the less urgent tasks off the dispatcher's plate, and we don't have to wait as long to get information either." Lee punched in the command for unit status. He immediately saw several power shift and graveyard officers assigned to a vehicle collision downtown, all on perimeter duty. Collision investigators were also on scene.

"Huh," he grunted.

"What?"

Lee hit a few keys. "Looks like there was an auto-ped a few hours ago downtown."

"Auto-ped?"

"Sorry," he said. "That means a collision where a vehicle hit a pedestrian."

"How badly hurt is the pedestrian?"

"Fatal."

"That's awful."

"Yeah," Lee said absently. "Our collision investigators will be out there for hours, taking measurements and conducting their investigation of the scene."

Since the intersection would be shut down and both streets were arterials, Lee made a mental note to take alternate routes to and from calls until the scene cleared. Luckily, his beat was further east and south, so it shouldn't impact him much.

As he dropped the car into gear and pulled out of the motor pool, his MDC pinged. He glanced down and saw he was being dispatched to the collision to relieve one of the patrol units on traffic control for the auto-ped.

Lee typed a message directly to the dispatcher.

NEG, HAVE RIDER.

He hit send and wound his way slowly through the parking lot. Just as he pulled onto the side street, his MDC beeped again. He looked down to see if the dispatcher had replied, but she hadn't. However, he was taken off the call.

Lee checked unit status for the sector. He was the only graveyard unit clear. That meant the next one that logged in would get perimeter duty.

He decided to address the elephant in the car. "So," Lee said as he turned onto Mallon Avenue, "my sergeant said you were part of the PRI."

"That's right. I'm on the board." Her statement rang with self-importance. "Is that a problem?"

Lee sensed the defensiveness in her voice. He'd heard people answer like that a thousand times, and it always meant the same thing—gearing up for a conflict. He needed to defuse things before they got there. "No. Should it be?"

"We're not exactly on the best of terms with the police department."

"True that."

"In fact, I'll bet he told you not to say anything or do anything."

"Who?"

"Your sergeant."

"She," Lee said, correcting her gently. "And not exactly."

"I'm sure," Weaver smirked. "It's no surprise. The department has a long history of being insular."

"Insular?"

"Closed off from the public," she explained.

Lee detected a lecturing tone that he didn't like. "I know

what it means."

Weaver shrugged but said nothing.

"Maybe that's true," he said, "and maybe it's not—"

"It's true."

"—but you're here, right?"

Weaver let out a short sigh. "Yeah, I'm here."

"That shows something, doesn't it?"

She hesitated, then nodded stiffly.

"Are you scheduled for a half shift or the entire one?" he asked, hoping. Five hours was a long time to endure with an unfriendly, but ten? Had to violate the prohibition against cruel and unusual punishment.

"Full shift."

He tried to keep his tone bright. "I always tell people that if they get tired and want to call it early, it's no problem."

"I'll be fine."

"Okay, no worries. All night, then."

Lee stopped at a traffic light. He thought of what he told his daughter when she had to go to the dentist, something strangely similar to how this shift was shaping up to be. But he knew that *I know it sucks but just get through it* wouldn't send the right message to a police-hating activist, so he adapted.

"Let's make the best of it," he said.

To his right, Weaver scowled.

Lee resisted the urge to sigh. He looked down at the MDC and punched up the calls-holding screen. Maybe if he could find something to do, the night would pass more quickly.

Chapter 2

MEL

When they were a block from the police station, Melody Weaver looked to her husband. "You're not understanding—I have to do this."

Her husband shook his head. "I'm telling you, you don't."

Melody puffed her cheeks and blew out a sigh. "You want me to go back on my word?"

David kept his eyes on the road. "Be honest. I don't think you agreed so much as Ellen convinced you."

Mel thought about it. Ellen Michaels, the PRI's secretary-treasurer, was the real power of the organization. Since Mel joined the board nineteen months ago, she had seen evidence of that first-hand. Ellen's force of will was considerable, and her conversation with Mel was further evidence.

"We need you in that patrol car," Ellen had stressed. "We need your eyes."

"I'm really busy, Ellen. I barely have time to come to our meetings and events, much less ride around with some aging jock for eight hours."

"Ten."

"What?"

"They work ten-hour shifts," Ellen said. "But don't worry, I'll get you a woman cop. It'll be a bonus. You can get that female perspective of the job, too."

"Why me?"

Ellen's eyebrows raised knowingly. "You don't think Chief Baumgartner is making sure to tell all his little minions to be on their best behavior when one of us is with them? Male or female?"

"I'm sure he is."

"Right. That way no one gets to see behind the curtain. It's the way it's always been in this town. The police are sewn up tighter than the KGB, consent decree or not."

"I know that," Mel agreed, "but why me?"

"Please. A white woman, and a teacher, too? You'll put them more at ease."

Melody clucked her tongue. "They know I'm on the board. You think they'll somehow show me what goes on behind that curtain? Because I don't."

"Neither do I. But if it's me, they'll be all like—" she assumed an uptight baritone voice— "What curtain, ma'am? There is no curtain.'"

Mel smiled at the impression.

"With you," Ellen said, "at least they'll admit that the curtain is there. Maybe you'll see some shapes moving behind it. Who knows, you might even get the chance to rip it aside and see what you can see."

"Which is?"

"The truth, sister. What else?"

Yeah, Mel thought as David turned into the parking lot next to the Public Safety Building. She hadn't so much volunteered as been coerced into the ride.

David wasn't finished, though. "Of course, I don't want you to go back on your word to Ellen. But you need to do what's best for you, babe."

Best for her? That equated to a glass of wine and making a dent in the papers she had to grade while a mildly interesting documentary played on the TV in the background. Or better yet, her head hitting the pillow for a solid eight hours of sleep.

David pulled to a stop near the entrance where she was supposed to meet her... what? Host? Escort? Mel didn't have the right word, something that always frustrated her when it happened. She taught English once upon a time. You'd think she'd be able to use it better.

"Look, I know some of this is about your dad, too," David said, breaking into her thoughts. "And that's another reason to call no joy if you want. I'll drive you home. Jana can drop the kids off early, or still keep them until tomorrow—"

"I'm fine." She bit the word off and immediately regretted it. He was only looking out for her.

David looked at her. "You sure?"

She nodded. "My dad's been gone twenty years. This isn't about him."

"Twenty years don't mean much when it's your folks." He motioned toward the police station. "And that's his world that you're stepping into."

"It's not about him," she repeated. She reached out and touched his face. "If anything, it's about us. And our kids. That's why I said yes to Ellen."

"You said yes to Ellen because no one says no to her."

She grunted. "That, too."

"I meant what I said. I'll take you home."

"No." She glanced down at her phone. "My... whoever they send will be here to pick me up any minute. It's too late to cancel."

"It's never too late if you don't want to do it."

"I have to," she said.

"Forget *have to*. Do you want to?"

"No."

"Then don't."

A tickle of irritation rose in her. "Life doesn't work that way. Sometimes we do things we don't want to do."

"Now you're talking to me like I'm one of your middle-schoolers."

"Then stop acting like one."

David just stared back at her.

She sighed. "Sorry."

He nodded with a concerned expression.

"Do I want to be here tonight?" She lifted her hands in frustration. "No. I wish things weren't so messed up in the world. I wish the police didn't do the shit they did, David. I wish I could get all my work done in a school day and didn't have to take work home every damn night. I wish a thousand other things, too, but none of them are true. And they won't get that way if all we do is bitch and wish and not do the hard things we don't want to do."

He pursed his lips. "Damn, girl. You're inspiring when you get all fired up."

"Stop."

"Sexy, too." His expression softened. "Listen, I hear everything you're saying. All I'm saying is that if you want me to, I'll take you home. That's all."

She shook her head. "It's fine. Besides, you'll miss your flight."

"Where they gonna go without me?" he joked. "My FO doesn't have the keys."

"Har-dee-har. I married Eddie Murphy over here."

He cocked his head. "I think I'm more of a Jamie Foxx."

"You wish." She reached out and rested her hand on his forearm. "I'm fine. Really."

He smiled at her. "No, you aren't. But you're going to do it, anyway, huh?"

"I am."

"All right, then." He leaned across and kissed her lightly. "I'm proud of you. But you be careful out there amongst the English, Mel."

She squeezed his forearm. "Have a safe flight. Text me when you land in Maui."

"Will do. You text when you get home."

"Roger that." She kissed him again. "I love you."

"I love you more," he replied.

"That's why our marriage works."

She slid out of the passenger seat. David watched her as she closed the door, his kind eyes never leaving hers. The smile on his lips was equal parts love and worry. Mel tried to return one filled with confidence but was unsure if she pulled it off. In front of thirty-five pre-teens, she could bullshit her way through just about anything she needed to. With David, though, the armor was off. She had little doubt he could read her frustration and trepidation as easily as if she'd scrawled the emotions on the white board in her classroom.

He lifted a hand in farewell. She lifted hers, and he slid away.

The bite of the evening October air immediately nipped at her. Mel zipped up her light jacket and flipped the thin strap of her small purse onto her shoulder. She moved to the nearby sidewalk. A concrete landing stood under a streetlamp. The fixture cast weak amber light onto the surroundings. The doors Ellen had described from the instructions the police department's Public Information Officer had given her stood fifteen yards away. A sign reading Employee Entrance was emblazoned in red letters on a yellow background, as unwelcome as a stop sign.

A man in a police uniform approached from the north along the building. His stride was confident and he watched her. When he neared the doors, he slowed then detoured toward her.

"You all right, ma'am?"

"I'm fine."

The officer cast a suspicious eye after David's car as it trailed away. "Who was that?"

"My husband. Why?"

At the word *husband*, the officer's eyes returned to her. "Looked like maybe you two were having an argument."

Mel's eyebrows furrowed. "An argument? No."

"You sure?"

"I'm absolutely sure we weren't arguing." She glanced down at the officer's nametag which read *M. Thornton*. She knew why the cop was insinuating such a thing. Suddenly, the prospect of spending the next ten hours in close confines with any officer loomed large. She wished she'd taken David up on his offer.

Thornton glanced after the departing SUV again. "I just want to make sure you were safe, is all."

"I'm fine," she repeated, not bothering to hide her contempt.

He smiled but it looked like an imitation to her. "Are you meeting someone here, or...?"

"I'm here for a ride-along."

"Oh." He pursed his lips. "Do you know the officer?"

She shook her head. "A woman on graveyard is all I know."

"Not sure who that would be. But I'm headed upstairs to drop off some paperwork. I'll let the sergeant know."

Mel nodded curtly. As Thornton turned away, she almost let it go, but couldn't. "Officer?"

He stopped and faced her, his brows raised questioningly.

"Why did you think we were arguing?" She allowed her tone to maintain its edge.

His expression became guarded. "Lots of factors."

"Lots? Or just one?"

"Several."

"Like what?"

Thornton paused a moment, as if debating whether or not to answer. Then he said, "You were moving your hands like you were angry."

"Did you notice us kissing, too?"

"I didn't, no."

Melody wanted to say that it wasn't a surprise, since that it didn't fit his narrative, but she simply looked at him like she would an unruly middle-schooler.

"But," the officer twirled his finger in the air, "this time of night, the only kind of people around here tend to be cops coming to work, or..." He shifted his finger to point toward the ugly building just to the north before finishing. "... criminals getting released from jail."

"So, you assumed we were criminals."

"Neither of you work for the department."

"You know that how?"

He scowled. "Because I know everyone who works here. What exactly is the problem?"

She returned his scowl. "I'm just wondering what other *factors* made you jump to your conclusion that I wasn't safe."

"I already told you."

"Yeah, you told me something."

Officer Thornton's scowl became a glare as he drew his shoulders back and thrust his chin out. "I'll let the sergeant know you're waiting. Have a nice night."

Without another word, he turned and stalked through the doors.

Mel watched him go.

That went well, she thought.

Absently, she rubbed her upper arms through her coat and waited under the sickly yellow light.

Over what seemed like the next thirty minutes, she stood with her hands in her jacket pockets and stamped her feet to keep warm. During that time, a half dozen uniformed cops streamed out of the building and walked north. All of them were white men and appeared to be in their late twenties. Each officer carried some incarnation of a black bag. Some looked like military duffel bags, others resembled the rolling briefcases she'd used herself when she subbed, years ago. A couple of the cops gave her a perfunctory nod. One asked if she needed anything. His voice was kinder than Thornton's but still tinged with suspicion and distance. Most simply ignored her.

Another five minutes passed. Then the doors swung open and another officer exited. He carried a bag slung over his shoulder. Unlike the others, he headed straight toward her. He was taller than her, though shorter than David. She guessed about five-ten. He appeared fit, and his uniform was crisp. He was, no surprise, white.

"Are you Ms. Weaver?"

"I am."

"I'm Officer Salter." He held out his hand.

Mel withdrew her own hand from the scant warmth of her pocket and gave him a quick handshake.

Salter adjusted his shoulder bag and glanced uncomfortably around.

"Can we wait inside?" She hated asking, especially after the confrontation with Officer Thornton. "It's cold out here."

Salter pointed north. "I need to grab my cruiser. You can come with or wait here."

"Wait. You're who I'm riding with?"

"I know you were expecting a female officer. But none were available tonight."

Right, she thought. This was probably the department's way of screwing with her. But she wouldn't be pushed around like that. "I'll come along."

Salter flashed a fake smile. It was the same one that Officer Thornton had given her thirty minutes ago.

Melody didn't smile back.

Salter turned and walked off. He appeared to be on a mission. She had to scramble to catch up. Once she did, she still had to stride more quickly than her natural gait just to keep pace with him. The entire time, he stared straight ahead and attempted some banal small talk. He marched past the squat jail building and toward a parking lot inside a chain-link fenced area.

All the cars looked the same—a stark black and white design highlighting the word Police, coupled with emergency lights on top. The only exceptions were a couple that were a solid dark color and no markings. Though these appeared sleeker, almost naked, without the lights on top, the heavy black push-bar at the front bumper and the thick radio antenna protruding from the trunk lid left no question as to their purpose.

Mel tried to remember if her father had ever driven one of those. He occasionally came home for lunch during his shift but all she remembered were police cars with lights on the roof. The irony was that the unmarked car was actually a better fit for his personality.

She swallowed past the lump in her throat. Just once, it'd

be nice to have a simple memory of him. But those were few and far between.

The cold seemed to be harsher now. All she wanted to do was get into the car and warm up. Then she could face the long shift with her robotic escort.

Salter had no difficulty finding his specific car. He opened the driver's door and dropped his bag onto the seat. Mel made her way to the passenger door. She waited for him to pop the lock, but he didn't. So, she waited there with the cold metal of the door handle pinched between her fingers.

He didn't notice her. Or he was purposefully ignoring her. She didn't know which but looked on in mild disbelief as he disengaged the trunk latch and moved to the rear of the car. After he'd clumped around in there for a few moments, she cleared her throat.

"Would you mind unlocking the door? It's cold."

He glanced around the trunk lid at her. His expression was as cold as her fingers. "In a minute. I need to show you something back here."

Mel's jaw dropped slightly. Irritated, she let go of the latch and stuffed her hand back into her pocket. She took a few steps so that she could see into the trunk.

Salter slowly and studiously pointed out the trunk's contents with the exception of his black duffel bag. Aside from the road flares and expandable cones, most of the same items were in the closet of her classroom. But he still insisted on reviewing each one as if she were an idiot.

Mel stood and nodded, hoping her silence sped the process along. She rubbed at her upper arms to emphasize how cold she was. Salter didn't seem to notice. Weren't cops supposed to be trained observers?

Finally, he finished his presentation and closed the trunk lid. When he moved toward the driver's door, Mel mirrored his action on the passenger side. Thankfully, he must have caught the hint because he unlocked her door. She got inside and closed it.

Salter left the driver's door wide open. The cold air streamed in while he busied himself checking the backseat for something.

"What are you looking for?" she asked.

"Contraband."

He slammed the rear door closed then dropped into the driver's seat and started the car.

Loud guitars blasted through the speakers. Some rocker who was probably about as mature as her seventh graders sang about a woman's ass.

Salter clicked off the radio. His attempt at a smile was forced. "Sorry. Last guy must have been into metal."

"No problem," she said, trying to paint on a smile. But she didn't mean it. She just wanted him to start the heater.

Salter pushed a button on the control console. There was a loud metallic clanking sound. He wrenched the shotgun from a rack between the seats and stepped outside with it. Mel stared out of the open driver's door while he pointed it at the ground and adjusted something on it.

When Salter returned to the front seat, he slammed the shotgun back into place and slapped the metal clasp shut. The gesture seemed like overkill to her, like some kind of uber-masculine display, but she stopped herself before that thought completely solidified. She knew hardly anything about guns. Maybe that was how things had to be done.

But probably not.

Salter leaned forward, his forearm brushing her leg as he reached for the glove compartment. Mel recoiled automatically, putting her knees together and turning them toward the door. He didn't apologize for the contact. He thrust a metal box roughly the same dimensions as a stenographer's notepad, only thicker, into the open glove compartment, then snapped it shut.

Mel started to return her knees forward when Salter reached into her space again. This time, he slapped a large black flashlight into a charger that was mounted on the left side of her seating area.

She often experienced the same way thing whenever she had to fly coach. David's status as a pilot meant they more often got to fly first class or at least sit together, but occasionally she joined him on flights that he piloted, which meant taking whatever seat she could get. Inevitably, she ended up next to someone, almost always a man, who sat knees wide, intruding in on her space without remorse. She debated with herself as to whether this was purposeful or if people were truly that unaware of their own behavior and came up with answers that were largely dependent on her mood at the time.

Salter finally closed the driver's door. Instead of turning on the heat, though, he lowered the window halfway down. She knew there wouldn't be heat coming from the vents yet, but rolling down the window seemed like some sort of sadism. She wondered if he was messing with her.

Despite the open window, Melody detected a strange scent in the car's interior. It seemed to waft forward from the back seat. She sniffed slightly, her senses trying to catalog the unfamiliar mix of smells—the chemical bite of too much plastic interlaced with body odor.

Salter appeared unaffected by the aroma. While she crossed her arms for warmth, he fiddled with the police radio. Then he played with the emergency lights. The colors danced and jumped in the reflection of the cars around them. Then the sudden, loud wail of the siren startled her.

Salter continued to ignore her, tapping keys on the keyboard.

She thought she understood what he was doing. Yes, he had to check his equipment. Maybe he did it habitually, like how David described performing his pre-flight checks. But the way he went about it was so very dismissive of her that it set her teeth on edge. And she was supposed to spend ten hours with this guy? This macho robot?

Another officer walked in front of the car. Salter turned on his headlights, switching on the high beams. "Gotta check the lights," he said through the still open window.

The other officer moved languidly, shifted his shouldered bag, and faced the car. Very deliberately, he grabbed his crotch with his free hand and thrusted his hips toward them.

"Check this!" he shouted back.

Mel watched with mild surprise. Apparently not all cops were robots—some were juveniles.

Salter turned off the headlights and the officer flipped them the bird before continuing on his way. Suddenly, Melody was reminded of being around the younger pilots in David's squadron back when they were first dating. Brash, alpha males who all thought they were in a real-life version of *Top Gun*.

"I know there's a lot of equipment in here," Salter said, not bothering to apologize for his colleague's crude behavior. "Always makes me feel like I'm a fighter pilot. But don't let it intimidate you."

His thinly veiled condescension irked her. "I'm not intimidated," she said coolly. "My husband *is* a pilot."

"Well, cool." Salter seemed unimpressed and rolled forward, using the same instructive tone he'd used while standing at the trunk. "This is the mobile data computer or MDC. It's where we get dispatched from and can access information."

She looked at him and wondered if he was gaslighting her.

"We can see what calls are holding and what everyone is up to." He punched a few keys. "Looks like there was an autoped a couple hours ago downtown.

"What's that?"

"That means a collision where a vehicle hit a pedestrian."

"How bad was the person hurt?"

"Looks like a fatal."

A small, sick feeling passed over her. She knew such things happened, of course. Hell, she was a teacher. They did lockdown drills for active shooter responses. She couldn't think of a more terrible event than some maniac targeting kids.

Besides that, her husband flew planes, and the reality was that planes sometimes crashed. But she'd been fortunate for most of her life to remain a step or two removed from these tragedies and others like them. True, they happened in the world, but there were always two or three layers of invisible skin between those events and her life. Now, one of those layers was missing somehow.

"That's awful," she whispered.

Salter grunted noncommittally. "Our guys will be out there for a long time doing an investigation."

She stared at him. Was that *really* his biggest concern? The workload?

He typed some more before he put the car in gear and left the fenced parking area.

The sick feeling didn't go away all at once. Part of the reason, she knew, was his reaction. She'd seen that exact affect before. Stone visage, flat tone. It was her dad's default, what she had called his "resting cop face."

Salter's voice broke into her thoughts. "So," he said, "my sergeant said you were part of the PRI."

He said it like they were a terrorist group, his monotone containing just a hint of a sneer.

"I serve on the board."

Salter grunted dismissively, keeping his eyes on the road as he drove.

"Is that going to be a problem?" Mel asked him.

"Not for me. Why?"

Mel let out an ironic chuckle. "Well, we haven't exactly had the best of relations with the police department lately. We've been... critical."

"That's one word for it."

"In fact, I bet your sergeant warned you. He probably told you not to say or do anything tonight."

"She didn't say that."

Mel smiled at the way he emphasized his sergeant's gender. Probably did it to show how "progressive" the SPD was.

"There's a long history of this department being overly insular. That's what we're trying to change."

"Insular, huh?"

"Closed off from the community."

"I know what it means," he said coldly. "And I don't know that it's true."

"It is."

"Even if it is," Salter said, "you have to admit one thing."

"What's that?"

"Things are changing."

"How so?"

"Well, you're here, for one. Ride-alongs are something we haven't done for years now, even before the pandemic."

"I am here," she admitted.

"There you go," he said, as if that settled the matter.

She resisted the urge to add how her presence was the result of pressure from groups like the PRI on councilmembers like Cody Lofton, who in turn pressured the mayor and the police chief. Or that the string of police-related scandals and resulting protests in the news over the past several years brought the full force of public opinion into the fray.

She wanted to say that it's not like the SPD flung open the doors to the PRI, but she bit her lip. If she'd learned one thing teaching middle school, it was how not to engage when it didn't serve any productive purpose.

"So, are you staying the whole tour?" he asked. "Or..." His voice turned slightly hopeful. "... am I dropping you off at the halfway point?"

"I'm here for all of it."

"You sure? Most people who don't work nights get pretty tired."

"I'll be fine. You're not getting rid of me that easily."

"I'm not trying to." She sensed a tinge of disappointment when he spoke. It sort of pleased her. "Anyway, if you get sleepy, you just let me know. I can drop you off whenever."

She didn't answer.

Salter cleared his throat. "Till then," he muttered, "I guess we'll just make the best of it."

Great attitude, Mel thought.

As he drove along, he glanced repeatedly down to the computer screen. His inattention made her nervous. It irritated her, too. There'd been a massive campaign not long ago on how distracted driving caused accidents. To go along with the public service announcements on television and radio, the police wrote a bunch of tickets. One of the teachers in her hall got one. But Salter blatantly violated the law right in front of her.

It was one of the major refrains she heard both in PRI board discussions and in testimony from the public. That cops think they're special, that they're above the law. The hypocrisy of it angered people, and here was a perfect example on casual display.

Mel opened her mouth to say something when Salter rolled to a stop at a red light.

"Here's something you don't see on graveyard very often," he said, tapping a few keys.

"What's that?"

"A shoplifter. Those are usually the bane of swing shift."

"Is that where we're going?" Mel asked.

He hit a final key, and the computer responded with a short series of beeps. "The call ain't gonna clear itself."

The light changed and he sped forward.

Chapter 3

LEE

He drove carefully, keeping his speed near the limit. Years ago, it had been his practice on graveyard to drive fast to everything. He reasoned that, with less traffic during those hours, speeding was easier and less dangerous and he got where he was needed more quickly. But it became a habit for most cops, including him. He'd been on the job for about a decade before he realized there was no need to rush to a non-emergency call.

Besides, there were plenty of calls on this shift that provided ample opportunity to drive fast.

Now, though, he almost wished he had a reason to speed. The sooner he got to this call—any call—the sooner he'd get a reprieve from the tense silence inside the car.

On the way, he scanned through the incident details on the MDC. The eighteen-year-old suspect was being detained by the store manager. Lee recognized the manager's name. Lonnie had been there for years and always worked the night shift.

Usually, stores employed their own loss prevention officers with limited commissions that allowed them to arrest for misdemeanors such as theft. This allowed most shoplifters to be cited and released, which streamlined the process for the store and kept from adding to the call load for the police. But if the suspect fought or if the value of the stolen merchandise amounted to a felony, they needed a fully commissioned officer to respond.

Lee saw nothing about an assault listed in the call. There wasn't any notation about felony-level theft either. So why was he going?

He scrolled a little further down the MDC, glancing back and forth to the road ahead as he drove. Then he found it.

Beer. The shoplifter stole beer, and he wasn't twenty-one.

When Lee arrived at the store, he parked at the curb in the front of the building. In smooth, quick succession, he punched the MDC's on-scene button, turned off the engine and pulled out the key, reached across and withdrew his ticket book from the glove compartment, and grabbed his flashlight from the charger.

Beside him, Weaver sat still. He ignored her, got out of the car, and stood in the open doorway. He slid his flashlight into his long, thigh pocket while he waited. Once Weaver was out of the car, he engaged the door locks and shut his. Then he headed toward the store entrance. He sensed, more than saw, Weaver following him.

The smell of the bakery hit his nostrils as soon as the automatic doors sprang open. The scent made him think of donuts. He half-expected Weaver to make the obligatory cops-and-donuts joke, then realized it was unlikely. She didn't seem the joking type.

A bored looking cashier manned the only active checkout lane. Her expression turned to mild surprise when she noticed Lee.

"Shoplifter?" he asked.

She pointed to the back of the store.

"Is Lonnie with him?"

The checker nodded. "He's the one who caught the kid."

"Kid? He's an adult."

She shrugged. "He looks young."

Lee thanked her and headed toward the rear of the store. Weaver trailed behind him. At the meat department, he walked along the cool case until he reached a pair of heavy swinging doors. He stepped through and hooked an immediate left up a short flight of stairs to the manager's office.

Lonnie Martin sat at the one desk in the room, his hulking frame hunched over some paperwork. Across from him sat the suspect, sullen and slouching in his chair. Despite his black jeans and ragged flannel, he appeared younger than eighteen years. He could see why the checker thought he was a juvenile. The suspect glanced up at him as he entered. As soon as he spotted Lee's uniform, his lip curled.

"Hey, Lee," Lonnie said. The manager rose to his feet and held out a hand. "Haven't seen you in a while."

Lee took his hand and shook it. "Most people think that's a good thing."

Lonnie chuckled. "I bet. Everything good?"

"Outstanding. How about you? Still killing it?"

"Murder City, baby." He motioned toward the suspect. "Got one for you."

"Felony theft?" Lee asked, hopeful that the details in the call had been wrong. He was doing paperwork either way, so it'd be nice to get a felony stat out of it.

"Naw. He swiped three brews, is all. But kid's only eighteen, so..."

Lee understood. "What happened?"

"It's your basic grab." Lonnie held up his paperwork. "You want to hear it, or should I make you a copy of the corporate report?"

Normally, Lee would have just reviewed Lonnie's narrative and determined probable cause from that. But he sensed Weaver standing in the doorway. That reminded him that tonight was no time to cut corners, even if it was more efficient.

"Better walk me through it," he said.

"Sure." Lonnie didn't miss a beat. He motioned toward the suspect. "Creighton here came in about forty-five minutes ago. I'm pretty sure he's burned us before, but we were always too slammed for me to keep an eye on him. Tonight was slow, though, so I managed to observe him without him being aware."

Lee made a sound of acknowledgment. Lonnie spoke naturally but with a touch of formality. This wasn't his first rodeo. Lee knew the night manager was completely familiar with what critical information he needed to share. As usual,

Lonnie omitted the location of his secret vantage points and Lee didn't ask. If the suspect learned that piece of intelligence, not only would he become more adept at stealing from the store next time, but that information would make its way through the whisper stream to all the other thieves out there.

"I had a clear view of him in the beer aisle when he took three cans of Icehouse and hid them underneath his jacket."

"That's bullshit," the suspect said. "You didn't—"

Lee held up his hand. "Wait. I'll talk to you next."

The suspect scowled and looked away, shaking his head and muttering.

"He walked around the store for a few minutes," Lonnie continued, "then headed for the doors. I stopped him just outside the entrance."

"Did he resist?"

Lonnie shrugged. "Not really."

Lee understood what that meant, too. Lonnie had played football in high school and then at Eastern Washington University. The ex-offensive lineman may have developed a grocer's paunch, but his arms still looked formidable. His 'not really' was coded explanation that the suspect's attempts to flee or fight were easily overcome, and he didn't want to push an assault beef over it.

"And he still had the beer?"

"All three cans." Lonnie pointed to three cans of Icehouse, neatly positioned at the corner of his desk.

"You got an ID?"

Lonnie handed him the suspect's ID card. Right away, Lee saw that it was a state identification card, not a driver's license. Working graveyard, he estimated at least a third of the people he contacted had IDs instead of a driver's license. That didn't count the significant number who simply didn't carry any ID at all.

He read the name from the card—Creighton Mackey. Eighteen years old last month. Probably used to how the system treated him as a juvenile. He was in for a shock now that he was an adult.

"Creighton," he said, "I'm a police officer."

"No duh."

"You have the right to remain silent," Lee continued, undeterred. "Anything you say can and will be held against you in a court of law. You have the right to an attorney, and if you can't afford an attorney, one will be provided for you. Do you understand these rights?"

"Yeah."

"Are you willing to waive these rights and speak to me?" Lee asked. Then he added, "Tell me your side of things?"

Creighton shrugged. "Sure."

"What happened?"

"Nothing."

Lee remained silent, staring at him.

Creighton squirmed in his seat. "What?"

"Nothing happened? Not a thing?"

"No."

"Did you hear what Mr. Martin just told me?"

"Obviously."

"And?"

"And it's not true."

"What part?"

"All of it."

"Enlighten me."

"Huh?"

"Tell me what *did* happen."

Creighton sniffed and shifted his position. "All right, check it. I came in, I looked around, couldn't find what I wanted, so I left. Then this big black dude grabbed me and started saying some crap about how I stole beer. And now you're here."

Lee waited a couple of beats. Then he pointed to the three cans on the desk. "You didn't take those?"

"Nuh-uh."

"So, what? Mr. Martin had a fever dream? He made this up?"

"I don't know. Maybe you all had to fill your quota or something. Like he said, slow night, so here I am."

Lee thought about it for a moment. Then he said, "Stand up."

"What?"

"Stand up. You're under arrest."

Creighton stared up at him in disbelief. "You can't do that."

Lee reached out and grabbed him by the upper arm and pulled him to his feet. He spun the suspect around. In one quick motion, he ratcheted on the handcuffs while Creighton stared over his shoulder. When the cuff tightened, Creighton winced.

"Ow, man. That hurts."

Lee didn't respond. He nudged Creighton's feet apart and proceeded to search him quickly. He found a wallet and key ring with two keys on it and put them on the desk. When he'd finished, he turned Creighton back around and sat him on the chair again. His cuffed hands forced him to sit near the edge of the chair and lean forward, striking a guilty pose.

Creighton's gaze found Weaver. "Are you seeing this?" he asked her. "This is police brutality. You're a witness."

Lee glanced at Weaver, but her expression was difficult to read.

"You're going to take me to jail over some bullshit I didn't do," Creighton complained.

"Be quiet," Lee directed him.

He was mildly surprised when Creighton obliged.

Lee opened his ticket book. With a practiced hand, he transcribed all of Creighton's information onto the criminal citation.

"I thought you guys had all that computerized now," Lonnie said.

He looked up at Lonnie while he wrote. "The other shifts get the nice toys. We're old school here on graves."

Lonnie chuckled. "I guess so."

Lee didn't add that some brilliant mind in the

administration decided that they should use up the last of the physical citations before they transitioned fully to digital. Sylvia, a records clerk he was friendly with, told him they still had a two-year supply of hard copy tickets to burn through. "I'll take that copy of your report, if you don't mind."

"Sure thing."

While Lonnie moved to the copier in the corner of the office, Lee filled in the two misdemeanor charges—theft and minor in possession of alcohol. By the time the night manager returned with his copies, he had completed the citation. He put it on the desk in front of where Creighton leaned forward. He replaced his personal pen in his breast pocket and withdrew one of the cheap plastic Bics he kept for suspects to use.

"This," he said, clicking the pen to expose the tip, "is a criminal citation for misdemeanor theft and for minor in possession of alcohol." He set the pen on top of the citation, the point of it resting in the signature block. "Signing this is not an admission of guilt, merely a promise to appear to answer to these charges within fifteen days. If you fail to appear, a warrant will be issued for your arrest."

Creighton stared at what Lee had written on the form. "Wait, you busting me for supposedly stealing brews and *then* for MIP, too?" He sounded both incredulous and indignant at the same time.

"That's correct."

"How the hell does *that* work?"

"Same way all laws do."

Creighton looked up at Lee. He could almost see the gears turning behind the suspect's eyes. First, he was processing how this was different than when he'd been busted as a juvenile. Then he was working out new ways to game the system. He'd seen this play out a thousand times before.

"I ain't signing that," Creighton finally said.

"No problem," Lee said. "Then I'll book you into jail instead."

"*What?*" Creighton blinked, surprise plain on his face.

"Stand up."

Creighton didn't move.

"Come on," Lee said. "Stand up so we can go to jail."

"Wait," Creighton said. "I'll... I'll sign it."

Lee remained quiet for a moment, as if considering. Then he said, "Turn around."

Creighton obeyed. Lee removed the handcuffs and stowed them in the case on his belt while Creighton rubbed his wrists.

"Sign," Lee directed him. "And press hard. There's four copies."

Hesitantly, Creighton reached for the pen. Lee could tell he was debating whether to refuse again. Thankfully, common sense won out. Creighton scrawled his looping signature in the block. Then he held out the pen to Lee.

"Keep it," Lee said. He tore out the defendant's copy from the ticket and extended it toward Creighton. "You have fifteen days to respond. If you don't, a warrant will be issued."

Creighton stared dumbly at the citation copy. "A warrant... how do I...?"

"Instructions are on the back," Lee said. He turned to Lonnie. "Are you trespassing him?"

"Already done," Lonnie said. He held up another piece of paper with Creighton's signature. "One year. I gave him a copy."

Lee turned back to Creighton. "You understand that? You can't come back here for a year. If you do, you'll be arrested for trespassing."

Creighton's brow scrunched. "Wait. I can't shop here?"

"No. Like I said, if you come back, you'll be arrested. If you come back and shoplift, you'll be arrested for burglary, which is a felony. Do you understand?"

Creighton shook his head but said nothing.

"Do you have any questions?"

"No," he muttered.

"You need anything else?" Lee asked Lonnie.

"Naw, we're good here. Thanks for coming out." He stuck

out his hand, and Lee shook it. "See you next time."

"Hopefully not too soon."

"I heard that."

"I'll escort him out," Lee said.

"Thanks."

"Come on," he told Creighton, jerking his head toward the door.

Creighton stood sullenly and headed for the door, muttering. Weaver stepped aside to allow him to pass. Lee followed, and the odd threesome made their way down the stairs and out onto the store floor. No one said a word as they walked through the coffee aisle. They passed by the gawking checker in silence. When they reached the front doors, they hissed open automatically. All three of them stepped out into the crisp night air.

"I ask you somethin'?" Creighton said.

"Sure."

"Is that for real, that I can't shop here no more?"

"Hundred percent."

Creighton took a deep breath, then muttered, "Man, that's messed up. This is the neighborhood store. Where am I supposed to get my groceries?"

"Go up to Safeway," Lee suggested. "Unless you're trespassed from there, too."

Creighton stared at him, his expression a cross between hurt and indignation. "That's cold." He turned and shuffled away.

Lee headed toward the car, a silent Weaver trailing him. He opened the driver's door and slid in, popping her lock as he did. While Weaver climbed into the passenger seat, he tore off the ticket, folded the copy of Lonnie's report in half and slipped the ticket between the folds. Then he slid it into the visor above him.

Weaver closed the door, rubbing her upper arms. Lee reached across and opened the glove compartment, placing his ticket book inside.

"Will you stop doing that?" she snapped.

He froze. "What?"

"Reaching everywhere. Infringing on my personal space."

Lee's jaw dropped. "Your..."

"It makes me uncomfortable," Weaver said.

He closed the latch on the glove box and sat back in his own seat. Weaver glared at him with her arms still crossed.

Irritation flared in him. *She* was uncomfortable? She should try driving around and trying to work while the Inquisition rides shotgun.

"I'm sorry." He spoke past a clenched jaw and his words sounded stiff to his own ears. "I didn't mean to make you uncomfortable."

Weaver pressed her lips together. Then she said, "How could you think it wouldn't?"

He motioned to the interior of the car. "This is my office. I'm used to working in here alone. You're sitting where my patrol bag usually is. Reaching around for things is just habit."

"It's still rude."

"It wasn't intentional."

"I believe you. Rudeness seems to be a habit with you."

Lee gawked at her. "What is that supposed to mean?"

She rubbed her upper arms with her hands, then let them drop to her lap. "That kid. You treated him like a criminal."

"He is a criminal."

"He shoplifted some beer."

"Which is a crime."

"I get that, but it's not exactly the crime of the century, is it?"

"Hey, I don't get to pick them. I take what comes my way and deal with it. That's the job. Do you have a problem with that?"

She stared at him. "You want an honest answer?"

"No," he snarled. "I want you to lie to me like everyone else out here does."

Her eyes flared open in surprise. It took a moment for her to regain her composure. Then, her tone milder, she said, "I do see a few problems with what just happened, yes. Do you want to hear them or should we just move on?"

"No, by all means." He gave her a wave of invitation.

She ignored his sarcasm. "First off, he's a kid. He—"

"He's eighteen. He's an adult."

"Technically, yes, but—"

"Not technically. *Legally*. And legally is how I have to approach things. I'm law enforcement. I enforce laws."

"Without discretion?"

"Sometimes, but not always."

"Did you have discretion back there?"

"What's your point?"

"Discretion is a choice. And you chose to handle that situation the way you did."

Lee stared at her in disbelief. *She* was lecturing *him* on how to do *his* job? It was unbelievable. He wondered if she'd appreciate it if he stopped by her workplace and offered a critique.

"I handled it like a professional," Lee said, his jaw clenching as he spoke. "He's a criminal. It's not like he was stealing a loaf of bread for his starving little brother or medicine for his sick mother, either. He stole beer."

"He's a product of the poverty he lives in."

Lee resisted the urge to roll his eyes. "Plenty of poor people don't steal."

"Either way, you and that other man were condescending. You threatened him with jail. You put handcuffs on him for no reason and you bullied him into signing that ticket. Then—"

"Is this how it's going to be all night?" Lee interrupted. "You think you're going to ride around with me and criticize everything I do? Because that's not how it works. You're an observer. You *observe*. That's all."

"You asked."

"I didn't ask for any of this. I was assigned."

"Trust me, I don't want to be here any more than you want me here."

Lee started the car and dropped it into gear. "Just say the word. I can take you back to the station right now."

A long, tense moment ensued. When she didn't reply, he slammed the gear lever back into Park and opened the door. Without a word, he got out of the car and swung the door shut. Anger gnawed on the edges of his composure.

I shouldn't have to put up with this, he thought.

Lee walked to the back of the car and stood for a moment. He reached for his phone, considering a call to Sergeant Gelabert. Then he stopped. What would be the point? He'd only seem like a whiner. Which, he had to admit, was exactly what it would be. Besides, he doubted there was anything the sergeant could do, other than to reassign Weaver to a different cop. There was no way he was passing a problem onto Murph or some other teammate.

Another consideration struck him. If he hauled Melody Weaver back to the station and dumped her off, he didn't want to face Gelabert's stern look of disappointment. On top of that, he'd put the sergeant in a tough spot. It'd look bad to the brass. The PRI and the newspaper would make a huge deal about it. Sergeant Gelabert would catch all that shit.

She didn't deserve that.

Gelabert had been a good sergeant. This was his third year working for her. She had a reputation of being solid long before he cast his shift bid to be on her team. He'd quickly discovered that the rep was well-earned. She ran a tight ship but cared for her people. She spent as much time in the field as the paperwork burden allowed, so she was available when he or one of his teammates needed her. Given that the department's promotional process was a crap shoot at best, Lee couldn't say that all sergeants were like Gelabert. Some were similar, but some let the power go to their heads, while others became house cats, rarely straying from the station. He'd learned early on in his career that when the annual shift bid came around, if you can find a good sergeant, it made for a good year. It was even worth it to work graveyard instead of an earlier shift if it meant sticking with Gelabert.

Loyalty was a two-way street. That was something his father used to say. It was one of the things that he had to admit the old man had completely right. Sergeant Gelabert was loyal to her people, including Lee. So, he was loyal in return.

And that meant not screwing her over with a public relations nightmare just because some rider pushed his buttons. She'd said she was counting on him, and he couldn't let her down.

His hand dropped to his belt as he was thinking. Weaver was essentially Cody Lofton's proxy. Between that and the DOJ consent decree, Lee knew he had no wiggle room here. He had to make this work. Gelabert had chosen him. She'd even brought up that he was a legacy cop, mentioning his father and grandfather in a roundabout way. Whether that was to stroke him or because she believed it, he wasn't sure.

"Shit," he muttered. All he wanted to do was be a patrol cop. Not brass, like his prick of a father, and certainly not a legend like his grandfather. But it seemed like other people weren't always willing to go along with the plan.

He glanced through the rear window to see that Weaver was on her phone.

Great, he thought, she was probably already complaining to Cody Lofton.

It didn't matter, he decided. She would report things how she viewed them, no matter what. He couldn't win. He felt like a closing pitcher brought in to save an unwinnable game. All he could do was play out the string. Do his best.

Lee took a deep breath. He waited for her to end her call, which took almost another minute.

After a while, he realized he'd been holding his breath and exhaled heavily. He shuffled toward the driver's door.

It was time to get back in the car and make it work.

And that meant he had to apologize.

Lee set his jaw and reached for the door handle.

Chapter 4

MEL

She wanted to shout, more than once. But feeling that way and not acting on it was a valuable skill she'd honed during her teaching career. There were times to be direct and times to avoid conflict. Over the years, there'd been plenty of things said or done that certainly merited screaming—by parents, administrators, other teachers, not to mention the kids. Mel usually found a way to engage without engaging or to deflect. On rare occasions, when she simply couldn't take it any longer, she'd let slip a sarcastic comment coated in honey. The passive-aggressive approach wasn't her style, but every once in a while, it was the only viable pressure release valve.

Even before they entered the store, everything the officer did grated on her nerves. First, he sped all the way to the store. She wondered if that was intentional—him rubbing her face in his presumed exemption from traffic law—or just a bad habit, a form of blue privilege he'd become accustomed to. She opened her mouth to say something but stopped herself. Fighting with this cop wasn't her purpose. It wasn't why Ellen asked her to be on this ride-along. So, she let it go.

But the irritation didn't end there. There was the way he swaggered into the store like some sort of uptight gunfighter. How he didn't greet the checker with any sort of courtesy, just barked out a request. And when the employee called the shoplifter a kid, he sternly corrected her before moving on. Mel offered her a sympathetic look as she passed by the checkout lane, hurrying to keep up with the officer.

It turned out the shoplifter *was* a kid, though. He sat, small in his chair, obviously scared and putting on a woefully transparent mask of toughness. She knew the look well. She saw it in some of her students, especially the so-called "hard" kids. They were the ones that many of the other teachers complained about or had no patience for, the stinky kids or the ones with behavior problems. Mel looked at them differently. The part about them that was hard wasn't their persona; it was their life. Without fail, their life was tough, full of difficulty or neglect, some of it unimaginable for a twelve- or thirteen-year-old to handle, and often it all came through in their behavior at school. They did what they did because of whatever situation they lived in. Negative attention was still attention.

The kid hunched in the store manager's office bore the same expression she'd seen on her middle-schoolers. The mask might have been slightly more practiced, but it was still the same disguise.

The cop acted buddy-buddy with the hulking manager, joking with him like they were in a locker room. He even asked the guy if he was "still crushing it," a reference she took as to whether he was getting laid regularly.

But it was the transitions that nudged her closer to the edge. First, the cop was remote and brusque. Then suddenly gregarious and charming. And when he turned on the kid, he just as swiftly became cold and menacing.

She'd seen that before, too.

It was exactly like her father.

Mel set her jaw, remembering. Her mother always called him a complicated man. She offered that explanation as if it somehow absolved his failings. Mel saw it differently. He wasn't complicated. But he was a contrast. Her dad managed to be well-loved in the neighborhood and throughout the community. He seemed to have time for everyone and managed to make them feel important, or make them laugh, or both. He seemed to genuinely care about them. The energy he put into other people left little for her, though. Outside of a precious few occasions, the man she got at home was cold and brusque, interspersed with short bursts of anger.

Complicated?

No. The only thing that was complicated was how she still felt about him. And that was painfully true as she watched

Officer Salter cycle through the same faces she'd seen her father wear.

By the time he bullied Creighton Mackey into a confession and put him in handcuffs, Mel's frustration neared its bursting point. The kid looked even younger and more vulnerable as he sat hunched over in his chair, waiting for the cop to take him to jail. Instead, Salter wrote him a ticket, lording the entire process over him like it was some kind of religious rite. The fact that Creighton didn't understand what was happening became painfully apparent, but the cop showed him no mercy, no compassion. He threatened to take him to jail again, bullying the kid into signing the ticket.

Still, Mel held her tongue. She was here to watch, to learn. This wasn't about her, it was about effecting change.

Mel managed to hold onto that as Salter stalked out of the store with her and Creighton in tow. But once they were outside, Creighton said something that broke her heart just a little.

"For real, I can't shop here no more?" he asked, his voice small and defeated.

"One hundred percent," the cop said, his voice uncaring.

Creighton seemed on the verge of tears. "Man, that's messed up. This is the neighborhood store. Where am I supposed to get my groceries?"

"Go to Safeway," Salter told him, pitiless. She knew the store he meant. It was at least a mile away. She doubted Creighton had a car. Then the cop added, "Unless you're trespassed from there, too."

That mask Creighton had tried to keep in place from the beginning fell away completely, revealing the deep hurt on the kid's face. "That's cold," he whispered huskily. Then he turned and walked away, beaten.

Salter seemed unaffected by the exchange. He returned to the car without a backward glance.

Mel joined him, getting in and closing the door. She teetered on the edge of speaking up. Was it her place? Was it professional? Would he even hear her? She tried to imagine how she'd feel if someone who wasn't in education came into her classroom and offered a critique. What did they know about teaching?

She shook her head slightly. That wasn't the same thing. She *did* know about the police. That's what the PRI was all about. She had a foundation of knowledge, so it was different.

Even so, she remained quiet a little longer.

Until he bumped her leg again while reaching for the glove box. Then she'd had enough.

"Will you stop doing that, please?" she asked, trying to keep the tension out of her voice.

He gave her a flat look. "Stop what?"

She motioned toward the glove box. "Reaching past me. Infringing on my personal space."

His expression turned to indignation. "Your *what?*"

"Please," she said, trying to keep things civil. "It makes me uncomfortable."

He stared at her. "I'm sorry I made you feel uncomfortable," he gritted, his tone unconvincing. "I didn't mean to."

"How could you not know that it would?"

"This is my office," he said, waving his hand around. "I usually work alone. In fact, you're sitting where my patrol bag usually goes. Me reaching around for things is just habit."

"That doesn't make it any less rude."

"It's not intentional," he asserted. He sounded angry and indignant now, almost petulant.

"I believe you," Mel said, softening her voice. "I think rudeness is something of a habit for you, though."

Slater stared at her. "What is *that* supposed to mean?"

Mel realized she was rubbing her upper arms and stopped herself. She gave him a forthright look. "I'm talking about that kid."

"What about him?"

"You treated him horribly. Like a criminal."

"That's because he *is* a criminal."

She rolled her eyes. "He shoplifted some beer. Not exactly the crime of the century."

"It's still a crime."

"I get that. But that doesn't mean you have to treat him that way."

"Listen," he snapped, "I don't get to choose my calls. I take them as they come. And I didn't tell him to steal from the store, either. He chose to do that; he got caught. I got the call; I handled it. That's the job. You see some kind of problem with that?"

"You really want me to answer that honestly?"

"No," he said coldly. "I want you to lie to me like all these people out here do."

Her eyes widened in surprise. The implied bias, even racism, in the uttered phrase of "these people startled her. She had no difficulty believing that most of the institutions in the country were riddled with racial bias. Health care, law enforcement, government... even education was. That didn't mean that the people toiling in those institutions were necessarily racist, at least not overtly. But his words rang with that familiar refrain, that dog whistle, that she'd heard all too often.

She hesitated. Now was the opportunity to disengage if she wanted to defuse the situation. Going forward might turn this brief exchange into a full-fledged argument.

Mel forced herself to speak in a milder tone. "I saw a few issues with what just happened. I'll share them if you want to hear what they are. But maybe we should just move on."

"No," he insisted. "By all means, enlighten me."

He's asking was her first thought. But she knew that wasn't really the case. He was in conversational battle mode right now, that was all. The best thing to do was to let it go.

Instead, she said, "All right. For starters, he was just a kid."

Salter scoffed. "He's over eighteen. That makes him an adult."

"Maybe legally, but—"

"There's no maybe about it. He's of legal age and that's how I have to treat him. That's what law enforcement does. We enforce laws."

"But you have discretion."

"Sometimes we do, but not always."

"Did you have discretion back there?"

"What's your point?"

"You always have discretion in how you treat people. It's a choice. And you chose to handle things the way you did."

"I handled it like a professional," Salter said, his jaw clenching as he spoke. "And he's not a kid, he's a criminal. He wasn't stealing bread because he was starving or medicine for his sick mom. He *stole beer*."

That was true enough, but his myopia still grated on her. "He's responding to the poverty he lives in."

"Lots of poor people don't steal."

Salter glared at her, but she was past the point of no return. "Either way, you and that other man were condescending and inappropriate. Then you threatened him."

"Threatened him?" Salter's anger was tinged with disbelief. "How?"

"You said you'd take him to jail. You handcuffed him. You bullied him into a confession and then again into signing that ticket. You arrested him for stealing beer and then somehow also for having it, which doesn't seem right. You didn't show him any compassion or asked if—"

He held up a hand. "Is this how it's going to be all night? You telling me how to do my job? I thought you were just an observer."

"You asked."

"I didn't *ask* for anything. I was assigned."

"Trust me," she said, "I don't want to be here any more than you want me here."

"Yeah?" Salter twisted the ignition key and the engine roared to life. He revved it once, like a snarl, then jerked the gear selector down. The car lurched forward slightly, then rocked back in place as he kept his foot on the brake. "Just say the word. I'll happily take you back to the station right now."

The tense silence hung between them. The police computer beeped and grinded its way through boot-up. Radio chatter filled the interior of the car. Salter stared flatly at her. She stared back, his face both foreign and familiar to her, both his and her father's all at once.

When she didn't respond, the officer slammed the car into park and got out. He shuffled toward the rear of the car, reached for something in his pocket, then stopped. His face twisted in anger and frustration.

I should just go home, she thought.

She pulled her phone from her purse. She paused, calculating where David would be right now. As best as she could guess, he wouldn't have started his pre-flight checks yet. She could interrupt without causing him any delays.

The phone rang three times before he picked up. "You okay, baby?"

"Not really," she said. Her voice cracked, and she was surprised at the rush of emotion that came with her admission.

"What happened?"

"Nothing. It's just... it's hard."

David didn't answer. He did as he always did when she needed to vent to him—he waited patiently.

"I don't want to be here," she said. "The cop they put me with alternates between being a robot and a jerk. He—"

"He? I thought you were going to ride with a lady cop?"

"So did I. But they put me with this guy who reminds me of..." She stopped.

"Your pops?"

Mel nodded. "Yeah," she whispered.

"You know you can go home if you want to."

"No, I can't. We already talked about this."

"Fixing the whole world isn't your responsibility, Melody. If this is too much, go home. You already do more than your part."

"He's just so... prickly. So defensive."

"Well, now, you've got to expect that, right?"

"I did, but not this bad."

"Can you work through it?"

She thought about it. She glanced over her shoulder to see Salter shaking his head at nothing in particular. "I don't know. Maybe."

"Knowing you like I do, my guess is that you can do it," David said. "I think the real question is whether it's worth the pain."

"Worth it for who?"

"That's for you to answer."

Was it worth it to her? She wasn't sure. But she knew good and well how important it was to Ellen and the rest of the PRI, not to mention Council President Lofton. And if she accepted that, that meant it was important to the rest of the city.

"You're no help," she chided him, but her tone was soft.

David chuckled slightly. "I'm no fool. I learned a long time ago that you're a woman who makes her own decisions."

"Okay. Have a safe flight. Sorry to bother you."

"Never a bother. I love you, babe."

"I love you, too."

They hung up.

Melody slid her phone back into her purse. Hearing his voice gave her a boost. It always did, no matter how difficult her day had been. The confidence he had in her helped remind her why she did what she did. As a teacher, it was all for the kids. With the PRI, it was all about reform. She couldn't let her own frustrations derail that effort.

She needed to be more diplomatic. And when Salter got back into the car—

The door swung open, and he clambered back inside. He adjusted his position in the seat and pulled the door closed. Then he turned to her.

"I'm sorry," he said.

She cocked her head, surprised. "What?"

"I shouldn't have barked at you like that. It was unprofessional."

"Okay." She didn't know how to respond further.

"I can take you back to the station if you want."

Mel swallowed. "I don't want to go back to the station. This is important."

Salter wasn't completely assuaged. "I agree, but I don't need you criticizing me all night, either."

She was about to respond when he added, "Especially when you don't really know what you're talking about."

Irritation flickered in her again, but she did her best to hold it at bay. "Look, we got off to a bad start. You don't want someone riding along. I get that. Believe it or not, I didn't volunteer for this, either. So maybe both of our attitudes aren't great."

Salter didn't reply. He stared at her, his flat expression unreadable.

"Maybe we can come to an agreement," she suggested.

"You mean like a truce?"

"If you want. I don't like to think of this as a war, though."

"What agreement?"

"Just some ground rules we can both live by."

He kept his gaze leveled at her, curious. "Like what?"

"Well, I'm here to learn about the police. I can do some of that by just watching, but I can learn a lot more with your help."

"Help?" His curiosity held more than a whisper of suspicion in it.

"If I can ask you questions, I'd learn more. And I'd be less likely to misconstrue anything."

"Questions, huh?"

She held up her hand. "Ask, not criticize. Okay?"

He nodded slowly. "I don't mind legitimate questions."

"But you have to promise me something, too."

His eyes grew suspicious again. "What?"

"Not to hear my questions as criticism. They're just questions. And I need you to be honest, not trot out the canned public relations response."

"That's two things."

She shrugged. "It's still fair, though, right?"

Salter watched her closely, as if trying to divine her true intentions. Even though she knew she wasn't hiding anything, his direct, penetrating gaze still made her want to squirm. Not because it was intimidating. Because she'd seen it before.

"A do-over, then?" he finally asked.

She nodded. "Can we do that?"

He considered a few moments longer. "On one condition."

"Name it."

"You tell me why you're really here. What you really want. You be honest about that, and I'll agree to your truce."

"Not a truce," she said. "If we're sticking with the war metaphor, I'm proposing something more like a treaty."

"I'll sign it, then. If you're honest with me."

Now it was her turn to consider. She had no way of knowing what he wanted to hear right then. Reassurances? Brutal truth? Anti-police vitriol? What would convince him?

Mel did the only thing she knew was always the right answer. She was honest.

"Okay, here it is. The PRI wants reform. That's no secret. And we're not huge fans of the department. That's no secret, either. But we're not blind to the need for a role for the police in our community. My purpose here is to learn as much as I can about the police to help make that role beneficial for everyone."

"Now, *that* sounds like a public relations answer."

"You're right," she admitted. She thought for a moment. "How about this, then? I want to know what's really going on with the police. Maybe you're as bad as some people say. Maybe they've got it wrong. I want to find out the truth."

"You really want the truth?"

"That's why I'm here."

"The truth isn't what you think it is."

"I could say the same thing to you."

A sardonic smile touched Salter's lips. "I know the truth. I'm out here every night."

"Then educate me," Mel said. "I'll listen to you if you listen to me."

"No punches thrown?"

She motioned to the inside of the car. "This is a safe place."

His smile was small and held a hint of mockery.

"I mean it," she said. "Ask anything, say anything. That's the deal."

"Ask anything, say anything," Salter murmured. He was quiet and seemed to think it over. After a few moments, he nodded. "Okay, you got it. But be careful what you wish for. Like I said, the truth isn't what you think it is."

It never is, she thought. But at least this was a start.

"We're in agreement, then?"

"Consider your treaty signed," Salter said. He let up on the brake pedal, and they rolled forward, out of the parking lot, and back onto the street.

Chapter 5

LEE

He pulled out of the grocery store parking lot. Out of habit, he drifted toward the various hot zones within his sector. Truthfully, he would have preferred to head back toward the station to drop off his rider.

Why didn't he, then?

It wasn't her first answer to his question, that was for sure. She'd rattled off some talking point that he was willing to bet he could find word-for-word on some PRI pamphlet or in their mission statement. But when he called her on that, he thought he detected a small ripple in her expression. Something real. Something genuine. And then when she laid it out openly and honestly for him, he knew she was being sincere.

Everybody hates you. I want to see if they're right or if they're wrong.

Those weren't her exact words, he knew, but it was what she meant. The stark, brutal directness of it was what he appreciated. That, and what seemed like an equally sincere desire to actually *learn*.

He believed her.

Or, at least, he was willing to give it a chance.

"You want coffee?" he asked Weaver. "I need coffee."

"Sure," she said.

Lee turned left and headed toward one of the few coffee stands he knew remained open past nine. "One thing I want to clear up, though."

"What's that?"

"I didn't double dip on that kid."

"What's that mean?"

"I didn't stack charges on him. The elements for theft and for minor in possession are different."

Weaver was quiet for a second, contemplating what he'd

said. "Still seems weird. He gets arrested for stealing beer *and* for having beer?"

"It's the law," Lee said.

"Kinda unfair, don't you think?"

"My job isn't to interpret the law," he said evenly. "It's to enforce it. And that, back there? That was what the law said."

"Okay," Weaver said, her tone noncommittal.

They drove on in silence.

Life's Bean Good was a shack-sized building on the corner of a gas station parking lot. Traffic on the normally bustling street was already growing sparse. Lee was able to cross the lane of oncoming traffic without waiting. He pulled in behind a battered El Camino, the only other customer in line. The driver held out cash and the barista took it.

"Sorry it's gotta be a drive-through," he said to Weaver while he typed. "I'm running the El Camino's plate, by the way."

"You do that often?"

"Anytime I can." He hit the return key on the MDC. "Hopefully we'll get a chance to get out of the car for some dinner or a decent break later on. But you never know."

The MDC dinged with the return. He examined the information. "The Camino's registration expires in three days. Bet you he rolls with expired tabs on day four."

"You should have some faith."

Lee smiled. "Uh-huh."

He considered checking the registered owner for warrants and driver's license status, but then a drink appeared through the coffee stand window, and the driver accepted it. The brake lights ahead flashed briefly, and the El Camino pulled away.

Lee let it go. If the tabs expired, that made for an easy reason to stop the car later down the line. Let the low hanging fruit ripen, he figured.

When he pulled up to the window, Sienna was working. The early-twenty-something had her auburn hair pulled back in a tight ponytail. She wore a gray, snug-fitting three-quarter

Seattle Mariners T-shirt that revealed a sliver of skin between the bottom hem and the beltline of her jeans.

"Hey, Lee," she said, giving him a smile as she wiped off the espresso machine. The small stone in her nose ring caught the light from the streetlamp. "How's it going?"

"Not bad," he lied. "Busy tonight?"

She held up her hand and waggled it. "*Mas o menos*. The usual for you?"

"Please. Oh, and..." He turned to Weaver expectantly.

"Chai latte," Weaver said. She held out a folded bill.

Lee shook his head. "My treat."

Weaver kept the money there between them, not relenting.

"Consider it a signing bonus," Lee said, forcing a slight smile. When she didn't react immediately, he added, "For the treaty."

Slowly, Weaver lowered the cash. "All right. Thanks."

Lee turned and relayed the order to Sienna.

The barista whipped through their orders, the equipment clanging and hissing.

"You come here a lot?" Weaver asked.

"A fair amount," he said, not looking away from Sienna while she worked. "In addition to the coffee, it's a good indicator of how busy the shift's going to be."

"Huh?"

He glanced at Weaver. "If she's getting slammed here, chances are pretty good there's going to be lots of calls. If the coffee stand is dead, it usually means I'm in for a quieter night."

"Not very scientific," Weaver observed.

Lee shrugged. "Maybe not, but it often bears out."

Less than three minutes later, Sienna handed him a pair of paper cups out of the coffee stand window. "Okay, one chai latte and one triple power Americano."

Lee took the cups, handing Weaver hers. Then he gave Sienna enough to cover the cost plus a healthy tip. "Keep it."

He set his cup in the cup holder as he pulled away. Weaver

glanced around, searching for someplace to put her own.

"Sorry," he said, lifting out his own cup. "There's only one in here. You can use it."

Weaver shook her head. "No. I can hold mine. You probably need both your hands, anyway."

That was true enough, so Lee didn't argue. He replaced his cup and turned out onto the street.

"She seems nice," Weaver said.

"Who, Sienna?" Lee nodded. "She's been there about a year and a half now. Working her way through college."

"Pretty, too. I can see why you'd go there."

Lee looked sidelong at her. Weaver held her cup close to her chest with both hands, as if trying to draw warmth from it. "Hey, I thought we had a truce."

"No, I don't mean it like that. It's just an observation. She's a pretty girl."

"She knows how to pull a shot," Lee said, a little defensive. "And she works at one of the only coffee stands open this late."

"Okay."

"If all I wanted was to gawk at a barista, there's one of those lingerie places a half mile away. They're open till eleven."

"You don't ever go there?"

"Their coffee tastes like burnt oil."

Weaver's nose crinkled. "So, you *have* been."

"Only on calls of customers bothering the baristas. But I got the intel on their brew."

Weaver held up a hand. "Okay, okay. I get it."

Lee thought about it for a minute. He knew more than a few patrol cops drove through the lingerie stand to stare and flirt. Some did the same at Life's Bean Good. Hell, if he was being honest, he supposed he was one of them, in some fashion. Nothing with intent, he simply enjoyed talking to Sienna, but...

"Maybe you're right," he admitted.

"About what?"

"I think part of the reason people go there is because of Sienna." He paused, then added, "Including me."

"Well... duh."

He glanced at her again, and thought he detected the hint of a smile. "Like I said, she brews a good cup."

"You said she knows how to pull a shot." Weaver sipped her chai latte. "Mmmm. Tasty."

Lee fought back a smile and pivoted the conversation. "So, you're a teacher, you said?"

"I am."

"What grade?"

"Seventh and eighth. I teach social studies."

Lee squinted. "That turns into government class in high school, right?"

"That, and history."

"You like it?"

"History?"

"No, teaching."

Weaver took a deep breath and let it out, nodding along with the exhale. "Yeah, I really do. It's hard but it's worth it."

"Sounds like my job."

"I don't think our two jobs are anything alike."

"I'm just saying the 'hard but worth it' part."

"Ah." She sipped her chai.

"What's your husband fly?"

Her eyes narrowed slightly. "How'd you know I was married?"

"You told me earlier," Lee said. "When I said the inside of the car was like a fighter jet."

"Oh."

"Besides," he motioned toward her left hand, wrapped around the cup. "Wedding ring."

She glanced down at her diamond band. "Ah."

"Kids?"

She nodded. "Two. Isaac is thirteen. Hattie's five."

"Kids are great. What's your husband fly?"

"Commercial, but he flew fighters in the Air Force."

"Out at Fairchild?"

"Yeah."

Lee eyed her. "Why'd he leave?"

"Because we had kids." The way she said it showed she was proud of her husband's decision.

"Huh." Lee didn't know if he would leave the job if his wife asked him to—even with all its ugliness. "And now he flies for an airline. Which one?"

"Alaska."

"How's he like that?"

"He loves to fly," Weaver said. "And Alaska's good to him."

"We flew with them when we went down to San Diego to visit my in-laws." He shrugged. "Seemed like a good airline." He honestly had no idea if there was a difference between any of the competing airlines, but the compliment cost him nothing.

"So you're married, then?"

"Yeah. We have a daughter, Olivia." He glanced over at her. "You sound surprised."

She gestured toward his left hand, resting at the twelve o'clock position on the steering wheel. "No ring."

"I take it off at work."

"Why?"

"A couple reasons."

"Like what?"

He shrugged a single shoulder. "It's a safety hazard, for one. Just like working in a factory."

"I don't follow."

Lee held up his left hand and tapped his ring finger with his thumb. "One time, an officer got into a foot pursuit through some backyards. As he was going over a tall chain link fence, his ring got caught up in it. When he landed, the ring stripped and tore the skin and muscle off his finger. De-gloved it, basically."

Weaver winced.

"And another time," Lee continued, "on a traffic stop, a guy climbed back into his car to take off. The cop reached out to stop him from getting away and the door slammed on his hand. His ring crushed onto the finger, and he couldn't pull free. Then the guy drove off with the cop stuck in the door. He got dragged for several blocks."

"That's horrible."

"It's what you call a life-threatening situation."

"What happened?"

"He pulled his gun and fired a round at the driver. That convinced him to stop."

Weaver took another sip of her chai. "That's frightening, but it doesn't sound like something that happens very often."

"Only takes once."

"I suppose." Weaver sounded unconvinced.

"Not wearing it gives me one less thing to worry about." Lee figured she thought that reason was a paranoid one. He imagined most people did. But most folks didn't know the sheer number of things that could go wrong in a single patrol shift. It wasn't paranoia if it was a real threat. But he didn't expect a civilian to understand that. "I also don't wear it to protect my family."

Her brow furrowed. "From?"

"Look," he said, "I deal with a lot of criminals out here. On every shift. Some of them are small time but not all. Some are so hardcore evil that you wouldn't believe it if I told you." He tapped his finger again with his thumb pad. "They see a ring here, and it gives them ammunition."

"For what?"

"Threats. If I had a dollar for every time someone has threatened to kill or rape my wife, I could have retired years ago."

"That happens?" she asked, seeming a little shocked.

"All the time."

"Even without your wedding band?"

"All the time," he repeated.

"That's awful."

"It gets worse. That's what people don't understand about this job. There are a thousand things like that out here, most of which we can't control. Cops get shot while sitting in their cars doing paperwork. Or sitting in uniform at a diner. The people we're trying to help spit on us. Or worse, they attack us. And yeah, on a rare occasion, we get a hand shut in a car door and dragged for half a mile down the road. The odds of any of those things happening might be low, but when there's a thousand of them that are possible, one will eventually hit."

Weaver watched him, her expression unreadable.

Lee turned onto Boone Avenue.

"There's more," he said. "But with all of that, we still have to do our job. So, we back into brightly lit places and look up every few seconds while we're doing paperwork. That way, nobody can sneak up on us. Everywhere we go, we sit with our backs to the wall, facing the entry. We stay on guard all the time and are vigilant with everyone. And," he gave his ring finger one final tap, "we leave the wedding band in the locker at the station. That way when some mope threatens to hurt my wife, I can flash my hand—" he lifted the bare hand toward her, "—and say I'm not married. It takes the wind out of their sails." He put his hand back on the steering wheel. "We control the things we can to mitigate the things we can't."

Weaver was quiet for a few moments. "I never thought of any of that."

Lee shrugged. Having the chance to express the sentiment gave him a sense of relief and one of darkness at the same time. "Most people don't, but they still think they know everything about my job."

"How's your wife feel about it?"

"She understands."

"Including the wedding band part?"

"She wants me to be safe, and she knows I love her."

Weaver made a thoughtful sound and sipped her chai. "Well, I'm sorry, then."

"For what?"

"If I'm being honest, my first thought was that you didn't wear the ring, so it'd be easier to flirt with women like what's her name back there."

"No," Lee asserted. "Not for me." Then, more softly, he admitted, "Maybe for some guys, though."

"Huh," Weaver said.

He glanced at her. "Huh, what?"

"That's some actual honesty. I kind of expected the blue wall to go up. All cops are heroes. That sort of thing."

Lee shrugged. "Cops are people. And some people are—" He started to say 'assholes' but shifted. "—are jerks. It only follows that some cops are going to be jerks, too."

Weaver didn't answer. Instead, she sipped her drink. Then she motioned toward his cup. "You haven't touched your coffee."

"It has to cool," Lee explained. "The Americano is super hot."

They drove in a tenuous silence for a few blocks. Lee scanned the streets and the cars he passed out of sheer habit. The feeling of dread in his gut had diminished slightly, but he still worried that their uneasy truce might fall apart any second.

Not a truce, he reminded himself.

A treaty.

Then Weaver said, "I guess maybe our jobs aren't so different."

Chapter 6

MEL

When he agreed to her treaty offer, she was moderately surprised. She'd expected him to jump at the chance to be rid of her.

Instead, he offered her coffee.

When he swung into the coffee stand, he focused on the car in front of them, explaining that he was running the license plate. She couldn't see any discernible reason for doing so but didn't ask him for one, either. Once more, the veil of resting cop face descended.

When they rolled up to the window, however, his demeanor changed completely. She sensed it first, rather than saw it, since she was digging some cash out of her small purse. But then Mel got a look at the barista, a cute young girl dressed in what she thought of as "casual provocative." She flashed Salter a practiced smile and called him by name, which explained a lot.

Still, the barista was fast, and the chai was good. She enjoyed it while Salter explained why he didn't wear his wedding band at work. "Most people don't understand," he said, his tone a little frustrated. "But they still think they know how to do my job."

That resonated with her. She experienced it all the time at work. But before she could examine the thought any further, Salter did something else to counter her expectations. Instead of throwing up the blue wall of silence regarding police behavior, he said, "Cops are people, too. That means some are—" He paused, then finished. "Jerks."

She didn't reply. His small honesty was refreshing. It gave her a spark of hope amidst a sea of suspicion.

More than that, his words got her thinking about his earlier comparison of their jobs. On the face of it, she didn't think the two were comparable at all. But something he'd said stuck in her head.

Most people don't understand. But they still think they know how to do my job.

"Maybe our jobs aren't so different, after all," she mused.

"Why? Some teachers are jerks, too?"

She laughed. "Oh yeah, but that's not why. It was something else you said. That people think they know how to do your job. I get the same thing."

"Yeah, huh?"

Mel nodded. "It's parents, most of the time. But the public in general, too. Everyone thinks they're experts on teaching just because they went to school themselves, or because they have kids in school. Even though I have a master's degree and have taught for eighteen years, they're somehow convinced they know how to do my job."

Salter grunted. "Sounds about right. It's the same for cops. I mean, minus the master's degree part. There's a lot people don't understand."

"The misconceptions about teachers are ridiculous. The only thing that's worse are the expectations that people have for us."

Now, Salter smirked.

"What?" Mel asked. "You don't believe me?"

He gave her the barest of shrugs, his eyes scanning the road. "No offense, but teaching seems like kind of a cake job. I mean, I get that people don't understand it but—"

"A *cake* job?"

"As in easy. Or at least not hard, you know?"

"So, you, too, huh?"

"I'm just saying. You work dayshift. You're done by three o'clock. You get weekends and holidays off. Christmas break, spring break, and that doesn't even count the fact that you get sum—"

"Don't say it."

"—mer's off. I mean, you're working nine months and

getting paid for twelve." Salter signaled and turned onto a residential side street. "Seems pretty cake to me. I mean, I work graveyard, ten hours plus mandatory overtime, and my so-called weekend rotates every quarter. I only get three weeks of vacation a year and due to staffing minimum requirements, I have to bid against my platoon mates for when I can take it."

Mel stared at him, unsure which part of all that bullshit she should unpack first. "You ever teach?"

"Not in the classroom, but I'm an FTO. That means Field Training Officer. We train the rookies out here on the street after the academy."

"I know what an FTO is."

Salter shrugged. "Anyway, it's teaching."

"So, you're instructing a motivated adult one-on-one, in a practical setting?"

"Exactly."

"Ever try to instruct thirty-five people at once?"

"Nope."

"It's completely different. Add in that they're kids at an age where all their hormones are freaking out and the classroom experience is a challenge. That doesn't speak to all the preparation that goes into the lesson ahead of time."

"I thought they gave you time for that."

Her eyes narrowed. "A single prep period—yeah. Less than an hour. Big deal. It's a fraction of what we need to do the job right. I spend evenings and weekends prepping for lessons. And grading. There's always grading. So, when you say I'm off at three, that's not the case. I leave the school around that time, but I'm not finished working."

"Okay."

"And all those breaks during the year that you're talking about? We need those. If you do my job right, it is exhausting. I'm talking about an absolutely crushing exhaustion. Kids need active, energetic engagement, not some robot droning at the front of the classroom."

Salter smiled a little. "Like that old movie? 'Anybody?

Anybody? Bueller?'"

"Something like that. If you meet that need for them, it completely drains you. Trust me, by the time we get to those breaks, they're not a luxury but an absolute necessity. We need it to recharge the batteries."

He seemed contemplative for a few seconds. "I guess I could see that. I'm pretty wiped after a four-week rotation with a rookie. And getting back-to-back recruits is murder."

Mel motioned with her hand in a *there-you-go* gesture. "And let me clear up something else for you—I don't get paid for summers off. I sign a contract to work a certain number of days in association with the school year. It ends up being about ten months—not nine—and it's the district that spreads the payments for those ten months out over twelve for their own accounting purposes."

Salter raised his brow slightly. "I didn't know that. So, you're basically on a year-to-year contract?"

"Yes."

"Huh," Salter grunted. "Not knowing if you're getting re-upped every year must be stressful."

"It is, for the first few years while you're on probation. Once you're tenured, it's a little harder for them to let you go."

"That sounds a lot like civil service," he said. "People think it's hard to fire a cop and they're right in some ways, but it isn't like cops are the only ones protected by civil service. Try firing a fireman sometime."

"Why would you want to?"

"Ha, ha."

Mel sipped her chai and looked out the window. She hadn't intended on the diatribe. Then again, if he could offer up a little education about his career field, then she could do the same about hers.

Salter sped up to drop in behind a Toyota pickup with a malfunctioning taillight. He followed a couple car lengths behind for a few blocks. He tapped a button on the MDC, then tapped several more keys.

"Entering the license plate?" Mel asked.

"Yeah."

"Going to stop them?"

"Maybe."

The Toyota approached an uncontrolled intersection and slowed before entering.

A beep emanated from the computer.

Salter motioned toward the MDC. "The registered owner lives a couple blocks up."

"So no stop?"

"Not unless he does something stupid."

The Toyota came to another uncontrolled intersection. It reduced its speed before proceeding through. Once it passed through, it turned into the first driveway on the right.

Salter didn't even bother looking at the driver as they passed by. Mel did, though, and the confused look from a citizen who'd just been followed by a cop for several blocks reflected back to her.

"Sounds like your job is harder than I thought."

She turned to him. Mel wanted to ask about what had just occurred—the random following of a citizen—but she'd been having a conversation with Salter. It seemed important to continue that.

"It's more than just hours or workload that makes it hard," she said. "If it was just teaching the kids and all the schooling and preparation that goes into that, it'd still be tough. But it'd be a whole lot easier without the other stuff."

"What other stuff?"

"You don't want to know."

"Actually, I do." Salter turned south but remained in a residential neighborhood. He constantly scanned out the windshield and side windows, glancing in the side and rearview mirrors regularly. His vigilance had the sense of practiced ease to it. "What do you mean by other stuff?"

"It'll sound like a rant."

"Ask anything, say anything." A trace of a smile lighted on

his lips. "Besides, I think we've already established that this car is an accepted rant zone." He held up his bare ring finger and tapped it with his thumb, repeating his gesture from earlier.

Mel hesitated. She was there to observe and learn about policing, not complain about her job. Besides, the truth was, she loved what she did. But some of the earlier tension between them was bleeding off as they spoke. That seemed like a positive development, one that might bear fruit as the night went on.

"I love the kids," she said. "They are the entire reason I'm there. But outside of them? There are some frustrations. Things they don't tell you about in college unless you get a professor who is willing to talk about the realities and not just the theories."

"Like what?"

"Parents are a big part of it. Not only do they think they know the job better than I do, but some like to remind me that 'I pay your salary.'" She air-quoted the last part and lowered her voice. "They expect me to jump at every request at the exact moment they make it."

Salter exhaled with something that might have been a grunt or a laugh.

"Seriously," Mel said. "Some will email me on a Saturday at ten o'clock at night about little Johnny's grade and expect an answer by ten-fifteen. And if they don't get one, then I'm being unresponsive and uncaring."

She glanced over at Salter. The corner of his mouth twitched upward. She took that as a good sign and continued.

"Ideally, our administration would run interference for us where the more difficult parents are concerned, and sometimes they do. But it seems like once teachers get promoted into admin, they start forgetting about what it's like in the classroom. Not just when it comes to parents but the work itself. They are constantly asking us to do 'one more small thing'," she air-quoted again, "not realizing that we've got about a hundred so-called small things on our plate already. If I used my prep period just to address all their small things, I still wouldn't have enough time to finish them, much less prepare lessons or grade."

Mel took a breath. She'd only scratched the surface but worried that she'd already said too much. Still, Salter's expression was receptive, even slightly amused. That encouraged her to finish her thought, at least.

"I'm supposed to be teaching kids. That's my job. But a lot of the time I'm expected to be more of a social worker, or a nutritionist, or a counselor. Essentially, a safety net for whatever the kids aren't getting elsewhere. Some parents expect me to not just teach their kids but to raise them, too. And yet some of these same parents bring up their kids not to like school or to respect teachers, so that just makes things more difficult. Some kids see me as a villain or a taskmaster. You hear it in the things they say. 'My mom makes me come to school,' and the like."

She shook her head.

"Worst of all," she continued, "I'm supposed to have this huge impact on this kid's life, right? And to accomplish this monumental feat, I get them for less than one hour a day in my class. Along with thirty-five other kids. That averages out to less than two minutes a day with a kid. And I'm supposed to fix their world?"

While she spoke, Salter's amused expression broadened unmistakably into a grin.

"What's so funny?" she asked, feeling like maybe he was mocking her. If he was, she decided it was her own fault for going off on a rant in the first place. Another teacher might understand, but she doubted he did. Most likely, she sounded ridiculous to him.

"Nothing's funny," Salter replied. He braked for a four-way stop, then continued straight ahead. "I just never thought about those dynamics in relation to teaching. I kinda thought it was a cake job, like I said."

"You're not alone." Mel sipped her chai and looked out the window at the passing houses. Maybe it had been a mistake to open up like that. She should have known better. A truce or a treaty was one thing. Holding forth on her own career was another. "Anyway, sorry for going off like that."

"Don't be. How long did you say you've been teaching?"

"Eighteen years."

Salter whistled. "I've only been on the job for fourteen."

She made a neutral sound and drank some more chai.

"You want to know why I was smiling?"

"I don't know. Making fun of me?"

"Not at all. I was commiserating."

Mel turned her head slightly and gave him a sideways glance. "With what?"

"Everything you said." Salter turned back onto an arterial. "It's all in police work, too. Point for point."

"It's not the same," she said automatically.

Salter nodded. "Oh, it pretty much is. Public demands. Unrealistic expectations. Out of touch bosses. A million 'just one more thing' tasks that have little or nothing to do with the core mission. That's my world, too. The details are different, but the big picture is exactly the same."

Mel didn't answer right away. She sorted through what she'd said and tried to work out the parallel. "I don't see it," she ventured weakly, no longer certain that was true.

"Trust me," he said. "It's almost identical. Right down to the 'I pay your salary' part. I get that one so often, I've had to come up with four or five good comebacks to keep my head from exploding."

She thought of several standard teacher responses to "I pay your salary."

"What's the comeback?" she asked.

"Sometimes, if I'm trying to keep things light, I'll say thanks," Salter said. "Then I'll add that my kids also thank them. That disarms some people. Pisses some off, too. Other times, I'll just ask them for a raise."

A smile crept onto her lips at that.

Salter chuckled a little. "If I'm feeling like a smart ass, then I offer to give them their nickel back if they'll shut up and go away."

Her smile faded. "You really say that to people?" She couldn't imagine saying that to a parent. If she did, she'd have her principal to contend with, or the district superintendent, depending on how far the outraged parent wanted to take things.

"Once in a while. You have to pick your moments if you don't want to end up with a complaint." Salter tapped a key on the computer and glanced down at the return. Then he said, "I get what you said about having an impact, too. People expect me to respond to a call and in the twenty minutes I spend there, I'm supposed to fix a problem that's been years in the making. Meanwhile, what are they doing except causing the problem in the first place?"

Mel thought about that. It closely resembled her opinion that parents had far more influence on a kid than she did as a teacher. Their expectations of what she could accomplish in the short time she had with each kid was out-sized.

"Sometimes," Salter said, "I feel like an overpaid babysitter rather than a cop, you want the truth."

"I think I'm in touch with that emotion."

"So, I suppose you're right," he said. "Our jobs aren't that similar."

She glanced at him, trying to detect sarcasm. "No?"

"Nope. Not similar. They're basically the same." He flashed her a smile, then looked back out to the road.

Mel sipped her chai and ran the conversation through her head. There were some parallels, she had to admit. Some of them were ones that she hadn't considered before. Then her mind snagged on something huge.

"You may be right," she said. "But there's one major difference."

"What's that?"

"You're not going to like it."

His confident, smiling expression didn't change. "I'm used to bad news," he said. "Hit me with it."

Mel took a measured breath. Then she said, "You don't see videos on the news of teachers killing an unarmed black man."

Salter's smiled faded. "You're right," he said flatly. The mask of resting cop face had fallen back into place. "I don't like that."

Chapter 7

LEE

For a short while there, he thought it might get better. After their initial flare-up, the air seemed to clear somewhat. Still uneasy but not as rife with tension. It was clear that she was making an effort, and that went a long way with him. Then she opened up some, sharing her own frustrations as a teacher. Teaching always seemed an easy gig to him, but as she piled up issue after issue, his perspective shifted. The entire exchange amused him because everything she said applied to his job as well. Perhaps they weren't so different after all.

He told her so.

She still didn't appear to like the idea very much. "They might be similar in some ways," she said, "but there's one huge difference."

"What's that?"

"You won't like it."

"I deal in bad news all day, every day," he said, smiling his assurance. "Hit me."

Weaver took a deep breath. Then she dropped the bomb on him. "You don't see videos on the news of teachers killing an unarmed black man."

Lee's smile slackened. A shimmer of anger lighted across his shoulders. His jaw flexed. The air between them seemed to crackle with tension again. "You're right," he said, struggling to keep his tone even. "I don't like that."

Weaver nodded slightly. "I know, but it's true."

Lee drove in silence. The massive wall that existed between what he experienced on the job and what the rest of society thought about the police seemed impenetrable. There were so many factors that he never knew for certain which ones to address first, even when talking with family and friends. In most instances, the topic was skirted, lumped in with politics and religion as territory strewn with relationship land mines.

As he drove, he could sense Weaver waiting. He knew it was his move. She was going to wait for his response, and that would define the rest of their time together. Maybe he was wrong about that, but he didn't think so.

He took his time. Several blocks of businesses rolled by outside his window. His frustration simmered while different lines of argument ran through his mind. None of them seemed likely to make a dent with someone who was a board member of the Police Reform Initiative.

But then he thought about how she seemed to listen to him when he explained about his wedding band. And hadn't her own career frustrations mirrored what he experienced in law enforcement? So maybe there was a chance.

Maybe he should just do what Gelabert suggested—work his shift and not talk about what didn't need to be talked about. Nothing good would come of it, anyway.

But he had to try to talk to her, didn't he? Because if he didn't try, then things definitely wouldn't change. Or they'd change in ways that didn't consider him or his profession.

"Let's put a pin in that for a little while," he said carefully.

"Put a pin in what, exactly?"

He listened closely to her tone, but it was difficult to interpret. Guarded? Resigned? A little on edge? It could be all three.

"The controversial videos. Let's come back around to those."

"Why don't you want to talk about them now?" Now her tone was unmistakable—sharp and confident, as if she knew exactly why he wanted to avoid the topic.

He kept his voice calm and even. "You teach history, right?"

"Yes."

"And to understand history, it's important to understand context. True?"

"Of course."

"So, let's talk about some context first. Because if all you want to do is glom onto one particular video or another and how the media has spun it, and then use that to characterize all of law enforcement, I'm not interested in having that conversation." He glanced over at her. "At least not yet."

"I wasn't going to do that," Weaver said. "But for the record, there are far, far more incidents to 'glom onto' than just one."

"I'm sure." Lee said, trying not to let too much sarcasm seep into his voice.

"And there's plenty to examine locally," she added. "Tyler Garrett, for example. Raymond Zielinski. And the ongoing consent decree."

Lee winced slightly. Garrett was an unquestionable blemish. He'd known the officer passingly and had respected him as much as everyone else. He was shocked at the revelations of his actions and felt almost personally betrayed by the man. In the quiet conversations he'd had with other officers, he wasn't alone in that. Garrett had dirtied the badge. Lee wanted nothing more than to write him off as a criminal.

Zielinski was another matter but no better from a public relations standpoint. He was seen as a cop who used his position inappropriately. There were some on the department who muttered that Zielinski's wrongdoings were at least directed at a criminal. Garrett's violations made him one himself.

And then there was the consent decree. Having DOJ hovering over the department, issuing orders disguised as suggestions, was a pain in the ass for everyone.

To avoid answering immediately, Lee homed in on an approaching Honda. He thought of the Accord as a truly egalitarian model, owned by everyone from college age kids to yuppies who couldn't afford a Subaru. But it was also a favorite of criminals. Usually, the year and condition of the car was a good indicator. If it was older and beat to hell, a struggling worker bee or a dirtbag criminal was in the driver's seat.

He felt Weaver's eyes on him as the Honda drew closer. A young woman in a waitressing uniform was behind the wheel. Satisfied, he glanced over at Weaver.

"I'm just asking for a bit of a reprieve," he said. "Save the tough sledding for a little later?"

Mel looked uncertain.

"Treaty, remember?"

She stared back at him, then slowly nodded. "All right. I can go along with that. What's the context you're referring to, then?"

That she relented surprised him a little, though maybe it shouldn't have. He shifted in his seat and took a moment to think. Out of habit, he checked the calls holding on the MDC. A cold burglary report had popped up on the other side of the sector. A suspicious circumstances call showed as well.

"Just a second," he murmured, and called up the details of the SUS-CIR. He scanned the text, glancing back and forth between the road and the screen, reading in short snatches. The complainant's description of three young white males in hoodies walking through the neighborhood and peering into cars left little to the imagination. Vehicle prowlers, searching for worthwhile targets. There'd been a spate of these in that area recently. Lee wondered if these were the same shitheads responsible. It was always possible.

He punched the self-dispatch button. The MDC beeped in response and assigned him to the call. He quickly added the notation "C4" so that the dispatcher and his fellow officers would know he was code four on the call, not requiring any back up.

Lee looked up at Weaver. "There are some possible vehicle prowlers over on Hartson that I'm going to check out."

Weaver nodded that she understood. "We can talk about this later."

"I can multi-task," he assured her. He drove for a few seconds, then said, "When I said context before, I meant it broadly. There's the context of every individual situation, but then there's also the context of policing in general. Does that make sense?"

"The first part does. I'm not exactly sure what you mean by the second part."

"Okay. Well, just to be clear, let me say this about the individual situation part. Whenever I see one of those videos play on the news, do you know what goes through my mind?"

Weaver didn't answer right away. Finally, she said, "I literally have no idea."

"My first thought is always the same," Lee said. "I wasn't there." He let the thought sit for a moment then repeated it. "I... wasn't... there. Therefore, I don't know all the facts about the situation. I don't know the details surrounding the call, what the officers knew going in, or what happened before the video started. I tell myself this because it reminds me to withhold judgment until I do know those things. If they're knowable."

Weaver sipped her drink. Then she said, "That sounds reasonable and maybe even scientific, in a way. But it is also a convenient way not to have to face the ugliness of some of those videos."

"That's not it."

"I think it might be," she said, and held up her thumb and forefinger slightly apart. "A little bit."

Lee shook his head. "It's simply the right approach—an investigator's approach. Look, you just said how people who never taught a day in their lives think they know all about your job and how you should teach, right?"

She nodded.

"Well," Lee said, "it's the same in police work, believe me. People don't always know what it is they saw."

"Some of it is pretty clear. A beating doesn't leave much to doubt."

"Maybe so, maybe not. All I'm saying is that I try not to jump to conclusions. I wait for the facts. Most of the media, people who are anti-police, they don't wait because those facts don't matter to them. They already have a desired outcome. They want it to be bad for the police. It's confirmation bias."

Weaver's eyes narrowed slightly. "Even if that's true, you don't think the police have confirmation bias, too? You want it to be justified, no matter what."

Lee hesitated, giving her statement some thought. "All right," he conceded. "Good point. Of course, I *hope* it's justified. But the point is, I wait for the facts."

"Facts are seen through the lens of our biases," Weaver said. "Knowing facts doesn't always pierce those biases, especially if the ideas are entrenched. Seemingly contrary evidence can even serve to reinforce them."

Lee narrowed his eyes. "I don't see how that could work. Facts are facts."

"If you don't believe me, try reasoning with a flat-earther sometime. Or any conspiracy theorist."

"I'm not talking about crazy people here. I'm talking about regular folks."

"And I'm talking about deep-seated beliefs that permeate someone's identity," Weaver said. "Beliefs that drive bias."

"I'm not biased."

"*Everyone* is biased," Weaver said. "It's the human condition."

"Fine, but that's not what I meant. I mean being prejudiced. Or racist." Suddenly, he felt like he was back in the academy class on cultural awareness. He remembered how he'd been excited for the lesson, hoping to learn different elements of the cultures present in the city so he could interact with those people better while on patrol. Instead, he got an eight-hour dose of being told by a rainbow coalition of instructors that, as a white male heterosexual, he was the reason for all the world's ills. The entire lesson seemed like one long accusation and the only thing Lee could remember getting out of it was a sense of resentment. Now, he realized he was throwing up some of the same defensive walls he'd used back then.

The realization irritated him. He shouldn't have to defend himself. He wasn't a racist. Or a misogynist. Or a homophobe. Yet, it seemed like a lot of people out there assumed all of that and more by default, somehow shifting the burden onto him to prove otherwise.

The sense of irritation put him on his heels. He simmered quietly for a moment.

"I never said you were a racist," Weaver continued. "I only said you were biased, like every other human. I'm biased, too. And one of your biases happens to be toward believing the police."

"That's because I should!" Lee said, forcefully. He took a left-hand turn, heading south.

"It's also because you want to." Weaver's tone was quiet but firm.

"What I want has nothing to do with it."

"Sure, it does. For fourteen years, you've been part of the police culture. Maybe longer if you had cops in the family."

"I did," Lee admitted, suddenly reluctant. When Weaver waited expectantly, he added, "My granddad. My father, too."

"Here, at this department?"

He nodded. "I'm third generation SPD."

"Even more to my point," Weaver said. "Your culture, your identity, is police. That creates bias, whether you intend it to or not. And that bias is a lens through which you see everything. *Especially* videos of police misconduct."

"Alleged," Lee said automatically.

"Fine. Alleged. Because you withhold judgment."

"You say that like it's a bad thing."

"Waiting for all the facts is obviously a good policy. We should all avoid jumping to conclusions. What I'm saying is that our own biases color how we see those facts, regardless of when they become available."

Lee shook his head. "My job is to be objective," he insisted. "Regardless of my opinion, I don't get to choose the facts. Facts are what they are. The truth is the truth."

"Yeah, but whose truth?"

He cocked his head. "The truth is objective. That's what makes it the truth."

"Okay," Weaver said easily. "We're going in circles a little bit here. You had a point about context?"

He paused, needing a moment to reset. He took a deep breath. Then he glanced down at the MDC to see if there was an update to the suspicious circumstances call. He saw nothing new.

"It's kind of a big concept," he admitted. "I don't know if I can get it across."

"Try me."

He forced a weak smile. "You won't like it."

She chuckled softly. "I'm used to getting bad news. I can take it."

He was glad for the small moment of banter that the callback provided. The temperature in the car had steadily risen, and the exchange, however minor, seemed to relieve some of the pressure.

"Like you said about teaching," Lee said, "people don't know as much as they think about police. They think they do, but they don't. They don't understand how we're trained or why we do things a certain way. They always *assume* malice."

Lee slowed and turned onto Hartson, a residential side street. He punched the on-scene button, making the MDC beep in response. He kept the car's speed down, rolling at a near crawl through the neighborhood. His eyes scanned the street and sidewalks while he spoke.

"We show up to a dynamic, rapidly evolving situation, usually with incomplete information, and we handle it in a reasonable manner according to our training and experience. These people, who have *no* training and *no* experience, who see one little snippet of the entire situation, make a snap judgment about not only what they saw out of context but also about the intent of the officer." Lee shook his head, not looking at Mel while he kept his eyes moving and searching for the suspects. "They don't understand the context of that situation, and they also don't understand the greater context of the profession that comes into each of those situations—the sum of all the knowledge and experience of the officers involved."

Lee peered in between the houses as he passed them. Sometimes vehicle prowlers saw headlights and hid, though it was a little early for that behavior. There was still enough reason for pedestrian traffic to make hiding in plain sight the better strategy. At four in the morning, when the only legitimate people moving at that time were newspaper delivery people, cops, and bakers, three young males walking around stood out more.

"If you see anyone suspicious," Lee said, "sing out."

"Suspicious," she mused. "What's that look like?"

"Someone busting into a car qualifies." He glanced at her and grinned slightly. "But, right now, suspicious means three young white males in hoodies."

"All right." They were quiet for a few seconds. Then Weaver said, "You know, there's some irony in what you just said."

"The three white males in hoodies part?"

"No. The no one understands the police part."

"They don't. They just think they do. How's that ironic?"

"Even if your statement is true, part of the reason people don't understand is because the police are so secretive, so closed to the public. You don't explain yourselves. You seem to bristle at the very idea. You certainly don't let people in to monitor or to learn. And then you complain that no one understands you."

He glanced at her again. "Blame the victim, huh?"

"Victim?"

"Just kidding," he said. "And what do you call DOJ being here for this consent decree?"

"I'd call that earned," she said.

Lee didn't respond right away. She had a point, he knew. A

lot of law enforcement's public relations wounds were self-inflicted. But the problem was the same one he faced with Weaver right now—explaining a complex situation that required ten thousand words or none. Some things couldn't accurately be condensed into a sound bite and still be true.

They were both silent for a few moments. Lee kept his eyes moving, looking for even a single white male in a hoodie. A middle-aged white male walked his dog with a kid in tow. The dog, a pit bull with a chain leash, strained to move forward and the man leaned back to compensate. On the other side of the street, two black males in puffy jackets stood, deep in conversation. He eyed both sets of people as he passed but neither group even approximated the description of the subjects in the call.

He tapped a few keys on the MDC again, double-checking the delay. The text showed the call was entered into the system fifteen minutes ago, so as these things go, it was fairly recent. But it was also plenty of time for the suspects to be well out of the area. People can move surprisingly fast on foot, even if they're pausing to look for easy opportunities to prowl a vehicle.

Lee turned off Hartson Avenue and went a block south to Seventh. He slowed almost to a stop in the middle of the uncontrolled intersection and looked up and down the street but saw nothing. He hooked to the left and rolled east, watching.

Her last words rang in his ears as he drove. Then the obvious thought struck him. "You said we don't let people in?"

"Not unless you have to."

"But you're here."

"You said that before."

He shrugged. "It bears repeating. You're here, a vocal critic of the police."

"There wasn't a lot of choice in it for you. Councilman Lofton had the slot and he used it."

"Maybe so, but we're talking, right?"

"We are."

"So that's something." He broke away from scanning for vehicle prowlers and met her gaze. "It's gotta be something, right?"

Chapter 8

MEL

"That's gotta be something, right?"

He sounded defensive.

She'd seen it often among her students, whenever their work or beliefs were challenged. Defense mechanisms were human nature, of course, and she knew she had some of her own. Unfortunately, they rarely proved easy obstacles.

Salter hadn't been joking when he said he could multitask. The officer drove purposefully toward his destination, guiding the car and operating the computer simultaneously. The seeming hypocrisy of the latter irked her once more. The recent public awareness campaign in the media was still fresh in her mind. For him to continually blatantly disregard the same rules that the public was browbeat over and received traffic citations for violating reeked of an 'above the law' mindset.

He seemed to be waiting for her reply, so she nodded slowly. "A ride-along like this is a good start."

"Yeah," he said. He seemed to think to himself for a moment, then repeated, "Yeah."

She decided to let it go at that, at least for a little while. Allow things to settle for a bit before tackling some more. She sipped her chai and watched the houses crawl by. Salter continued his methodical search, turning down several side streets.

Mel saw a few pedestrians. None came close to the description Salter gave. "You said you were a third-generation cop?" she asked.

"That's right."

"That's quite a tradition."

He looked sideways at her, as if searching for hidden sarcasm. Mel returned his gaze with an open expression. "You

---

could say that," he finally said. "It comes with expectations."

"How so?"

Salter shifted in his seat. "My dad climbed the ranks. He was a captain when he retired." He shrugged. "But that's not for me."

"No?"

"I like patrol. It's where I can do the most good. And I don't have to deal with politics." His eyes flicked to her and away again. "Most of the time."

She let the comment pass. "What about your grandfather?"

"He made captain, too, right at the end of his career. But his biggest role was as a sergeant and lieutenant. He headed up all the best units in the department. Hell, he helped found several of them—SWAT, K-9, Hostage Negotiators." Salter drummed the steering wheel briefly. His mask slipped a little as a wistful expression crossed his face. "He really was a legend. A cop's cop, for sure."

Mel was surprised she'd never heard of either of them. Then again, her interest in what her father did for a living began and ended with the fact that he was an authority figure to rebel against. And her study of the police department since joining the PRI was focused more on current affairs than its history.

"Anyway," Salter said, "it's a lot to live up to."

"Sounds like it."

"What about you? Were your parents teachers?"

"My mother," she answered. "My father was a police officer."

Surprise registered on Salter's face. "Really?"

She nodded.

"Where at?"

"Here in Spokane."

"SPD?"

She nodded again.

"Who was he?"

"Roy Hurst."

Salter's eyebrows went up. He drove in silence for a few moments. Then he muttered, "Roy Hurst... no kidding."

"Did you know him?"

He shook his head. "No, he was years before my time. But I remember the funeral. I went with my dad and grandad. There were a lot of cops there, especially since he died on duty."

"It was a heart attack," she said. "He just happened to be in uniform when it occurred."

"I know. He was in the middle of writing a ticket on a traffic stop, wasn't he?"

"Something like that."

"I'm sorry," Salter said.

She waved a hand. "It was a long time ago."

"It was a big deal back then, as I recall. The police officer's union set up a scholarship award in his memory." He glanced at her. "Probably helped you get through college, huh?"

"I never applied for it."

Salter opened his mouth to reply, then the officer's attention locked on to something outside the car. She followed his gaze to a single kid in a blue hoodie striding down the sidewalk, backpack slung over one shoulder. He pulled up closer, eyeing the kid from behind as they approached. When he'd pulled even with him, the kid glanced over. He started to look away, then did a double take. His eyes widened.

Salter lowered the passenger window. He leaned in her direction to peer out at the kid, whose pace had slowed to a near stop.

"Evening," Salter said. The greeting boomed with authority.

"Huh... hi," the kid squeaked.

"You live around here?"

"Yeah." The kid cleared his throat and pointed to a house halfway up the block. "Right there."

Salter nodded his understanding. "What's your name?"

"Dan."

"Dan what?"

"Dan Quince."

"You're out a little late, Dan."

The kid just stared back at him.

"Coming from a friend's house or something?" Salter asked.

"No, sir. I just got off work."

"Yeah, huh? Where do you work?"

Dan pointed back the direction he'd come. "Fratello's Pizza."

"Over on Freya?"

Dan nodded.

"They've got good pies," Salter said. "You like working there?"

He shrugged. "It's a job. I get free pizza, so yeah, I guess."

"Well, good for you, Dan. Hey, you see a group of three or so kids about your age, wearing hoodies like yours, wandering around the neighborhood? Maybe checking cars?"

Dan shook his head. "No, nothing like that."

"All right. Well, thanks for your help."

Dan gave him an unsure expression. "You're welcome."

"Have a good night."

As Salter rolled up the window and started forward, Dan raised a tentative hand and mouthed, "You, too."

Salter continued his search.

The conversation played over in her head. It wasn't so much a conversation, though. More of a veiled interrogation.

"You really ever eat at Fratello's?" she asked him.

"Only occasional takeout."

"Can I ask you something else?"

"Ask anything, say anything," he reminded her.

"You talked to that kid because he...?"

He shrugged a single shoulder. "Because he matched the description in the call."

"But he was alone."

"Criminals do this thing sometimes," Salter said dryly,

"where they split up."

"I don't think he was a criminal."

"Neither do I."

"But you talked to him because he matched the description."

"Why is that so hard to understand?"

"It's not. But what I don't understand is this: a few blocks back, there was a pair of black kids standing on the sidewalk, remember?"

"Yes."

"And you gave them a long look."

"A long look?" He shook his head. "I don't think so."

"You checked them out."

"Yeah. So?"

"So, they don't match the description. They weren't wearing hoodies. They weren't white. And there were only two of them."

"That's why I didn't stop to talk to them."

"But you still checked them out."

Salter lifted his hand from the wheel. "What do you want from me? I can't know that they don't fit the description if I don't check them out first. See, that right there is the problem with a lot of the criticism we get."

"That problem being…?"

"You look at a situation *after* the fact with all the available information. Then you want to go back and hold us to some kind of standard or judge our intent as if we had all of that same information beforehand. Not only is that unfair, it's unrealistic." He jerked his thumb toward the rear of the car. "I'm looking for vehicle prowlers on foot. Three of them. While in the area, I see two figures walking down the street. Of *course*, I looked at them. Once I see they don't match the clothing or race description, I move on. Because now I know *those* facts. But people like you take that knowledge and try to go back and somehow find fault with me looking at them in the first place because they're black and don't fit the

---

90

description. Like I'm being racist or profiling."

She absorbed his point. "All right," she said carefully. "But had you stopped to talk to those two, would you see why I might question the motivation?"

"No."

Her brow scrunched. "Why not?"

"First off, I didn't. I drove on. Because I focus on facts and behavior. I don't have a hidden agenda to target a certain race."

"I said *if*."

"Fine, *if* I had stopped to talk to them, what's the problem with that? Maybe they saw our suspects roaming around."

"That's not what I meant, and I think you know it."

"I only know what you're saying, so help me out here."

"All too often," Mel said, "young black men are stopped by police, supposedly randomly or on flimsy suspicion. Can you see why people have a problem with that?"

"I have a problem with the premise," Salter said. He turned down another side street. "I don't think it's accurate."

"Studies have proven it."

"What studies?"

Mel motioned toward her purse. "I can pull them up on my phone if you want. But study after study has shown that people of color are disproportionately stopped by police. It's a statistical fact."

"You can do pretty much anything you want with statistics," Salter said, but his voice lacked conviction.

"If it was just one study, that argument might have some merit. But it's been replicated multiple times. How do you explain that?"

Salter shrugged. "I don't have to. It's not my job to explain what some social scientist thinks he figured out in some study. I can only speak to my own actions and experience."

"What about the broader context of policing?" Mel asked. "You were just expounding on that a few minutes ago."

Salter was quiet for a moment. Then he said, "What I'm hearing from you is that you think cops are motivated by race.

That we stop people because of the color of their skin."

"I'm absolutely saying that because it's true."

"No, it's not. At least, not in the vast majority of the cases."

"That's not what the research has found."

"Researchers have biases, too, and research can be flawed. All it takes is for there to be one variable that they don't account for, and the results get skewed."

Mel frowned, dubious. "The sheer volume of the research would argue against that."

"The sheer volume of the situation is the problem." Salter waved his hand vaguely toward the windshield. "It's not a laboratory out there. It's messy and there are lots of moving parts. Even if you accept the statistics, and I'm not sure I do, the conclusion is bullshit."

"Bullshit?" She raised a brow at the word.

He glanced sideways at her. "They take their numbers, and they infer intent. That's one hell of a leap, and believe me, getting inside someone's head is not easy to do. It's tricky. Proving intent is hard. For example, some charges require intent as an element of the crime, and it can be a big hurdle."

"Fine," she agreed. "But we're not talking about an individual here. We're talking about a much larger group and a pattern of behavior across that group. And those patterns are easier to draw conclusions from."

"That cops are racist," Salter stated flatly.

"No, not exactly." She considered for a moment. "Maybe a better way to put it is that police take action based upon race."

"Which is, by definition, racist."

"True," she conceded. "But I think you could argue that in some cases the biases are implicit, not overt."

He thought about that while he drove. Finally, he sighed. "I don't think we're finding these little vehicle prowlers." He punched a button on the computer terminal. After another few moments, he said, "Implicit, huh? So, we're racist but we don't know it?"

That actually made her smile slightly. "That's one way to

look at implicit bias, I suppose. I mean, the reality is that policing is a racist institution. Anyone operating in that system helps promulgate that racism. But that doesn't necessarily mean each of those individual members are overtly racist."

"They just don't know better."

"Ehhhhhhh... they're unaware. Or clouded by their own biases."

"All of that sounds like someone's master's thesis, if you want the truth."

She pressed her lips together and lifted her shoulders slightly. "It probably was. More than one, I'm sure. But that doesn't make it untrue."

Salter shook his head. "I'm going back to what I said before. I reject the premise. Policing is a racist institution? Come on."

Mel blinked at that. She stared at Salter in silent disbelief.

It took him several long seconds to notice. Then his eyes narrowed slightly. "What?"

"Seriously?" Mel asked. "Do you not know the history of policing?"

"Of course, I do. Sir Robert Peel was my grandfather's personal hero. He made me memorize Peel's Principles of Policing while I was still in middle school."

"Peel was British."

"I know."

"I'm talking about American policing."

"Peel has had a huge influence on police in America."

"Less than he should," Mel said.

"Times change but principles don't."

Mel suppressed a tickle of irritation. Did he really not know, or was he being purposefully argumentative?

"You know the two biggest roles the police have had in early American history?" she asked, struggling to keep her voice neutral.

"Protect and serve?"

She considered, then nodded. "Exactly."

Salter rode in silence for a few seconds. When she didn't follow up, he glanced over at her. "That's it? I figured you had something more to say."

"Nope, you hit it on the head. Protect and serve." She waited a beat before she spoke again. "Of course, what they protected was the institution of slavery—"

"Whoa!"

"— and they served the direct interests of the political bosses."

Salter shook his head. "Come on, that's insane."

"It's true. Early police departments in this country were regularly deployed as slave catchers."

"Maybe in the deep south but—"

"Everywhere. And it wasn't a one-off, either. It was part of their primary mission."

Salter's mouth was a hard line. "Look, I don't agree with slavery. Let's be clear about that."

"But?"

"But nothing. Even if what you're saying is true, it happened when slavery was the law of the land. The police didn't create the law. They enforced it."

"Yet those laws were racist. By vigorously enforcing them, policing was a racist institution. And it didn't stop once slavery ended, thanks to decades of Jim Crow laws."

"Society made those laws."

"You're right. And the police enforced them."

"That was a long time ago."

"Not as long as we'd all like to think. And the hangover effects of those hundreds of years are still driving events today." She paused, sipping her nearly empty cup of chai. Next to her, Salter was silent again, though she couldn't tell if he was considering her words or merely fuming over them. "You make a good point, though," she offered. "The police didn't create the laws. The problem is a much wider one."

"We're not the only racists?" Salter's voice was slathered with sarcasm.

Mel ignored his tone. "Not even close. Our entire political system is inherently racist. So is health care, religion, and—"

"Education?"

She didn't hesitate. "Of course, education."

"But teachers aren't racist. Only cops."

"I didn't say that."

"Sounded like it."

"Then let me put it this way—teachers are no more or less racist than cops." She lifted her hands. "Okay?"

He nodded grudgingly. "I still don't know if that means you think we're all racist or what."

"The *institution* is clearly racist," Mel explained. "Any objective examination bears that out, time and again. But the individuals who are part of that institution? They're people, so it depends. Some might be overtly racist but not the majority. Everyone has implicit bias though. And our society reinforces those biases."

Salter cocked his head. "I'm not sure I buy all of that. It's not what I see every day."

"That's part of your bias."

"You're making a circular argument."

"I can show you the studies. I can show you the history."

"I might take you up on that, but it sounds like you're saying every public institution in America is inherently racist."

"I am, whether explicitly or implicitly."

"To-may-to, to-mah-to," Salter said. "But if that's the case, then why are you so focused on us? Why not address the issues in politics or health care or education?"

"We need to. And in my work life, I do focus on education."

"This is your fun life?"

She smiled slightly. "The answer to your question is one word—power."

"If you worked my job for a week, you'd see how little power I truly have. You have more as a teacher."

Mel shook her head. "No. I have *influence*. You have power. I can guide a student, try to influence them to learn, to take a particular path. I can't force them to do anything."

"You can fail them."

"True. But up until high school, they still get promoted to the next grade. And even if they don't graduate high school, there are other options available to them. GED programs, for instance. And some people have managed to do just fine without a high school diploma."

Salter's eyebrows went up. "I thought getting a diploma was pretty important."

"It is. It's a major predictor of future success. The impact is huge." She finished the last of her chai which caused a brief gurgle inside the cup. "But I can't force a diploma on a kid. I can only influence them. And whether that influence is large or small, it still doesn't match up to the power of the police. Your ability to take away someone's freedom is unrivaled in our society. You have the authority to take someone's life without a trial or a judge being involved. That's power. Compared to that, what do I have? The ability to give someone a D-minus?"

He pursed his lips. "You don't give F's?"

"That's not the point. You asked why start with the police? I'm telling you the reason is power."

"I get it, but you can't act like that power doesn't come with a ton of limitations and responsibilities."

"As it should."

"As it should," he repeated, agreeing.

They both fell silent for a few seconds. Melody stared out the front windshield as they drove, wondering if any of what she'd said was getting through to Salter. She sensed his resistance. She also sensed some consideration, though it was impossible to know for sure, especially when that mask dropped over his face intermittently.

Up ahead, they approached a four-way stop. From the left cross-street, a late model Mazda 6 slowed briefly, then drove straight through the intersection.

Salter accelerated slightly. He slowed as he neared the

intersection, then rolled through it as well. Accelerating again, he punched a button on his console. Suddenly, the night was awash with red and blue lights from above the police car. A distinct *fwick fwick* sound emanated from the mechanism.

Salter's voice was clipped and professional as he spoke into the microphone.

"Charlie-411, a traffic stop."

Chapter 9

LEE

"Charlie-411, a traffic stop," Lee intoned, turning on his overhead rotators.

"Eleven, go ahead," the dispatcher replied.

He rattled off the location and the license plate of the car in front of them. While Lee spoke, the brake lights ahead flashed. A moment later, the driver pulled to the side of the street. Lee adjusted the patrol car's spotlight to shine directly on the Mazda as they both came to a stop. His actions were automatic, the result of hundreds of traffic stops he'd made. In one fluid motion, Lee put the car into park, brushed the headlights forward to high beam, released his seat belt, grabbed his flashlight, and opened the door.

Then he hesitated. He glanced at Weaver. "You can get out but stay at the front bumper of my car. For safety."

Weaver nodded woodenly.

Lee exited the car. He snapped on his mag light, holding it in his left hand out of habit—his right hand free to quickly reach for his gun if needed. As he neared the rear of the car, he touched the trunk, giving it a slight tug to ensure it was latched normally. He noted the driver's hands were both placed on the wheel at ten and two. The driver stared straight ahead.

Lee shone his flashlight through the rear and the driver's side windows, sweeping the powerful beam around the back seat.

Empty.

He stopped just prior to the door post, illuminating the driver, a black man of roughly forty, dressed casually.

"Good evening, sir," Lee said. "Do you know why I stopped you tonight?"

"No idea," the driver said, his tone clipped.

"You rolled through that stop sign back there."

The man glanced over his shoulder and winced as if noticing the spotlight. He faced forward again.

"Did you mean to do that?" Lee asked. He clarified his question by adding, "Roll through the intersection?"

"I didn't say I did it."

"Okay. I need to see your license, registration, and proof of insurance."

"They're in the glove box."

"All right."

The man leaned and reached with exaggerated slowness. Lee followed his motion with his flashlight. When the glove box popped open, it was strewn with papers and a couple of travel-size tissue containers. The man rummaged for a few moments, eventually finding the documents he was looking for. He closed the glove box and extended the papers toward Lee.

"Hang onto them until you have your license out, too," Lee said.

The man frowned. He kept the proffered paperwork in place while he shifted in his seat to reach into his back pocket. Lee leaned forward, following his right hand with his light. The man's hand emerged with a wallet of worn brown leather. He flipped it open and fished out his driver's license. Then he handed all three documents to Lee.

"You gonna write me a ticket?"

Lee glanced at the paperwork to make sure all were correct. "I haven't determined that yet."

The man grunted.

"Wait here. I'll be back in a few."

Lee backed away, keeping his attention on the driver until he'd reached the rear of the Mazda, then turned and strode quickly to his patrol vehicle. On the way, he cast a couple of backward glances toward the driver.

Weaver stood by the front tire on her side of the car, watching him intently. When Lee climbed into the cruiser, she joined him there. He ignored her, focusing on the task at hand. First, he downgraded his overhead rotators to simple back-and-forth flashers. Then he held up the driver's license so that he could inspect it while keeping the car in front of him in view at the same time. Satisfied that the license was real, he pulled up the appropriate application on the MDC. Lee entered the driver's name and date of birth into the computer, glancing up every few keystrokes to monitor the driver.

"I thought you had scanners for that," Weaver said. "There was something on the news about it."

"We do," Lee said as he continued to type. "Just not everyone yet."

"And graveyard gets it last? Like you told the store manager?"

"Exactly," Lee said.

To be honest, Lee preferred this older method. Scanning the license and printing out a ticket in a few seconds seemed too easy, like a grocery checkout. The process of typing the driver's information into the computer manually gave him time to consider whether to write the infraction or not. And despite the manual nature of it, the operation still went quickly enough.

The local criminal database return was immediate, advising him with a terse beep. Lee examined the man's record. "He has several minor entries," he said for Weaver's benefit. "But his role in all of them is either as victim or witness. His only criminal entry was a dismissed assault charge from twelve years ago. Probably a mutual fight, I'd guess."

In his peripheral vision, Weaver nodded that she understood.

The Department of License database kicked back a return a few moments later. "Valid license with no moving violations within the prior twenty-four months," he reported.

Lee noticed that the dispatcher had already run the registration for him and appended the information to the call in CAD. This served as a convenience for him but also as an additional safeguard in case a traffic stop ever went to hell in a fast way. If that happened, the information was already there, saving the dispatcher valuable seconds in getting the information out to other officers.

"The vehicle reg is clear and matches the driver." He quickly examined the insurance card. "Insurance is a match, too." Then he noticed that the card had expired over a month ago.

Lee considered his course of action but not for long. He decided to issue a verbal warning.

He gathered the documents together and exited the car. Behind him, he heard Weaver follow suit. He kept his focus on the vehicle, repeating the approach with the same caution as he had before. Second approaches could be more dangerous than the initial one, as the driver's anxiety level likely grew as he waited for the outcome of the stop while the officer tended to relax more as the contact went on. He always made a point to remain vigilant.

At the driver's door post, he stopped. The man sat in the same rigid position he'd maintained throughout the stop—hands on the wheel at ten and two, staring straight forward, frowning.

"Sir?" Lee said. "I noticed your insurance card is expired."

The driver's frown deepened. "I got insurance."

"But the card is expired. Do you have another one in the glove box?"

The man shook his head. "The insurance company sent out a new one. It's probably at home on the counter. I forgot to put it in the car."

"All right," Lee said. "I'm not going to issue you any infractions tonight. If I did, it'd be for failing to stop for a stop sign and no proof of current insurance."

"I got insurance," the man repeated.

"I believe you, but do me a favor and swap out the old card with the new one, okay?"

The man hesitated, then nodded. "I will."

"And make sure you come to a complete stop for the four-ways. I know there's not a lot of traffic this late, but it's still an issue of traffic safety."

This time, there was more hesitation before the man gave Lee a grudging nod.

Lee held out the paperwork. "I appreciate your cooperation tonight. You're free to go. Have a good evening."

The man took his papers from him and set about returning them to their proper location. "Yeah, you, too," he muttered.

Lee retreated from the window and back to his patrol car in the same fashion as before. Once inside the car, he shut off the spotlight and dimmed his high beams. He left the flashers on until the man had signaled and pulled away. Then he turned those off as well. He punched his disposition—1D, meaning officer contact, no citation—into the computer and hit send. The MDC beeped, and his status showed clear.

"No ticket?" Weaver asked.

"Nope." Lee pulled away from the curb. Up ahead, the driver he'd just stopped turned left at the next intersection, so he made a point to go straight.

"Can I ask why not?"

"The short answer is discretion," Lee said.

"I get that, but I'm curious about the decision-making process."

"You want me to explain why I didn't write the guy?"

"That a problem?"

"No, but let me ask you something first." He kept his eyes on the road while he drove, considering his words. "Did you see whether that car stopped for the stop sign?"

"I saw him slow down."

"But not stop."

"No, he didn't stop."

"That's right. He rolled right through," Lee said. "Did you notice the driver's race?"

"He was black."

"When did you notice?"

"As soon as I saw him."

"And when exactly was that?"

Weaver hesitated.

Lee waited a few moments, then said, "Let me put it another way. We watched the car go through the stop sign, right? Then I caught up to the car, turned on all my lights, and stopped him. We both got out of the car. I contacted the driver at his door. He gave me his paperwork." He glanced over at her. "Now, my question is, at what point in all of that did you first become aware of the color of his skin?"

Weaver furrowed her brow, thinking.

While he waited, he checked the MDC to see if any calls had queued up during his traffic stop. Units were still out on the fatal collision downtown. A few other calls had disappeared but a new one showed. The label was U-GUEST—an unwanted guest. Lee punched the button to bring up the details.

"I can't say for sure," Weaver finally said.

"I can," Lee replied. "The moment I became aware that the driver was a black man was when I walked up to his window."

He let that sit for a few moments. The MDC beeped but he ignored it.

Weaver didn't answer right away. He wondered if she were going over it in her mind, trying to recreate the events to see if what he said was true. Lee didn't worry about that. The one thing he was fairly certain of at this point was that Weaver was honest. He doubted she would purposefully manufacture a lie that she had noticed the man's race before he did.

When the silence had gone on long enough, Lee decided to emphasize his point. "I didn't know his race when he rolled through the stop sign, or when I decided to initiate a traffic stop. So even if I wanted to target someone because of their race—and I definitely don't—how could I here? I didn't know any more than you did. Unless you remember it differently?"

"No," Weaver said, her tone thoughtful. "I don't remember noticing until I got out of the car to watch you talk to him."

"That's why I get annoyed at the whole 'driving while black' accusation. It assumes I'm targeting drivers because of some racist tendencies inherent within me. I don't. I target behavior. What people *do*. Like running a stop sign."

Weaver cleared her throat. "It didn't seem that egregious," she said. "Him rolling through the intersection this time of night."

"That's a different conversation," Lee said, "and we can have that one, too. But do you know what the number one cause of collisions is in this city?"

"You're going to say stop signs?"

"No," Lee admitted. "It's actually distracted driving. But ignoring a traffic signal—and that includes stop signs—is number two."

"Not drunk driving?"

"Not even in the top three. Speeding is, though." He tapped the wheel momentarily. "All of those are behaviors that are dangerous and likely to cause a crash. That's why they're against the law. So, do I target drivers? You bet. But I target them based on their behavior, not their race. And you just witnessed a perfect example of that."

Weaver was quiet for a few seconds. Then she said, "But you didn't give him a ticket."

"That's the other conversation I mentioned. It's a matter of discretion." Lee took a moment to scan through the unwanted guest call.

Weaver's voice broke in. "Discretion, you were saying?"

"Just a sec." Lee pushed the button to put himself en route to the call, adding a quick notation that he was code four. When he'd finished, he looked over at Weaver. "We're heading to handle an unwanted guest call."

She nodded that she understood but looked at him expectantly.

"Okay," he said, "So here it is: some cops would have written him the ticket, but I chose not to. I took in the totality of the circumstances, and I made a judgment call."

"Are you going to tell me why, or do I need to interrogate you?"

That made Lee smile. "No, I'll explain. Did he commit a violation? Yes. Two, in fact—his insurance card was expired, though I'm pretty sure he's covered. Was his violation a dangerous one? Technically, yes. But in this instance, as you point out, it wasn't reckless. More of a bad habit that could lead to unwanted results down the road."

"So, not egregious."

Lee lifted the corner of his mouth. "*Touché*. Not egregious. And his record was pretty clean. He's not a criminal, just a guy. And in my book, regular people with clean records deserve a break."

"That's it?"

He considered. "No, there's one more thing on top of all that. The way I look at it, some people hardly ever interact with the police. So, if everything else points toward no ticket, and allows me to take a situation like this one and make it a positive experience, that goes a long way toward forming how this person sees us."

Weaver nodded slowly. "I understand."

"Good. That's what I was hoping for."

Hell, he thought, it's what we need.

They rode in silence for several blocks. Then Weaver said, "You make a good point."

"Thanks."

"In fact," she said, "it pretty much validates what I was saying before."

He frowned. "Which was what, exactly?"

"Before, when I said that while individual members might not be racist, but the institution is? I think you just proved it."

Lee stared at her, shaking his head. "How the hell did I do that?"

Chapter 10

MEL

"How the hell did I do that?" Salter almost choked on his words.

She could see he was surprised by what she said. This was another symptom of the problem. His defense mechanism looked to be gearing up again, too. She'd need to walk him through it.

"Let's start with the man you stopped," she said. "How do you think the experience was for him?"

Salter considered. Then he shrugged. "No one likes being stopped by us, but outside of that, I figure overall, things went well."

"You said part of the reason you decided not to write him a ticket had to do with making it a good experience."

"Because it *was* part of the reason," he insisted. "A regular citizen might only have contact with the police once every five years or more. I want them to leave with a positive attitude if I can."

"That's admirable," Melody said.

"Are you being sarcastic?"

"No. I'm reasonably sure there are neighborhoods where your operating theory plays out exactly as you plan."

"But not this neighborhood, you're saying?"

"Let me ask you this— how did the driver act while you talked to him?"

Salter turned left. He checked the rearview mirror before he spoke. "He was a little gruff."

"Did he seem relaxed to you?"

"Not really. Kept his hands on the wheel and stared straight ahead most of the time." Salter glanced at her. "Honestly, I appreciate that. It makes the stop safer for me."

"For him, too."

Salter's eyes narrowed. "He was never in any danger."

"I wonder if he thought so."

"Seeing as how we can't ask him, I guess we'll never know."

Mel nodded slowly. "Not for sure. But do you think it's possible that he kept his hands on the wheel, limited his interaction with you, and moved slowly because it was a learned behavior?"

"Learned how?"

"The same way people learn most things—repetition."

Salter thought as he drove. "You're saying he's been stopped before."

"My guess is that he's been stopped a lot. Him and other black men like him. Over time, he's learned how to navigate that process in the safest way possible."

"You can't know that."

"Not for sure, no. But I think it's a reasonable conclusion."

"I didn't stop him because he's black," Salter insisted, his tone hardening. "You saw. I targeted the stop sign violation. The *behavior*."

"I know."

"So, what exactly is your point? That this guy might have been stopped a lot? How is that my fault?'

"It's not."

"I didn't even write him a ticket."

Mel wondered if that was a decision he made for her benefit. She decided it probably wasn't. At least, not entirely. But it had to be a factor, if only subconsciously.

"Did he seem happy about that?" she asked.

"He wasn't *unhappy* about it."

"You know what I mean."

Salter pursed his lips in thought. "He was a little gruff through the whole stop, like I said. And he didn't seem exactly appreciative for the break I gave him, either."

"If you'd been stopped ten times already this year, how grateful would you feel?"

"Now it's ten times?" Salter scoffed. "You're making some leaps here. For all we know, that was the first time he's been stopped in years."

Mel fiddled with the empty coffee container. "Let's come at this a little differently. Do you have an assigned area to patrol?"

"Sure. Charlie sector. All of the south side of Spokane."

"That's more than a quarter of the city. Do you spend your time equally across all the neighborhoods?"

"No. I respond to calls wherever they happen, and when I patrol, I focus on higher crime areas."

"Like where?"

Salter turned up his hand with a flourish and gestured outside the windshield.

Mel twisted the plastic top slowly. "This neighborhood has a higher population of black and Hispanic residents than most of the city."

"That doesn't matter. It's a high crime area. Crime is a behavior, and I focus on behaviors, remember?"

"Would you say you patrol more in a high crime area than a lower crime area?"

"Of course. That's just smart deployment. Otherwise, we'd spend most of our time driving from the lower crime areas to get to calls in the higher crime areas."

"So, if someone lives in a high crime area, the chances of getting stopped for a minor infraction are greater than elsewhere."

"I suppose."

She looked over at him. "Considerably higher?"

He shrugged.

"I guarantee you the man you stopped just now has been stopped multiple times before."

"I don't know about that," Salter said. "But the fact is, he ran the stop sign."

"He did. And it's possible that every time he's been stopped, it was for a legitimate reason. But you said his record was clean. It factored into your decision to not write him a ticket. You said he was not a criminal, just a guy. Right?" She stared at him for confirmation.

"I said that," he admitted. "So what?"

"So, if you're just a guy and not a criminal, how many times does it take getting stopped for minor infractions before it starts to feel like something more is going on? That the reason isn't just the stop sign or whatever but you and the color of your skin?"

Salter scowled. "I didn't write him," he repeated. "He ran the four-way, but I gave him a warning. That's it."

"If this was the sixth or eighth or tenth time this year he's been stopped, you can understand why he wasn't falling all over himself to thank you for the break."

"Even if it was," Salter said, "and you have no proof of that, but even if it was, he should be happy I'm patrolling here. It's a high crime area."

"Based on what?"

"Statistics. Crime Analysis pulls all the data. They make fancy heat maps, predictive models, the whole shmear. And if you looked at one of those maps, you'd see that where we are driving around right now is in the center of a big red blob." He raised his brows slightly. "A hot spot in the middle of a high crime area."

Mel was aware of this already. The department's crime figures were made public, albeit delayed by more than a month. The data was available to police operations much sooner but held back for what Chief Baumgartner called "pressing strategic reasons." She expected that to be one of many things that the consent decree forced to change.

"What makes it a high crime area?" she asked.

"I just told you. Crime statistics."

"All crimes?"

Salter nodded.

"Which includes citizen report calls and officer-initiated stops."

"Yes, both."

Mel glanced at a late-night jogger as they passed by. "Are the citizen calls for service higher in this neighborhood than elsewhere in the city?"

Salter seemed to think about it then shrugged. "I assume so, but I don't know. Do you?"

"I do. Last month, the citizen calls here were the second highest citywide."

"There you go."

"By four percent," she added. "Four percent more than the number three neighborhood, and only six percent higher than the mean. Not an overwhelming number."

"Still higher."

"The rest of the statistics driving the high crime area designator were officer-initiated."

Salter slowed to look at a pair of men working on a car in the street. Even to Melody, it was clearly not suspicious. The open hood, bright work lights, the car up on jack stands, all marked it as above board.

He seemed to reach the same conclusion. Salter gave the men a small wave as they drove past. One of the men stared back. The other returned the wave.

"Sounds to me like patrol officers working hard," he said. "What's the problem?"

"The problem is that the police cause this to become a high crime area by over-patrolling here."

Salter squinted. "You're saying our stops skew the numbers?"

"I'm saying your very presence does."

"No way. We don't create the crime. We respond to it."

"Really? Are you up near Moran Prairie much?"

"Once in a while. There's not much crime there."

"If you patrolled there as much as you patrol here, you might find out there's more crime than you think."

Salter shook his head. "No. We're talking about reported crime. This is a higher crime area, so this is where I need to be."

"And by your presence, this becomes an even higher crime area," Mel said. "And that necessitates your continued presence, which guarantees that the high crime area designation will also continue."

"What are you saying? We should just bail on this neighborhood, where there's more crime happening, and go patrol in low crime areas so that, what? People can't call us racist anymore?"

"I'm asking you to recognize that the way the entire mechanism works inherently focuses on neighborhoods like this, which are traditionally ones of color. That systematically targeting these neighborhoods creates a self-perpetuating result. That's the policing institution and what I meant when I said the institution itself is racist."

They drove in silence for several blocks. Then Salter said, "I patrol here more often than places like Moran Prairie because there's plenty of good people in this neighborhood that deserve police protection, too."

"They do, but they pay a price for it. And I don't mean just in taxes."

Salter stewed while he drove. "This is the problem with what you're saying: we can't win. If we don't patrol here, then we're scrimping on service because the population is black and brown. But if we focus on it because it's a high crime area, then we're over-policing minorities. Either way, we're wrong, so I figure the best thing to do is follow the statistics."

"That's fine. But don't be surprised that you're not met with appreciation when someone gets stopped for the umpteenth time, even if you don't write a ticket."

"Again with this." Salter waved his hand. "You don't know how many times that guy's been stopped. Maybe he just doesn't like cops. Or he had a bad day. Or he read on the internet how to act when he gets pulled over. You don't know."

"I don't know his specific experience, but I've seen the

dynamic."

"How?"

"My husband, David. He's black, and he's gone through almost exactly what I described."

Salter's eyes flicked toward her, then back to the road. "Your husband's black?"

"Yes."

"And he's been stopped a lot?"

"Not as much as I imagine the man tonight has been, but more than what is usual."

"What's that?"

"At least once every couple of months," Mel said. "But we live in a nice neighborhood."

"Where's that?"

She smiled tightly. "Moran Prairie."

He scowled. "That feels a little bit like you're setting traps for me."

"Not intentionally."

Salter continued to drive. He checked his computer. Then he said, "So why does he get stopped? Your husband."

"Traffic infractions."

"Like running stop signs?"

"No. He's a careful driver. Much smaller stuff."

"Give me an example."

She tried to remember. "The last time, I think it was for not signaling soon enough before changing lanes."

"That's a legitimate stop."

"I didn't say it wasn't. But I'm willing to bet it's something that happens all day long, all across the city. It's not exactly egregious."

Salter shrugged. "That doesn't make it racist."

"It's not just traffic stops," Mel said. "I told you he's a pilot for Alaska, right? That means he's going through security at different airports all the time. He gets stopped for so-called random checks at least three times more often than his white co-workers."

Salter managed a weak smile. "TSA, you know?"

"It's a widespread problem. It's not just the police." She paused, then added, "And we've recently had to have the talk with our son, Isaac, so that he stays safe. Do you have any idea how hard that is? To talk about that? To explain it to a thirteen-year-old?"

They rode a few blocks. Mel twisted the top to her empty coffee cup while Salter checked the computer and scanned outside the patrol car.

Salter broke the silence. "Say anything, right?"

"Sure. That was the deal."

"I'm sorry about your son. That's hard."

"Thanks. But that's not what you wanted to say."

"Not entirely, no," he said. "It's sad that you had to tell your son how to behave when contacted by the police. But the reality is that it's also smart. Everyone should take that same advice. It'd make the situation safer for them and for me."

"I'd rather we work toward a world where people didn't have to act a certain way to avoid being killed by the police. We shouldn't have to walk on eggshells around the people who are supposed to be there for protection."

Salter remained silent for several moments, his lips compressed into a thin line. Finally, he said, "Not having to worry if the next person I talk to is going to try to kill me would be a wonderful reality. Unfortunately, I don't have that luxury. I have to take things as they really exist."

Melody leaned back slightly, surprised at the cynical defeatism in what he said. "Do you even want things to change?"

"Of course, I do." He glanced sideways at her, his expression tight. "But that requires people to trust each other."

"Obviously." Then she caught something in his tone. Something almost accusatory. "Meaning what, exactly?"

"I feel like you ambushed me with the Moran Prairie thing." Salter bobbed his head a couple of times before adding, "And your husband being black."

"How is that an ambush?"

"You withheld the information to see if I said something you could use against me."

"I didn't."

"It felt that way."

Mel took a deep breath and let it out. A thought occurred to her, and she faced Salter. "What color is your wife?"

His brow wrinkled. "What's that got to do with anything?"

"You never told me. Are you withholding it to see if I say something?"

"It's not the same."

"Why? Because she's white?"

Salter rolled his eyes. "No, because I'm not trying to play a game of gotcha with a teacher."

"Okay." She allowed herself a small smile. "I guess I feel like it shouldn't matter where I live or who my husband is. That's how I approach things."

Salter shook his head. "Everything matters. I wish we lived in a world where it didn't, but we don't."

Mel made an expression of agreement. "But I wasn't trying to trap you. I promise."

He turned down a residential street, slowing the car. Then he looked over at her. "All right. I believe you."

"Good."

He punched a key on the computer, and it beeped. "Anyway, we're here."

Chapter 11

LEE

Lee punched the on-scene button on the MDC, resulting in a beep of confirmation. "Anyway," he said, "we're here."

It annoyed him that Weaver had withheld the information about her husband being black. It felt like a trap, or a test, or... what, exactly?

Suspicion.

A lack of trust.

All of which he expected when it came to the public, but he thought they had reached a truce.

A *treaty*, he corrected.

Then she tried to minimize it with the stupid joke about his wife's color.

"What's this call again?" she asked.

"Unwanted guest," he explained tersely. "Most of the time, these calls are pretty tame. Occasionally, they get mislabeled and are actually DVs." He paused and glanced at her. "Domestic violence. But this one seems straightforward enough."

"How's that?"

"The woman, Doris Beech, wants the man, Jonathan Hite, to leave. Both black, by the way, since we're keeping track."

Her face registered offense. "We're not keeping track."

He paused and thought about arguing the point. Instead, he simply said, "Let's go."

Lee exited the patrol car, easing the door shut out of habit, pushing it hard at the last to close it. When Weaver swung her door shut, it thunked loudly. Lee winced and admonished himself for not addressing it sooner. The conversation had distracted him, which wasn't a place he wanted to be mentally.

The address for the call was technically a single residence, but the entire block was strewn with strips of squat, ground level apartments. Most of them shared at least one wall with another unit. The layout reminded Lee of an old-style campus dormitory.

Weaver trailed him by a few steps as he made his way to the caller's door. He verified the numbers off to the side by illuminating them with his flashlight. Satisfied, he stood next to the door and knocked firmly.

A few seconds later, a black woman opened the door and peered out. She appeared to be in her late forties. She wore a long-sleeved red flannel nightgown that hung past her knees and a pair of fuzzy white slippers. Her face was creased with frustration.

"Ms. Beech?" Lee asked.

"Yes."

"Police, ma'am. You called?"

"I did," she said, swinging the door wider. "Come on in and get this piece of shit out of my house."

"Where's he at?" Lee asked before moving.

"In the kitchen." She pointed almost directly behind herself. "He's drunk."

Lee started forward and Weaver followed.

"Wait. Who are you?" Beech asked Weaver.

"She's with me," Lee said and left it at that.

Beech didn't argue and stood aside for Weaver as well.

Lee saw into the kitchen immediately. In the small apartment, it was only a few strides away. A man, presumably Jonathan Hite, lounged on a dining room chair that was turned outward, facing away from the table. A tall can of beer next to him. Several others were grouped together a little further away. A cigarette dangled from his hand. He raised it to his lips and inhaled as he watched Lee approach.

"Well, will you look at that," he croaked, exhaling the smoke. "She went and called the po-lice on me."

Lee stopped several feet away from him. He scanned for weapons, but aside from the cutlery in the kitchen, none were immediately visible. Part of Hite's waistline was obscured by the chair back. One hand held the dangling cigarette and the other was empty, hanging down as the man rested his elbow on the table. Lee automatically stood with his body bladed, gun side away. He reached for his pen and notepad. He might not need to take many notes, but holding the two items allowed him to keep his hands high without appearing as if he were on guard.

"What's going on here tonight?" Lee asked benignly. When no one answered right away, he eyed Beech expectantly.

She waved her hand at Hite. "He won't leave. We had ourselves a little party, and it's over. Time for him to go. I have to work in the morning."

Lee nodded that he understood. "That true, sir?" he asked Hite.

Hite took a deep drag from the cigarette. When he blew out the smoke, it billowed toward Lee. The bite of cigarette odor washed over him.

"Some of it," Hite said.

"Which part?"

Hite stared back at him, not answering.

"Do you live here?" Lee asked.

Hite continued to stare and smoke.

Lee turned to Beech. "Does he live here?"

"No, sir," she said. "This is *my* house. *I* pay the rent."

"Has he ever lived here?"

"Never."

"Does he stay over often?"

"No." Beech was adamant.

Hite chuckled. "Girl, that ain't true, and you know it."

"You sleep here, then?" Lee asked him.

"On occasion."

Lee should have known this wouldn't be easy. If Hite had established residency, Lee couldn't just boot him out of the house. "What's your side of things?" he asked Hite.

"Side?" Hite shook his head. "Ain't no side, other than Doris here treating me ugly like this, now that she done had her fun."

"She wants you to leave."

"No shit."

"You stay here?" Lee asked again.

"I do."

"How often?"

"That's between me and the lady."

"Not tonight. I need to know."

"Needing ain't getting, as they say."

Lee forged ahead. "Do you keep any clothes here?"

Hite simply stared at him.

"He's got no clothes here," Beech offered. "And he don't stay the night. Ever."

"Bullshit, I don't."

"Do you get mail at this address?" Lee asked.

"I got a box at the post office for that."

"What's the address on your driver's license?"

"My old address. I ain't changed it yet."

"This is not his house," Beech insisted. "And he needs to go. I got work in the morning."

"Then go on to bed," Hite told her. "I'll be in after I finish my beer."

"Don't you tell me what to do under my own roof," she snapped at him. "I don't see your name on no lease."

"I'm not telling." Hite smirked. "I'm suggesting."

"You be careful," Beech said and pointed at him, "or you'll find yourself getting suggested right upside your head."

"Okay, okay," Lee intervened. "Let's take it down a notch."

"I want him out of my house," Beech continued, her tone insistent. "That's what I called you people for. Now do your job."

"I understand, but I need to work something out first, okay?" He waited until Beech nodded begrudgingly, then turned back to Hite. "How long have you lived here?"

"He doesn't live here!" Beech's tone was exasperated.

Lee held up his hand toward her. She scowled and crossed

her arms.

"How long?" he asked Hite.

"Three, four months."

"Do you have a toothbrush here?"

"What're you, my dentist?"

Lee pointed in the only direction the bathroom could be. "If I go into that bathroom and take a look around, am I going to find two toothbrushes?"

Hite stared back. He took his time sucking on the cigarette. Then he said, "You know what? Fuck you, motherfucker. Get outta my house."

"Okay," Lee said. He motioned toward Beech. "Ma'am, can I ask you to step over there into the living room and have a seat for me?"

Beech glared at him with her arms still crossed. "Why you telling me to go sit down when I'm in my own house?"

"You want him gone?" Lee asked. "If so, I need to know you're in a safe place while I deal with him."

Beech hesitated a moment. Then she wheeled and stalked to the loveseat and dropped into it. "Now get outta here so I can go to bed!" she yelled at Hite.

Lee turned his attention back to Hite. "Sir, you need to get up and leave the house now."

Hite made no effort to comply. He gazed back at Lee, smoking.

"I mean it, sir," Lee said. "It's time to go."

Hite blew out smoke. "Or what?"

"Let's not explore those options."

"No, let's. I don't get up, what're you going to do about it?"

"If you don't leave voluntarily, I'll be forced to arrest you and remove you from the premises."

Hite let out a barking laugh. "I'd like to see that. Maybe instead I kick your white ass. How'd you like that?"

"If things get physical, neither of us are going to like it," Lee said, keeping his voice even.

"Maybe after I get done beating your ass, I'll slap you with a lawsuit for trying to throw me out of my own house."

"You don't live here!" Beech shouted from the couch.

Hite raised a finger. "I do. And I want that shit on the record." He dropped his finger to point at Lee. "You're fixing to make a man leave his own house. That ain't right."

"You don't live here," Lee said.

"My house!" Hite snapped.

Lee shook his head. "Okay, well, I'm not here to argue about that. Here's your choice: leave on your own or get arrested."

Hite glared at him, his finger pointing directly at his chest. "You *want* to arrest me, don't you?"

"No, I don't."

"Sure, you do. Make you feel like a big shot to throw a black man in jail over some *bullshit*."

"Trust me," Lee said, "I don't want to arrest you. What I would like is for you to leave on your own."

"I bet." Hite took another drag of his cigarette, almost finishing it. "I bet," he repeated. "Worried about getting your ass kicked, ain't ya?"

"Sir, it's time for you to leave. If you don't go now, then I'll have to arrest you. I don't want to, but I will. I don't want to fight with you, either, but if that happens, you know you'll end up losing no matter what. Whether it's me that arrests you or if I have to call three more cops in here to get it done, you'll still end up arrested. But then you trade a trespassing misdemeanor for a felony assault on a police officer. That's an ugly upgrade and trouble you don't need." Lee slid his pen and notebook into his breast pocket. He spread his hands wide, beseeching Hite. "Of course, if you leave on your own, you get no charges and you're free to come back someday if the lady invites you."

"That's not happening," Beech muttered. "Believe that."

"Regardless," Lee continued, keeping his eyes on Hite. "Those are your options. A free walk out of here with no trouble at all, or..." He shrugged. "Or trouble you don't need."

Hite stared at him.

"*Charlie-Four-Eleven, status check*," his radio crackled.

Lee cocked his head to the left and spoke into his shoulder mic. "Stand by," he said.

Depending on Hite's answer, he prepared to request back-up. If he'd known earlier what he was going to be dealing with on this call, he'd have got someone rolling before even knocking on the door.

"What's it going to be, sir?" Lee asked.

Hite's glare remained for several long seconds. Then he took a final drag of his cigarette, leaned over the table, and dropped the butt into one of the empty beer cans. There was abbreviated hiss as it landed in the remains of the brew.

"I'll go," Hite said. "But you haven't heard the last of this, I promise you."

"Okay."

"I mean it. You'll hear from my lawyer, cracker."

Lee fought the desire to make a snarky comeback. This contact had already taken longer than he wanted. Had Mel not been there, he might have said something like, "The complaint line forms to the right, my friend. Plan on experiencing longer than normal wait times as all our agents are busy with other customers." But his rider was there, and he held the comment in check.

Instead, he said, "Time to go."

"Yeah, whatever." Hite stood. He loaded his cigarettes into one pocket, then put his lighter in another. "I'll go because I *want* to go."

"Does he have a coat?" Lee asked Beech.

Beech pointed toward the kitchen table.

Lee spotted a jacket over the back of one of the chairs on the other side of the table. Hite was already reaching for it. Ideally, Lee would have checked the coat for weapons first. That was standard safety protocol. But at this point, he wondered if it would only serve to make Hite angry and possibly reverse his cooperation. He watched on carefully as the man shrugged himself into the jacket.

Once his coat was on, Hite grabbed a beer can, popped the top, and started for the door. That was another violation about to occur—open and consume alcohol in public—but Lee let that go, too. His gut told him it was either let the man walk while drinking his beer or fight with him. He chose the lesser of two evils.

Hite pulled open the door. He paused, giving Lee another glare. "*Adios*, motherfucker," he said. Then he glanced at Beech. "See you later, girl."

"No, you won't," Beech called after him, but Hite was already slamming the door.

Lee waited a moment to see if he decided to come back inside. When he didn't, he depressed the button on his shoulder mic and said, "Charlie-411, code four. Clearing shortly."

"*Four-Eleven, copy.*"

Lee turned his attention to Beech. "Everything good here?"

She nodded. "Now I can go to bed."

"If he comes back, don't let him in."

"No shit. I got work in the morning."

"Are you done with him, or is this temporary?"

Beech shrugged. "Everything's temporary, isn't it?"

"I suppose it is," Lee said. He gave her a formal nod. "Have a good night, ma'am."

Chapter 12

MEL

She waited until they were back in the car to ask him the question that was on her mind. "Why'd you kick him out?"

Salter turned the key in the ignition, and the engine rumbled to life. The electronics inside the car booted up. He flashed her a look of disbelief. "Seriously?"

"I'm curious." She clicked her seat belt into place. "He said it was his house."

"He lied."

"You just decided that?"

Salter's disbelief faded into an irritated scowl. "Yes. That's my job."

Mel held up her hands. "I'm only asking."

Salter grunted. "Yeah, okay." He punched a key on the computer, causing it to beep. Then he hit another and stared at the screen. "Looks like things are light now. Nothing holding above a priority three. Might be a good time to grab a cup of coffee so I can knock out this shoplifting report."

"Okay."

"I like to get them done early if I can," he explained. "Writing reports goes slower at four in the morning, you know?"

She thought of paper-grading marathons and nodded knowingly—the third hour into them was always the worst. But something else gnawed on her.

Emotional disguises. Masks, basically.

She knew everyone wore them, but the startling way Salter slipped in and out of his unsettled her. Some of the reason had to do with her father's masks, but even accounting for that, his shifts bothered her in a way she couldn't quite pinpoint.

Initially, she thought his approach with the couple in the apartment was brusque. He stood in the center of the woman's home like he owned the space. She sensed his cynicism beneath the cold, professional veneer of his words. It was no surprise that the man sitting at the kitchen table resented this.

As the conversation continued, though, she noticed something. Salter deflected several of the man's direct challenges. She'd seen kids in her classroom working themselves up to test her or otherwise act out. This man seemed to be doing the same, gearing himself up for a fight. Yet Salter talked him out of it. He ignored the insults, kept calm, and gave the man options. Ultimately, he chose the peaceful one.

"You going to answer my question?" she pressed.

"Sure." He put the car in gear and started forward. "The law says she can kick him out if he doesn't live there. If he doesn't leave, it's trespassing."

"But if he *does* live there..."

"Then it's a completely different situation. So, I had to figure out whether or not he had established legal residency so I could know whether to treat this as an unwanted guest or as a domestic dispute." He glanced over at her. "Way different set of circumstances."

"Makes sense." She was generally aware of the domestic violence laws, but even common sense supported what Salter said. That wasn't the part that she wondered about.

"In this situation," he continued, "you've got two different people telling me two different things that are mutually exclusive. Somebody's lying. In this case, it was him."

"When did you decide that?"

"I knew right away."

"How?"

Salter gave her an indulgent smile. "People lie to me all the time. Constantly. It's gotten to the point where the only way I can tell when someone is telling the truth is because it feels weird."

She detected the same cynicism underneath his words as when he spoke inside the house. "So, you kicked the guy out based on gut instinct?"

"No. See, it doesn't matter what I *know*. What matters is what I can prove. That's why I asked the questions I did." He ticked off the details by lifting a finger for each point. "He claims he lives there, but he doesn't get his mail at the address, and doesn't list the address on his identification. He doesn't have clothing or even basic toiletries there. Plus, she says he doesn't live there. All of that taken together..." He trailed off and shrugged. "Seemed clear to me."

Mel thought about it objectively. Did those factors add up to a reasonable conclusion that he didn't live there? She supposed so.

So, what was her problem then?

Masks.

It was the masks.

"Okay," she said. "I understand."

"Would you have wanted me to do something different? I mean, she deserves some peace in her own house, doesn't she?"

"I have no issue with it." She rode in silence for a few seconds. "You seemed very on guard with him."

"Habit. You have a problem with me being safe now?"

She frowned. He was *so* defensive. "It's just an observation. One of the complaints people levy against police is that you are stand-offish. Cold. Rude, even."

"I wasn't rude."

"You were a little brusque."

"Trust me—out here, you can't always go around with a soft tone. People need to hear some authority in the way I speak. Otherwise, they don't listen. Sometimes they don't anyway."

"It wasn't a criticism. I actually thought you were very patient with Mr. Hite."

He cast a sidelong glance at her. "Yeah?"

"I did. Patient but brusque."

He shrugged. "That's the job. You have to be firm with

people. It's what they expect. It's what they want."

"And being on guard like that?"

"That's for me. My own safety. You never know when something might happen, or who might be the person that snaps. That guy back there could have just as easily stood up and charged at me as leave peacefully, regardless of what I said or did. And when that happens, and we're in the middle of it, maybe the woman has a sudden change of heart and jumps in on his side."

"I don't think that's likely."

"You'd be surprised. I've had more than one woman jump on my back after I arrested the man who just beat her."

Mel was shocked by that. Would a person really attack the person sent to defend them? Had her father lived with that same constant tension in his life? Or had times been different then?

"But that's the grind," Salter continued. "A lot of people like to say that policing isn't the most dangerous job out there—"

"It isn't," she said automatically. "It's not even in the top ten."

"I know. Ironically, garbage collectors are, though."

"Garbage collectors?"

"Sorry. Inside joke."

"Not so hard to decipher that one."

Salter cleared his throat. "The thing is, maybe it isn't the most dangerous job every second of every day. We're not in constant danger. You've seen that already tonight. But we're under the constant *threat* of danger. And that constant threat is why I must be vigilant. It's also why this job is so stressful."

Melody nodded. "I can see that, but it's no different than any of those other jobs in the top ten. Or take someone not in the top ten. A bank teller never knows when he might be robbed. How stressful is that job?"

"It's not the same."

"You're right. You have a gun, a badge, training... a bank

126

teller has an alarm button."

Salter rolled his eyes. "Come on."

"I'm serious. The lack of control is what causes people more stress than almost anything else."

"That's what I'm saying. I can't control who goes bug shit on me in any situation."

Mel shifted in her seat. "Fair enough, but with your training and tools at your disposal, you have a lot more control than that poor teller. All he has is a red button."

"And all he's responsible for is pushing it, too. And handing over the money."

"I imagine getting robbed is a terrifying experience."

"I'm sure it is. So is being shot at, stabbed, or fighting with a suspect."

"It isn't a zero-sum game here," Mel said. "Both things can be stressful. I'm just pointing out that policing is less dangerous than the police seem to think it is. But because you all perceive it that way, you take measures, both physical and social, to combat that overblown danger, which leads to community estrangement and to unnecessary uses of force."

Salter was quiet for several long seconds. Then he said, "That sounds like it came right out of the PRI handbook."

Melody frowned. "You're deflecting."

He didn't answer immediately. Then he said, "Think about this: how many bank tellers worry about getting held up when they're not at work, huh? None. Do they have to worry about running into some customer off duty who is going to threaten them and their family at a restaurant because of an overdrawn checking account or denied loan?"

"That would be pretty rare," she admitted.

"It's an everyday reality for cops."

"Every *day*?"

He shrugged. "The threat of it happening is constant. And the odds are not about *if* but *when*."

"I'm sorry, but that sounds a little paranoid."

Salter gave her a tight smile. "I'm sure it does."

She didn't answer.

His mask remained firmly in place.

Mel tried to lighten the mood. "I thought you might make one of those comments we talked about earlier."

His eyebrows raised, but he didn't bother looking at her. "Yeah? When."

"Back at the house. When that guy was going off about calling his lawyer. It seemed like you had about enough." She forced a smile. "I thought you might offer to let him use your phone or something."

Salter rolled his lip down and shook his head. "Didn't seem the time or place for a joke." He eyed her. "I don't think Mr. Hite would have received it too well."

"Probably not."

Salter swung the patrol car into a convenience store lot, then backed into a space.

"More coffee?" he asked.

She glanced at her watch. She'd finished her chai less than an hour ago.

He reached up into the visor and withdrew the ticket from earlier. "I know what you're thinking, but trust me, coffee is the rocket fuel of a graveyard cop. Let's go."

Then he exited the car, not waiting for her reply.

Melody was annoyed as she got out and walked toward the convenience store. For a while there, she thought Salter might be a reasonable person, and that their tentative agreement to talk and to listen might yield results. But she saw the telltale signs of him shutting down under the pressure of criticism. She even tried to lighten the mood right before they arrived, but it failed. It didn't bode well for the remainder of the evening.

Even so, the officer stopped at the entrance to the convenience store and held the door open for her. She strode through into the open interior. A friendly clerk waved at the two of them.

"Hey, Randy," Salter greeted him, his friendly mask back on.

Another officer sat in the bench seats along one wall, facing outward toward the door. Salter made his way toward him, and she followed. She recognized the man from earlier in the night. He'd been the one who grabbed his crotch when Salter highlighted him. He lifted his chin to them as they approached.

Salter paused at the table, standing and waiting for her. When they drew closer, he motioned with his hand, indicating she should slide in first.

She gave him a questioning look.

"In case I have to move quickly," he explained.

Mel suppressed a frown. Her father always had to have his back to the door. Pity the hostess who brought her family to a table in the middle of a restaurant because that would not do.

She slid into the booth, moving all the way to the wall.

"This is Officer Colm Murphy," Salter said, his tone clipped.

A polite, mostly sincere smile crossed Murphy's craggy face.

"Murph," Salter continued, "this is Melody Weaver."

Murphy held out his hand to her, past the portable radio that sat on the table in front of him.

"You met earlier," Salter told him. "In a way."

Murphy's gaze turned quizzical.

"When I spotlighted you."

Murphy winced slightly, then his smile turned sheepish. "Sorry about that. I didn't know Lee had a rider."

"No problem." She accepted his hand and shook it.

"She's with the PRI," Salter finished.

To his credit, the falter in Murphy's expression was only a flicker. She wasn't sure what she saw in that moment— dismay, distrust, or disgust—but it was gone before she could catalog it.

"Nice to meet you," Murphy said.

She let go of his hand. "You, too."

"I'm getting a coffee," Salter said. "Anyone want anything?"

Murphy lifted his foam cup. "I'm good."

"I'm fine, too," she said.

"All right, but you might want to grab a granola bar or something while we're here, in case we get stuck on a long call later on."

"Noted."

Salter wandered off toward the coffee stand behind the cash register.

"So," Murphy said. "Seriously... sorry about the Mötley Crüe imitation. I was just messing around."

"It's not a problem. Really."

"All right." He gave her a questioning look. "Good night so far?"

Mel almost laughed. How was she supposed to sum up her evening to this point? The blow-up, the treaty, the conversations both cautious and contentious? She didn't know how she felt about it yet, so trying to describe it, especially to one of Salter's partners, seemed impossible.

"Something funny?" Murphy asked. He adjusted the volume on his portable radio down.

"No," she said quickly. "Not at all."

"Oh." He pursed his lips. "So, it's *not* been good, then?"

Murphy looked like a veteran cop. His closely cropped strawberry-blond hair was speckled with gray. The quintessential cop mustache he wore was slightly darker and also had gray splashed through it. But it was looking into his light green eyes that convinced her that he had years on the job. The combination of world-weary cynicism, curiosity, and humor was unmistakable.

"It's been fine," she told him. "We've actually covered some interesting ground."

"Interesting?" Murphy smirked playfully. "Lee?"

"Why do you say that?"

"Most nights, he's about as interesting as dry toast."

She smiled slightly. "Well, he's been honest about things."

"Yeah, he's foolish that way."

That did make her laugh. Murphy's expression didn't change, though.

"What kind of calls you been on?" he asked. "Anything good?"

"It's all good to me. Everything's an education."

Murphy nodded knowingly. He glanced over at Salter, who was filling a cup of coffee from a pump carafe. "He's a little intense sometimes, but he's a good cop."

Mel didn't answer.

"Comes from a long line of cops. His dad and grandad were both on the job."

"I heard."

"Yeah?" Murphy turned back to her. "Well, both are basically legends around here. But that guy over there? He might be the best of the three. Just don't tell him I said that."

She mimed zipping her lips shut.

Murphy raised his cup toward her in salute and then sipped.

"Why do you say he's the best?" she asked.

Murphy set the cup down again. "The short answer is ambition. But where the other two had ambition to climb the ranks, Lee's ambition is just to do the job."

"You're right," she said. "That is a pretty short answer. What's the long one?"

"The long one is for another time, when I know you better."

"Okay." She motioned toward the paperwork in front of him. "What are you working on?"

"Nothing special—a run-of-the-mill burglary report. I caught it as soon as I cleared the auto-ped." He grinned at her. "I'm pretty sure I was on perimeter duty so that you and the all-star didn't have to be."

"Oh. I'm sorry."

"Don't be. It's all part of the job."

"Was it bad?" she asked.

Murphy shrugged. "Anytime a car hits a human at speed, it's ugly." He picked up his pen and returned his attention to the paper in front of him.

"I thought all police reports were typed now," Mel said. "I mean, didn't the department recently spend a bunch of money buying some new software to streamline the process?"

Murphy looked up. He appeared both amused and irritated at the same time as he spoke. "They did."

They? She found that a curious, perhaps even telling, word choice.

"But you're not using it?"

"Only when I have to."

"I don't understand. Why not?"

"I'd like to say it's because I'm old school," Murphy said. "And, in a way, I guess that's true."

"You can just decide whether or not to use the reporting system? I thought it was mandatory."

She probably sounded like she was nit-picking, but the tickle of irritation from her conversation with Salter hadn't diminished yet, and this tendency increased it. Assistant Chief Hatcher had spearheaded the push for extra funds to purchase new software to replace the existing, supposedly outdated, broken system that was in place at the time.

Hatcher hedged her bets by referencing the consent decree, citing the importance of a robust reporting system. To avoid anyone on the council or the public getting lost in the technobabble of the proposal, she likened it to the rest of the criminal justice system using the newest Apple iteration while the police department was still using Windows 95. It was a smart analogy. The council appropriated the funds.

All that money, and yet here was Officer Murphy still handwriting a police report.

Murphy took his time responding. He filled in a couple of boxes on the form before he said, "The new reporting system is about eighty-five percent implemented. Which shift do you think gets the new stuff last?"

She thought about her earlier exchanges with Salter on similar matters. "Graveyard."

"Exactly." Murphy put down his pen. "For any reports

longer than a couple paragraphs, I hold off until I can get into a neighborhood substation. Those computers have the software installed on them. But for a quick burg report like this one? It's easier to scratch it out and let them scan it in records."

Mel didn't press the issue. An image of a lone data entry clerk flashed in her mind, with a massive stack of paperwork to one side, frantically entering data as the pile next to him grew.

"There are hiccups every time the system changes," Murphy said, as if he could see the same image. "The kinks will work themselves out. Especially if the brass stay out of the way."

Without waiting for her reaction, Murphy turned back to his report.

Salter settled into the seat beside her. "What're we talking about?"

"Our flawless transition to Qual-Report," Murphy intoned, not looking up.

Salter snorted. "You mean like the one to Qual-Scan?" He dropped the document he'd taken from the car onto the table, flipped it open and started writing on the back.

Mel leaned forward slightly. "Is that from the shoplifting?"

"Yep."

"You write the report on the citation?"

He shook his head. "No. I have to do a complete report in Qual-Report. But the prosecutor requires us to put a summary of the facts with all the elements of the crime in the citation narrative, too."

The duplication of effort seemed a waste to her. "Why?"

A thin, rueful smile creased his lips. "In case the paperwork is lost. At least that's the official reason."

"You think it's something else?"

He shrugged. "I'm sure lost paperwork is part of why they first asked."

Murphy grunted. "Demanded, you mean?"

Salter raised and dropped his brow in response, then turned

back to Melody. "The word we got was that if the paperwork was unavailable when the prosecutor was in court, at least the probable cause was there. He—or she—could make the case off the summary rather than be forced to dismiss."

"That sounds reasonable."

"I'm sure they thought so, too." Salter continued writing while he spoke. "But we're pretty sure that it's devolved into the prosecutors just using the ticket all the time instead of the report, and then complaining when there isn't enough detail in the summary. The result is we end up writing the same report twice because without fail, whichever one we don't put enough detail into will be the one the prosecutor uses."

Mel watched him write, soaking in what he'd said. Bureaucracy was nothing new to her; education was rife with it. But Salter's description reminded her of some of the foolish things that David used to joke about the Army doing when he was counting the reasons that he was grateful he'd chosen the Air Force instead. No institution was immune to bureaucratic mishaps, but David's examples of the Army way versus the Air Force way drove home the point to her that these things existed by degree.

Even so, writing the same report twice seemed like a poor use of a police officer's time, especially when both Chief Baumgartner and Assistant Chief Hatcher were constantly harping on the police department being understaffed. In fact, it was one of the few points that both the Chief's Office and the Police Union seemed to agree upon... which was actually why Melody and most PRI members were suspicious of the assertion.

As a teacher, she knew the fallacy of the 'do more with less' mantra that leadership tried unsuccessfully to trot out every so often. This philosophy had been dressed up in more attractive clothing as "work smarter, not harder," even though the eventual expectations were the same as doing more with less. But here, it seemed like there was a more efficient way to do things.

Then another thought occurred to her.

"Is this for all citations, or just the ones you write by hand?"

Salter scowled. "Just the handwritten ones. Anything that goes through Qual-Scan is auto-populated in Qual-Report and linked."

"Supposedly," Murphy added.

"Supposedly," Salter agreed. He shrugged. "Once the system is one hundred percent in place, we won't have to do things this way anymore."

"When will that be?" Mel asked.

Salter's tight, ironic grin bordered on a sneer. "About six months ago, last I heard."

"They're saying by the end of the year now," Murphy said. Then he added, "Supposedly."

Some of the sneer left Salter's face but his short chuckle lost none of the irony. "And I'm sure we'll have a contract by then, too." He glanced at Mel. "Everything is always just a few months away. It's like that sports team that is always rebuilding."

Melody fell silent. She didn't know how much criticism the strained mood between them could take before everything shut down. While the equipment complaint seemed safe enough— it wasn't like she didn't experience the same issues in her classroom—she didn't want to touch the union contract squabbles at the moment. Maybe later when they were in a better place.

If they were ever in a better place.

And Tyler Garrett? Or Ray Zielinski? The consent decree? She wondered if those topics might have to remain untouched. Or spark another battle between them.

The two men wrote quietly for a few minutes. Mel wished she had gotten something to drink but didn't want to disturb Salter's scribbling. She pulled out her phone and saw a thirty-minute old text from David.

ON TIME. LOVE YOU.

She smiled to herself, imagining him passing ten thousand

feet by now, in his element, and in command. He was an easy man to be proud of.

She scrolled through one of her teacher groups on Facebook, skimming a couple of conversations but finding nothing new. Then, almost simultaneously, both officers stopped writing, collected their paperwork together, and leaned back. Murphy adjusted the volume knob on his portable radio. The sound of crackling voices and radio static increased slightly.

"Shoplifter, huh?" Murphy said to Salter.

Salter shrugged. "It was on the screen. Besides, I didn't want to keep Lonnie waiting forever. He's a good guy."

"He still making scratch on his side hustle?"

"Sounds like it."

Mel glanced up from her phone. "Side hustle?"

"He's a day trader," Murphy said.

"As in stocks?"

Murphy nodded. "He does it for fun. Strictly low stakes."

Salter blew on his coffee, then sipped. "I don't know. Last time I was in there, he said he was clearing a few hundred bucks a month at it. He said he was still doing well when we talked tonight."

Mel stared, recalling the conversation. She'd thought the two men were talking about sexual conquests when Salter asked Lonnie if he was "killing it."

Murphy made an appreciative face. "Pretty nice when your hobby earns you beer money." He motioned toward Salter. "Maybe you could find a way to do that with *Call of Duty*."

"Shut up."

"That's a video game," Murphy told her.

"I know what *Call of Duty* is," Mel said. "I teach middle school."

A broad smile spread across Murphy's face. "Hear that?" he said to Salter. "Middle school. Maybe you know some of her kids from playing online."

"I said, shut up. I only play with guys from work. And my

cousins."

"Afraid her kids might beat you?" Murphy teased.

"Sorry my recreation doesn't meet with your approval. I should be more like you. Take up woodworking or some other old man gig."

"Working with wood is grounding, my boy."

"We all have our own ways to relieve stress. You make sawdust, I shoot pixels." Salter spread his hands, his tone mockingly philosophical. "We're each on our own journey."

Murphy clucked his tongue but didn't argue further. Instead, he turned to Melody. "How about you? What does a teacher do for fun?"

Mel took a deep breath, considering. Then she lifted her hands. "This, I suppose."

"Ride around with a graveyard cop? See the worst humanity has to offer and with bad hours, to boot?" He shook his head slowly. "You've got a strange definition of fun."

"Honestly, I don't have much time for fun during the school year." She looked back and forth between the two of them. "There's only so many hours, and between the classroom, lesson-planning, and grading, and then some family time…"

"And the PRI," Salter said quietly.

"That, too. It's important work."

Neither man replied. After a few awkward moments, Murphy said, "I guess you do do this for fun."

"Kinda."

Murphy grunted lightly but said nothing more. He turned his cup slowly in front of him. Mel noticed the gold band on his finger.

"So, you wear yours," she said, flicking her eyes toward the ring.

Murphy followed her glance. "The ring? Of course."

"Why?"

"Because I'm married."

"No, I mean—"

Murphy smiled and lifted his hand. "I know what you

mean. Some guys don't, and they have their reasons."

"Good reasons," Salter added.

"No argument."

"But you do," Mel said. "Why is that?"

"Because my wife would murder me if I took it off."

She watched him carefully, trying to discern if he meant what he said. Murphy stared at her in return, as if he were curious to see if she could determine it, too. After a little while, she decided she couldn't. So, she just asked, "Really?"

"Well, not murder. But a serious ass-kicking would be in the offing." Murphy drank some of his coffee, then pursed his lips thoughtfully. "I guess it's more important to me to have it on than to worry about what some mope threatens to do. He doesn't know me or her, so what do I care?" He shrugged. "Also, it keeps women from hitting on me constantly."

She caught the sly glint when he said the last. "Ah, then you're paranoid, too," she joked. "Just in a different way."

Murphy started to answer but Salter sprang from his seat. Mel looked around to see what was happening, but nothing seemed out of the ordinary. Salter strode purposefully toward the restroom.

"Uh…" Murphy said. "You might want to tread lightly on that topic."

"What topic?" All she did was join in the banter a little. Why was that so upsetting?

Murphy scratched at his thick mustache, then smoothed it. "Look, every cop out here takes officer safety seriously. But Lee probably does more than others, so teasing about it strikes a nerve for him."

Mel looked back at him. Why was Salter so delicate about this?

Murphy seemed to sense her question. He lowered his voice slightly. "A few years ago, a guy attacked him with a knife. Sliced his arm pretty good." Murphy traced a line across his triceps. "Made him a true believer in the twenty-one-foot rule."

She shook her head in confusion. "I don't know what that is."

"A group of defensive tactics experts conducted a series of experiments years ago when there was some backlash over a cop shooting some guy with a knife or whatever. Basically, what their research showed was that a person with an edged weapon can cover twenty-one feet in the time it takes an officer to draw his weapon from its holster and bring it up on target."

"Seems like a lot of distance," she said, trying to envision twenty-one feet in her head.

"It's only seven yards, if that helps you picture it."

"That doesn't."

"Helped me," Murphy said with a smile, "but I played football. Anyway, a lot of cops were doubters, too. So, they repeated their research with cameras and encouraged DT instructors to try it at their own academies. The research held up. Turns out, if someone has a blade in their hand, they're a lot more dangerous than you think from a lot further away than you think."

Mel squinted a little. "I'd be interested to see that research."

"I could probably get it to you," Murphy said. Then he motioned with his head toward Salter's departed form. "Point is, when it comes to being vigilant, let's just say he doesn't take well to anyone poo-pooing the idea."

"I didn't know," she said.

Murphy waved it off. "It didn't get a lot of coverage, since we didn't end up shooting the guy."

"What happened, then?"

"The guy was left-handed, see? So, when he slashed Lee, the cut was across his right arm. Like a lot of us, Lee wears his Taser for a left-hand draw and deployment. That's to avoid confusion between our gun and the Taser. Since his left arm still worked, he drew his Taser after the second slice and fired it into the guy's chest. The suspect fell over and hit his head on the coffee table, knocking him out cold. Lee kicked the knife away and by then, more of us arrived on scene and put the suspect in cuffs."

Melody stared at him. "That's… horrible."

Murphy raised his eyebrows in agreement. "It wasn't pretty. But you can understand why he takes things so seriously."

She swallowed, nodding. "Thanks… thanks for telling me."

"He probably wouldn't want me to. But I didn't want you to think he was an asshole or something." Murphy flashed her a small grin. "Not because of that, anyway."

They sat quietly for a little while. Mel digested what Murphy told her, trying to imagine what Salter went through. It took her very little time to realize that she simply couldn't. Not exactly, anyway.

Murphy's radio crackled. At first, she only half-listened to the dispatcher's voice, not following some of the codes. But she picked up the description of the call.

"*Complainant is female,*" he reported evenly. "*She reports that a strange child has wandered into her home. The child is currently sitting in her living room. She is requesting a police response.*"

Murphy stared down at his radio, frowning. "This call was already holding when I cleared the perimeter of the auto-ped earlier."

Melody sat back in surprise. That meant this woman had been waiting for hours. The callous way Murphy mentioned it surprised her. "It sounds like an emergency," she ventured. "Why hasn't anyone gone yet?"

Murphy shook his head slightly. "Because there is no kid."

Mel looked at him, perplexed. Why would someone call the police about a nonexistent child?

Murphy raised his radio to his mouth. "Charlie-409, any one-oh-five entries?"

"*Four-oh-nine, negative.*"

Murphy appeared mildly surprised at the reply. "One-oh-five means mental health issues," he told her.

140

"You can talk about that over the air?" she asked. "What about HIPAA?"

He opened his mouth to speak again, but someone else beat him to it. Mel recognized Salter's voice. It came through Murphy's radio, tinged with static, but also from across the convenience store as he walked toward them.

"Charlie-Four-Eleven, I'll be en route."

Salter arrived at the table, picking up his coffee cup.

"I can grab this," Murphy said.

"I got it. Finish your coffee."

"I'm done. You want back up?"

"Why?" Salter asked. "There's no kid." He glanced over at Mel. "You ready?"

Chapter 13

LEE

The blocks flitted past as he drove in silence.

He should have known better.

Just work your shift. That had been Sergeant Gelabert's advice. Now, it rang in his ears in an 'I told you so' tone. He'd been a cop for fourteen years and he was still learning that sometimes you should just listen to your sergeant.

Weaver had kept up her end of the silence so far. He imagined she could sense his... what? Frustration?

No, he decided. Frustration was a slow burn. Right now, he was pissed off.

And tired.

Tired of all those people in the world who thought they knew a damn thing about being a cop. They understood none of the rigors. None of the dangers. And yet they passed judgment.

Usually, he could shut out these emotions. But having a living, breathing example of those exact people riding with him and passing those judgments made that impossible.

As if on cue, Weaver cleared her throat. "Murphy said there wasn't any child on this call. You said the same thing."

"So?"

"I'm wondering why."

His eyes slid to the right and caught her earnest expression. He was unmoved. "Because there's no kid."

"How do you know? Why would anyone—"

"There's no kid," he repeated.

She frowned. "All right, you don't want to explain. Then tell me why you're mad at me."

Lee didn't answer.

"Is it because I said you're paranoid?"

"I'm not paranoid."

"I understand."

He eyed her. "I'm not. It's the other way around. Most people are oblivious."

"I don't know if that's true."

"Paranoia is being concerned about things that don't exist." He tapped the steering wheel for emphasis. "Danger exists."

"I know it does, but paranoia can also be about inflating likelihoods. Or the breadth of an issue."

"What?"

"Danger exists, like you said, but paranoia inflates how likely it is that the danger will actually occur. Or from how many sources."

"Listen to you," he said sourly. "You've been out here for what? A couple of hours?"

"I understand," she said again.

"No, you don't. This is my job, every night. You work in a classroom."

Weaver didn't reply immediately, but he could sense her fuming.

"I'm not paranoid," he repeated and tried to force calm into his voice. "I see the world as it is. And I do that so that most everyone else in this city can go on living in their blissful little bubble."

He regretted the last three words almost immediately. They weren't necessary.

She shook her head. "That's so condescending."

They fell silent again. Lee exited the arterial, taking a short cut to get up to Rockwell. He drove automatically, his mind whirring. Their fragile truce was disintegrating, but it had probably been doomed from the start. Yet he still wanted to get his point across. Whether she wanted to hear it was another question.

He inhaled deeply before beginning. "The world is a dark and dirty place with broken edges, and full of danger. Most people don't ever see it for what it is. Those of us that do keep that ugliness in check. We hold the darkness at bay so that

143

everyone else can live a brighter life. Maybe sometimes that ugly reality intrudes on their lives but only on rare occasions."

"If you think the rest of the world is living in a blissful little bubble, you're not seeing things clearly."

He shook his head. He shouldn't have uttered those words, but now she wasn't letting them go. That left Salter only two viable courses of action—apologize or lean into the words. He wasn't about to say he was sorry. "Are you kidding me? Look around. People have no idea what's going on because of cops, firefighters, and other emergency responders. We protect their blissful little bubbles." He shook his head. He'd said the words again, but he wasn't about to back off. "Here's what chaps my ass. I don't want people to make a big deal about what we do. I don't even need a thank you. But it would be nice if people at least stayed out of the damn way while I did it."

"Do you seriously believe that horse shit?"

"Horse shit? Listen, being unappreciated is one thing—"

"Unappreciated?" she scoffed. "Chief Baumgartner is constantly trotting out heroes for this community and people eat it up."

He ignored her and continued. "Being unappreciated is one thing. You get used to that. But providing a critical service to the public at great personal risk and then being persecuted for it? *That's* horse shit."

Weaver shook her head in disbelief. "That is the most sanctimonious, deluded, self-righteous pile of crap I've ever heard."

"I guess you don't make it to many PRI meetings, then."

She glared at him. "I don't know what happened here. I thought we were getting along. I thought we were talking."

"So did I."

"Then what is this?" Weaver waved her hand at him.

"It's me being tired of getting kicked in the face," Lee said. "You and your little committee are going to think and do the same thing no matter what I say or do here tonight, so I guess I don't see the point of riding around with your judgment and your misinformed, so-called facts."

"All of this because I said you seemed paranoid?"

Lee glanced sideways at her again. Weaver appeared genuinely hurt and baffled, and his ire sagged. He forced his tone to soften. "Look, I'm sorry I snapped at you."

"But not for what you said."

He shrugged. "Ask anything, say anything."

"So that's still a thing? Because it's supposed to be constructive, not feel like a free-for-all full of cheap shots."

"Calling me paranoid was a cheap shot."

"It wasn't meant that way." Weaver was quiet for a moment. Then she said, "Look, I know this is a tough situation. For both of us. And I want you to know that I have respect for some of what I've seen you do tonight. But you have to see that part of what is wrong with policing is right there in that rant you just let fly."

"I didn't rant."

"Yes, you did. It was a full-on Jack Nicholson, 'You want me on that wall' rant."

Lee halted the car for a four-way stop. There were no other cars at the intersection, so he looked over at her. "I know the movie you're talking about. And while he took it too far, there's truth in what he was saying. It's frustrating to be the sheep dog, protecting the flock from the wolves, only to have the sheep tell you—"

"The *sheep*?"

"It's an analogy."

"It's an insulting one. Are you saying people like me are sheep?"

"In the analogy, yes."

"I'm *not* a sheep," she snarled.

Lee was taken aback. Now, she was truly angry. "It wasn't meant to be offensive."

"Are you fucking kidding me? How can calling someone a sheep *not* be offensive? The absolute arrogance of it is appalling." She shook her head. "Do you even hear yourself?

I mean, do you ever step outside of your blue world and just listen to what you're saying?"

His flagging frustration welled up again. He clenched his jaw and drove forward.

Just work your shift, he thought. Yet that seemed impossible tonight.

"You know what I think?" he said, biting off each word.

"At this point, I have no idea what goes on inside your head."

"I think our world experience is so radically different that we don't have any common frame of reference."

"I don't know if—"

"And I think," he interrupted, "that without that common ground, all we're doing here is making things worse." He pulled to the side of the road, a couple of houses down from the complainant's address. As he punched the on-scene button on the MDC, he said, "So the best thing for both of us might be for me to take you back to the station after I clear this call."

He didn't wait for Weaver to answer. He snatched his flashlight from the charger and got out of the car. As he quietly shut the door, he was surprised to see Weaver exiting the passenger side. He was tempted to tell her to wait for him in the cruiser but let it go. This was already a disaster. He didn't need to make it worse.

Then she angrily slammed her door shut as if they were having a lover's quarrel.

Lee stared at her. He was as angry at her for how she closed the door as he was at himself for forgetting to tell how to properly do it.

"What?" she asked.

"We need to be quiet as we approach the house."

"Why? You said there was no kid."

His face flattened, but his anger was barely contained.

"Whatever," she whispered. "I'll be quiet."

He turned and strode down the sidewalk. Parking two houses away was habit, part of the practice of silent and invisible deployment that had been drilled into him since the academy. Sometimes it mattered, sometimes it didn't. On a call like this, it probably didn't. But he never knew when it would, so he always did it.

Behind him, Weaver hurried to keep up. He cut across the front yard of the house next to the complainant's, expecting Weaver would balk at that and keep to the sidewalk. She stayed at his heels, however.

At the front door, Lee stood to one side. He took a deep breath before knocking. He had to focus on the call. A distracted cop is a dead cop, his grandfather always said. And while people like Weaver might find that to be extreme, he knew it was true. The concept extended to all facets of the job. Police work was a detail-oriented endeavor. A distracted cop might not end up dead, but he was going to miss things, and that resulted in a substandard job. He'd already been distracted enough tonight.

So, he focused.

And then he knocked.

Chapter 14

MEL

Part of her was furious. Salter was being a jerk, and she didn't know if it was an atypical response from him or the curtain parting to show who he really was. Either way, there was a mask involved. That created its own set of mixed emotions for her.

But another part of her was legitimately confused. His reaction to the term paranoid seemed out of proportion. And how could he not see how offensive the term 'sheep' would be to anyone?

She stood behind him as he knocked on the front door of the house. He stood to the side of the frame, ramrod straight.

This is hopeless, she thought. Would it have been better with a different officer? Would a female cop have been more receptive to actually conversing with her as opposed to bouts of lecturing?

When no one answered the door, Salter knocked a second time. Another ten seconds passed before the lock rattled. A crack appeared in the doorway. A white woman in her fifties peered out cautiously.

"Police, ma'am," Salter said. "You called about a child?"

"Yes," she said, and swung the door open.

The woman wore a sleeveless pale blue night gown that hung past her knees. She stood aside and beckoned them to enter. Salter strode in confidently, looking around. Mel followed. The woman offered no objection to her presence or even questioned it. She latched the door behind them.

"In there," she told Salter.

Salter motioned for her to lead the way. The woman headed deeper into the house, and he walked after her. In just a few strides, they arrived in the darkened living room. Light from the entryway sliced across the floor, and the porch light leaked in through the partially open blinds, creating sharp shadows in places.

"Right there," the woman pointed. "Sitting in that chair."

Mel followed her finger. Aside from a couple of coats draped haphazardly across it, the chair was empty. In fact, except for the three of them, the entire room was empty.

She felt a momentary chagrin. Immediately afterward, Mel wondered if there was a child that had perhaps wandered off. But she recognized that as faulty thinking. The woman was pointing at nothing.

Salter remained unfazed. He shined his flashlight on the chair.

"Ma'am, there's no child in that chair."

The woman blinked in confusion and lowered her arm.

"Would you mind turning on the light?" Salter asked.

She reached for the wall switch. Light flooded the room and shadows retreated.

Salter snapped off his flashlight. "See?" he said, his tone landing somewhere between gentle and matter-of-fact. "No child."

The woman stared at the chair, working her mouth for a moment. Then she looked at Salter. "She... she must have snuck out while I was calling you."

"What's your name, ma'am?"

"Heather."

"Heather, who is this child? Do you know her?"

The woman shook her head. "She just wandered in. Through the front door."

"When was that?"

"A few hours ago."

"Okay, I understand. Tell me, what did she look like?"

Heather glanced back at the chair. "About seven. Pigtails. A yellow dress with little blue bows." She traced a line from her throat to her midsection. "All in a row."

"That's a good description," Salter said.

"She... she was just here." She fixed him with a pleading

stare. "Please, you have to find her. It's cold out, and she wasn't wearing a coat. That's why I let her stay. To get warm."

"All right. Why don't we start by checking through the house?"

Heather considered, then nodded slowly. "Yes. That's a good idea." She waved her hand. "Go ahead. You have my permission."

"Would you mind showing me around?" Salter asked. "You know your house better than I do. You can point out places to check that I might miss."

"Oh. Yes, that makes sense."

"I'll look in here first," he said.

Salter methodically checked the entire living room. His movements were unhurried, sure and efficient. While he searched, he asked her innocuous questions.

"How long have you lived here, Heather?" He peered under the couch and then behind it.

"All my life. This was my parents' house."

Salter checked behind the chair where the coats rested. "They're gone now?"

"Yes. About ten years ago."

He opened the closet door near the entry way. "Sorry for your loss."

"Thank you."

Salter pushed aside jackets. "Seems a little young to pass."

"I was a late baby," Heather said.

Salter shined his light up onto the shelf above the rack. "Are you retired yourself?"

"No."

He closed the closet door. "But you get a pension of some kind, right?"

"From the railroad, yes. My husband worked for the Union Pacific. He died in an accident."

"I'm sorry to hear that." Salter paused at a table strewn with framed photographs. His gaze swept over them. He leaned in and touched one of them. "Do you get any help from the state?"

Heather crossed her arms. "What's with all the questions? I didn't do anything wrong, Officer. That child wandered into my house."

"I know." Salter squatted and looked underneath. "I'm just making conversation."

"Oh." Heather pursed her lips. Then she let her hands fall to her sides. "Well, I don't mean to be rude."

"You're not being rude at all, Heather." Salter stood. "I think this room is clear. How about we move on?"

Heather nodded. She led them to the sparse dining room. Mel stopped in the doorway. Salter looked around but there really wasn't anywhere a child could have hidden.

"The kitchen?" he asked.

"Of course." She turned and headed through the doorway. Salter kept close, turning on his flashlight until she flicked the switch.

The kitchen was small. The two-seater table was clear of anything save a place mat and a partially filled napkin rack. The sink had a single plate and some utensils in it. Several bottles of wine rested on the counter.

Salter leaned over and peered under the table. When he stood up, he said, "Smells good in here. What'd you cook for dinner?"

"Beef Stroganoff."

"Homemade?"

Heather let out a sputtering laugh. "What, I should eat it from a box?"

That made Melody smile. Even Salter seemed to allow a hint of a smile to touch the corners of his mouth.

He pointed to the wine. "Have you been drinking a little tonight?"

She shrugged. "Just to help me sleep."

Salter motioned toward one of the bottles. "I like that Pepperwood. It's good stuff." He glanced around. "I think we're okay in here. Where to next?"

Heather led them down a short hall. The first door was to the bathroom. Salter stepped inside, turning on the light. He pulled aside the shower curtain, revealing an empty bathtub. Then he opened the closet door and shined his light on each shelf. Finally, he paused. He picked up the small trash can, looking down at its contents.

"What is it?" Heather asked.

Salter glanced up at her. "Nothing. I noticed you've thrown away a lot of prescription bottles is all. Are all of these empty?"

"Of course, they are. Who would throw away perfectly good prescriptions?"

"What medications are you taking, Heather?"

She waved her hands dismissively. "Just this and that."

Salter kept looking at her, waiting.

Heather shifted her feet. "Xanex."

Salter nodded. "What else?"

"Olanzipine."

"And you've been taking these consistently?"

"Of course." She shifted her feet and looked away.

"But you ran out?"

Heather nodded. "A couple of days ago."

Salter replaced the small garbage can. "Shall we check the bedrooms?"

Heather nodded and led them further down the hall. Mel stood in the hallway while Salter went through the complete ritual of looking under the bed and in the closets of both the master bedroom and the guest bedroom. Halfway through, his radio crackled.

"*Charlie-Four-Eleven, a status check.*"

Salter keyed the mic. "Code four."

"*Copy.*"

Once he finished with the second bedroom, he suggested they return to the living room. The three of them trailed through the house, past the kitchen toward their destination. On the way, Heather asked, "What are you going to do now?"

Salter didn't answer until they reached the living room. Then he asked, "Heather, do you know what your diagnosis is?"

She shook her head. "That doesn't matter. Are you going to go search for the little girl?" She pointed at the front window. "It's cold out there, Officer."

"Lee," Salter said.

Heather's brow scrunched. "What?"

Salter tapped his chest. "My name is Lee, Heather. And yes, I'm going to find that little girl. I'll make sure she gets home safe, all right?"

Relief swept across her features. "Thank you," she breathed. "I've been so worried."

"I understand. Heather, who is your MHP caseworker?"

"Lindsay Wagner," she answered immediately. "But he can't prescribe. Only my doctor can do that. And he's on vacation."

"I understand." Salter took out his small notebook and jotted something down. Then he tilted his head toward the kitchen. "Since your meds ran out, you've been using the wine to help?"

"Yes."

"Does it help you sleep?"

"Some."

"And does it help with the anxiety?"

Heather nodded, then shrugged. "Not really. Not completely."

"You're doing the best you can," Salter said. He replaced his notebook in his breast pocket and smoothed it. "I'm going to leave now and go find this little girl. But can I ask you to do something for me?"

"What is it?"

"Two things," Salter said. He raised his first finger. "Call your caseworker tomorrow morning. Let him know about your meds and your doctor being on vacation. He can take care of it."

"I told you, he can't prescribe."

"No, but they have doctors who can fill in for times like this."

"I don't want to see a different doctor. Dr. Haggerty is the only one I trust."

"I hear you. I'm sure your caseworker knows that, too. But this will just be to fill your scrips. Then you can talk to your own doctor when he gets back from vacation. Okay?"

Slowly, Heather nodded.

"Good," said Salter. He raised his second finger and turned them toward her as if flashing her the peace sign. "The other thing is to go to bed. Get a good night's sleep. Don't worry about this child because I'm going to take care of it. Okay?"

Heather considered. Then she nodded again. "Thank you," she said. She stepped forward and took Salter's hand in both of hers. Her voice wavered with emotion. "Thank you so much."

Salter gave her another smile and patted her hands. "It's going to be all right," he said. "Call Lindsay in the morning, okay?"

"I will."

"Good." Salter patted her hands one last time and turned toward the front door. Heather followed them, taking hold of the knob as Salter swung it open. "Good night, ma'am."

"Good night," Heather said. "And thank you."

Salter headed down the steps. Mel followed. Heather fixed her with a look as she passed, bobbing her head slightly. "Thank you," she repeated.

Mel returned the gesture, then went down the stairs behind Salter.

At the patrol car, Salter opened his door and popped the lock for her. He started the car and waited for the computer to boot up. As Melody settled into her seat, she glanced back toward the house. Heather still stood in the doorway, watching them. The woman waved.

Mel waved back.

Heather closed the door. A few moments later, the light in the living room window went dark.

"No kid," she muttered, without looking away. "You were right. How'd you know?"

It seemed like Salter wasn't going to answer at first. Then he said, "There was a kid, actually."

Mel turned to him. "What?"

His voice remained cool and distant. "There's a picture of a little girl in that exact dress she described, mixed in with all the others on the table in the living room."

"Her daughter?"

He shrugged. "Or her, when she was young. Who knows? She's a mental."

Chapter 15

LEE

"Who really knows?" Lee said. "She's a mental."

Weaver's confusion melted into a scowl. "That isn't very kind."

"It's a statement of fact. She's got mental issues and she's off her meds, using booze to take the edge off. Who can say what goes on in her mind?"

She shook her head. "I don't get you."

"What's to get?" Lee dropped the patrol car into gear and pulled away from the curb.

"You were nice to her, but now—"

"Why wouldn't I be? What, are you disappointed I wasn't a jerk? Doesn't fit the narrative for you?"

She leaned away. "No, I'm not disappointed. Pleasantly surprised, actually."

Lee brought up the call on the MDC, glancing down while he drove. "I'm sure."

Weaver didn't respond.

Lee punched in his clearance code from the previous call and hit SEND. The MDC beeped in response. Less than three seconds later, the dispatcher's voice broke into the tense silence of the patrol cruiser.

"Charlie-409 and Charlie-411?"

Lee reached for the mic, waiting until Murph answered up before following suit. "Four-eleven, go ahead."

The dispatcher rattled off an address. Lee immediately adjusted his route to start that direction before she'd finished describing the call.

"Possible domestic order violation. Female caller stated 'he is here' before leaving the line open. Nine-one-one operators can hear a discussion between a male and a female in the background." The dispatcher broke the transmission for

a full second, then continued. *"The address shows a Marsha Gold and Timothy Colton. Several DV entries over the past two years. Gold is the petitioner of a current DVOP with Colton as the respondent."*

Murph copied the call, then asked the dispatcher to have records pull the order and confirm it. Once the dispatcher copied the request, Lee added his own acknowledgment.

"I need to take this call before I can drop you off," he said evenly. "Unless you want to stay, that is."

"I wasn't the one who wanted to end our ride. I told you I'm in it for the long haul."

Salter already felt like a fool for losing his cool in front of a schoolteacher. He really didn't want Mel to ride with him all night, but he'd be damned if he was going to quit when she wasn't.

"Fine," he said.

"So, where are we headed? A domestic abuse call?"

"Order violation."

She didn't reply. He knew she was waiting for him to fill in some of the gaps, to educate her on the call, to explain the nuances of it. But he wasn't ready to fully embrace their treaty again. So, he kept quiet and drove.

Murph checked out on-scene about twenty seconds before they arrived.

The turn before the address, Lee shut off all the patrol car's lights and hit the MDC's on-scene button. He parked a few yards behind Murph's car. As Lee climbed out of the car, he noticed Weaver doing the same.

"You can wait here if you want."

She seemed offended at his suggestion. "I'm not waiting in the car."

"It's not safe."

"I'm *not* waiting."

Lee hesitated. Murph was waiting for him, likely already posted up outside the door of the residence, listening for any signs of an ongoing assault. Arguing with Weaver was a waste of time. She was supposed to follow his directives without dispute, but he wasn't surprised by this. The problem was how to deal with it. Another verbal command would only net another refusal. Short of physically forcing her into the back of the cruiser, he didn't see another option.

"Fine, but you need to listen to me and follow directions."

She held up her hands in supplication. "I won't get in the way."

"Don't slam your door," he muttered. Now wasn't the time to go into a longer explanation. He locked the car door and closed it, setting off toward the target house. He cut through the open front yards from the corner to the house itself, three lots in. As he expected, Murph was already in place. The veteran officer caught his eye on approach. He flapped his hand to mimic people talking and then lowered the same hand to indicate the voices hadn't been above a mild argument. The temperature of the scene somewhat dictated their response, although with an order in place, the caller's statement, and a male voice inside, Lee knew they were going inside one way or another.

Lee moved to the side of the front door. He was aware of Weaver a few feet behind him. At least she had the sense to stick close to the house.

Once Lee was in position, Murph knocked. The sound of his fist echoed through the night. After a hushed exchange and a pause that was almost long enough to merit a second knock, the knob rattled and the door swung open. A white woman stood in the doorway. She wore a pair of dark blue yoga pants and an oversized T-shirt with Tweety Bird on it.

"Police, ma'am," Murph said before Lee could say anything. "Mind if we come in?"

The woman swallowed but stepped aside to let them enter. Murph went in first, ignoring the woman and sweeping visually for the male half of the couple. Lee kept the woman in view while he also watched for the man. Behind him, Weaver followed. She stepped inside just far enough to allow the woman to close the door, then backed up close to it.

"What's your name, ma'am?" Lee asked.

"Marsha."

"Marsha Gold?"

She nodded.

"Where's Timothy?" Lee asked.

Marsha licked her lips and swallowed before answering. "He's not here." Her voice was louder than it needed to be. "Why are you?"

Lee stared at her for a brief second, already tired of this game. "Are you alone in the house?"

"Yes."

Lee resisted a frown at the thin charade, but the woman had been the caller, so he knew it was possible she was acting now out of fear.

He glanced at Murph as he re-entered the living room. Murph returned the look and shook his head. To an outsider, Lee guessed his partner's expression seemed flat, but he read the nuance to it. Colton was hiding somewhere not immediately accessible on a safety sweep.

"Okay," Lee said evenly. "Has anyone hit you tonight?"

As he asked the question, he nodded in a slow, exaggerated bob, signaling her that she could give him a true answer with body language.

Marsha stared. "No," she said, shaking her head. "I'm alone. Who called you?"

"It doesn't matter. We're just here to make sure you're safe."

"I'm fine. You can leave."

"All right." Lee removed his pocket notebook. "But I need to confirm some information with you first."

"Why?"

"It's protocol, ma'am."

Lee scrawled out the words *where is he?* on a blank page. "Can you confirm the spelling of your name?" He held out the pad and pen to her.

Marsha took them hesitantly, reading the message.

"I know how to spell Gold," Lee clarified, "but how do you spell Marsha?"

Marsha gripped the pen but didn't immediately write anything. "M-A-R-S-H-A," she recited.

Lee pointed toward the notepad and mimed writing with his finger in the air. "See, I would have gone with the other spelling. C-I-A."

"No," Marsha said.

"Your date of birth?"

Marsha rattled off her birthdate in rote fashion.

"Phone number?" Lee asked.

In the same flat tone, Marsha recited it to him. As she spoke, though, she began to write something on the notepad.

"Are you working?"

"Yes."

"Where?"

"I tend bar at the Happy Time Tavern."

"Oh yeah? Pamela still work there?"

Marsha nodded. "Of course. She's dating the owner."

She handed the notepad back to him. Lee glanced down at her flowing script.

Bedroom closet.

Lee tilted the notepad toward Murph so he could read it. Then he said, "Well, here's the thing, Marsha. There's a domestic violence protection order in place that protects you from Timothy Colton. Have you seen Timothy?"

"No," Marsha said.

"Do you mind if we look around to make sure he isn't here?"

"He's not here," she said loudly. "I already told you."

"I know. But sometimes people lie to us about these things."

"I'm not."

"All right." Lee sighed, more for the benefit of the performance. But he was surprised at how much actual pent-up pressure rushed out of him. He sensed Weaver's eyes on him from where she stood vigil at the door. He showed her the writing on his notepad. Weaver cocked her head questioningly then quickly nodded with understanding.

Lee refocused on Marsha. "The truth is, Miss Gold, my asking for permission is just a matter of courtesy. With the order in place, we need to make sure you're safe."

"You don't have probable cause," Marsha said. "An order isn't a warrant."

"Ma'am—"

"You don't have the authority," she insisted.

Lee waited until he was sure she was finished before resuming himself. "It's not a question of authority, ma'am. It's a matter of obligation. Where these orders are concerned, we're mandated to take action."

Marsha had no response to that.

"Wait over there." Lee pointed to the couch. "We'll do a quick check and be out of your hair."

Marsha moved toward the couch and sat. Lee got her attention and pointed toward the bedroom. She nodded back. He formed a gun with his thumb and forefinger and raised his brows questioningly. Marsha's eyes widened momentarily. Then she shook her head.

That was good. Of course, a knife was every bit as dangerous, something he could personally attest to. But at least they didn't have to worry about Colton shooting at them through the closet door.

Unless she was lying.

Or wrong.

Lee met Murph's eyes again and wordlessly, they began the search.

Instead of going straight toward the closet in the bedroom, the two officers worked their way in that direction with a methodical search. Part of the reason was to maintain the fragile pretense for Marsha's benefit. The majority of the reason, though, was pure tactical caution. It wasn't uncommon for victims to lie in these cases. The overwhelming psychological weight of the abusive relationship could outweigh everything else. If Colton was able to ambush them because Marsha gave them bad intel, he was sure she'd be remorseful later. But that didn't change the outcome today.

Marsha could just as easily be wrong. Perhaps Colton told her he was going to hide in the bedroom closet but didn't. Or initially did so but moved when she went to answer the door. There were too many possibilities for things to go sideways if they blithely strode to the bedroom closet door and opened it.

Guns drawn and at the low ready, Lee and Murph moved through the house, clearing each location before moving on. In less than a minute, they stood on opposite sides of the bedroom door. Lee turned the knob and pushed it open. Both officers peered around the entryway. The room appeared empty. The sliding closet doors were shut. Aside from under the bed, Lee saw nowhere else to hide.

"Timothy Colton," Lee announced. "This is the Spokane Police Department. We know you're in there. Come out now with your hands where I can see them."

There was a short silence.

"If you don't come out," Lee warned, "we'll call for the K-9. He will find you and when he does, he will bite you."

Lee noticed movement in his peripheral vision and started to turn. Then he realized it was Weaver, following them. He shot her a warning look and jerked his head back toward the living room. Before Weaver could react, the sound of a sliding closet door filled the air.

"Screw it," a man's voice echoed from within the closet. "I don't want to get bit. I'm coming out."

Lee swiveled his attention back to the bedroom. A stocky man with greasy shoulder-length hair emerged from the closet. He wore a gray tank top and loose-fitting black shorts. He held his hands up in front of him as he stepped forward.

"Stop there!" Lee ordered.

Colton stopped.

"Turn away from me."

Colton turned a slow one-eighty.

Lee slid his gun into his holster and secured the safety straps over the weapon. Next to him came the clack and snap of Murph doing the same. Together, the two officers stepped into the room and moved toward Colton.

The bedroom was small, and the bed took up much of the space, allowing only a narrow corridor at the foot to reach the far side where Colton stood waiting in front of the open closet. Lee was closer and ended up first in line. By the time he reached Colton, he could see there wouldn't be room for both him and Murph to go hands-on at the same time. He reached out to take control of Colton's nearest arm.

The moment his fingers made contact, Colton wheeled and spun away. Lee charged forward but Colton leapt and rolled across the bed. Then the burly suspect made a dash for the door. Murph moved to intercept him. As Colton swept past him, Murph grasped in vain. Colton used one arm to deflect the grab, shooting toward the door like a running back breaking a tackle.

As Colton burst through the doorway and into the hall, a shocked and strangled cry came from Weaver. Without missing a beat, Murph ran after the suspect. Lee followed. His mind raced with the possibility that Colton may latch onto Weaver as a hostage. Footsteps trampled down the hall. A moment later, Lee was out the bedroom door and racing past Weaver, who stood with her back flattened against the wall to allow them through.

Lee rumbled down the hall as Murph quickly gained ground on Colton. After a few more steps, Murph launched himself forward, tackling him. The two men crashed to the floor, sliding forward into the living room.

Marsha screamed in surprise, then hopped onto the couch as if she'd spotted a mouse skittering across the floor. Lee kept his focus on Murph and Colton, both struggling on the ground.

"Stop resisting!" he bellowed, then jumped into the fray.

"Let me go!" Colton hollered. He jerked his arms and legs wildly, bucking and dancing in all different directions. Murph tried to grasp his right arm, but Colton's frenetic thrashing made it difficult.

Lee dropped his knee forcefully onto the back of Colton's thigh, trying to pin him to one place. The suspect howled in pain. His frantic movements increased. Lee's knee slid off Colton's leg and banged against the ground.

He grunted and tried again. Keeping his hands up to deflect any wayward kicks, Lee shuffled across Colton's body to the opposite side as Murph. Then he dropped his weight down onto Colton's back as the man started to press himself off the ground. The suspect let out a whoof as Lee's torso landed and collapsed to his stomach. Lee immediately reached for the suspect's right wrist and elbow.

Colton had other ideas. He managed to get both hands free and on the ground to his sides. With a guttural exhale, he pushed upward again.

Lee wavered slightly, his balance thrown as Colton did a pushup with him perched on the man's back. He tried once more to get a grip on the suspect's wrist, but it was now out of reach. He spotted Murph trying to wrest Colton's left arm with no success, either.

"Stop fighting!" Lee said. He pushed himself up then drove his entire body downward again onto Colton's back. The shift in weight made the stocky man waver, but he recovered. Lee felt the motion of Colton trying to get his knees underneath him.

"Clear," Murph said through gritted teeth.

Lee moved without thinking, sliding off Colton's back toward his right. A moment later, Murph landed a thundering knee strike to Colton's side.

"On the ground!" Lee ordered.

Colton grunted when the blow landed. He tilted and leaned away. His left arm came up and flailed at Murph, bouncing off his shoulder once, then tearing away the shoulder mic from the epaulet.

Murph threw another knee strike. This one landed more solidly. Colton rolled into Lee, curling up to protect his midsection. Lee grabbed onto his nearest wrist and elbow and tried to pry it free. Colton's arms were rock hard and had no give. Murph grabbed the suspect's other arm in a similar grip but couldn't budge it either.

"My way," Murph said.

Lee let go and started to push Colton over onto his stomach again. Murph released his grasp, reaching across to Colton's left wrist again. As the suspect rolled toward Murph, his right fist shot up, thudding against Murph's exposed midsection. His knuckles thumped against the police vest beneath Murph's uniform.

Enough of this, Lee thought.

He snaked his arm around Colton's neck, snugging his own chest to the man's back. Colton's elbow shot backward, grazing Lee's side but still delivering a surprising amount of force. Lee ignored the pain. He worked his forearm under Colton's chin and hoisted upward. The man resisted, but Murph delivered a sledgehammer blow to the solar plexus that caused him to momentarily weaken. Lee took full advantage, sliding his arm all the way around Colton's neck. The sides of the suspect's neck were now pinched between Lee's forearm and his bicep. As intended, his windpipe was largely unaffected in the open space created in the crook of Lee's arm.

Colton reached up with both hands to flail at Lee's arm. Lee countered by clasping his hands together for greater leverage. Colton's hands shifted, clawing at Lee's face. Lee tucked his chin, turned his face aside and squeezed. As soon as he compressed the sides of Colton's throat, the man tapped frantically at his arms, signaling surrender.

Lee considered rendering him unconscious anyway, just to be safe. But he took a chance and let up the pressure.

"Hands out to the side," he started to say, but before he could get the words out, Colton twisted violently in his grasp, trying to get free.

Lee held on, throwing a leg around Colton's waist for even better purchase. Once he got his arm in good position, he clamped down again. A moment later, Colton resumed his frantic tapping. Lee ignored the gesture this time and continued to squeeze. After a few seconds, Colton went limp in his arms.

"Out," he said. Murph was already slipping a handcuff over one wrist.

Lee kept the hold on for a five-count before he released it. He slid off Colton and rolled the man onto his belly. Then he grabbed the remaining free wrist and pulled it toward the small of his back for Murph to cuff.

It didn't reach.

Colton's thick body and short arms didn't allow his wrists to get close enough to handcuff. As soon as he recognized that, Lee shifted his position so that one knee rested on Colton's upper back, pinning the man to the ground. He kept his hold on the free wrist. Meanwhile, Murph withdrew a second pair of handcuffs from his belt. Expertly, the veteran officer connected one cuff to the other, then reached for Colton's unrestrained wrist.

That was when Colton woke up and came out fighting.

The stocky man angrily cried out and rocked back and forth against Lee's knee. Without his hands on the ground, he lacked significant support, but that didn't stop him from struggling. He slid his knees up and tried to get them underneath himself to push up. Meanwhile, he strained his arms against both Lee's and Murph's grasp.

Lee held on for all he was worth. He rocked back and forth with Colton's writhing, struggling to keep his wrist in place. His arms quivered with effort. Then he heard the cuffs ratchet into place.

"They're on," Murph grunted.

Almost as one, all three men sagged.

Lee waited a moment, panting heavily from exertion. Then

he shifted his weight off Colton warily, half-expecting another escape attempt. Colton lay still and wheezed laboriously. His face was hidden behind a wall of greasy hair.

"You're under arrest," Lee said, catching his breath. He looked up to see Marsha still standing on the couch, staring down at them in horror. Then he glanced around for Weaver. He spotted her a few feet away, standing at the hallway entrance. She stared, too, wide-eyed and slightly confused, her hand to her face. Lee had seen that look before.

It was the expression of the uninitiated.

"Hey, dude," Colton said, his tone unperturbed. "Can you get my hair out of my face?"

Chapter 16

MEL

It all happened too fast for her to process.

First, she was in the hallway, determined to witness the arrest.

Then a flurry of movement sounded from inside the bedroom. A man with a solid frame and long greasy hair burst through the doorway and barreled toward her. Before she could move or react, the palm of his hand lashed out and struck her in the mouth, driving her back into the wall. The force reverberated through her shoulder blades. Her face throbbed, not yet in pain but almost like a bass note singing out.

Officer Murphy darted out of the doorway and flashed past her. Right on his heels came Salter. Mel pressed her back to the wall to create as much space for them as possible. Then, holding her hand to her face, she stumbled after them.

A pile of humanity struggled on the living room floor while the woman—Mel suddenly couldn't remember her name—stood on her couch, looking on in horror. Mel watched, too, trying to follow the rapid shift of movement in the mass of arms and legs. Salter yelled several orders, but the man didn't obey. He tried to get up, but Murphy kneed him violently in the sides. Then Salter wrapped his arm around the man's throat in a chokehold.

She took a breath to yell. Before she could, the man went still. Salter released the man and flipped him on his stomach. The officers took forever to handcuff him, but once the ratcheting sound of the cuffs going on filled the room, the three men seemed to relax all at once, almost as if an unseen official had blown the play dead.

"You're under arrest," Salter grunted.

Mel realized she'd been holding the breath she'd taken to yell with. She let it out in a long whoosh. Salter looked up at the other woman—Mel still couldn't remember her name. Then Salter looked to her. His gaze settled on her for a long moment, but he said nothing.

"Dude, can you get my hair out of my face?" the man asked in a neutral tone.

Now, Mel tried to remember the man's name. She knew she'd heard it after they'd entered the house.

Salter appraised the man on the ground. "You going to bite me, Tim?"

Timothy Colton, she thought. That was it.

"No, man." Colton blew out a puff of air that rippled his hair but did nothing to clear it away from his field of vision. "Game over."

Surprisingly, Salter reached down and hooked some of Colton's long hair with his index finger. He flipped it so that it landed on the side of his head.

"Thanks."

Salter grunted. He rolled the man onto his side and said, "Stand up."

"I've got no hands."

"Use your legs," Salter said, getting his own feet underneath him. "Push against me."

"It won't work."

"Trust me. Engage your core."

Colton blew out air again, forcing aside some stray strands of hair still across his face. "Fucking yoga cop here," he muttered. But then he made an attempt. He stood far more easily than Mel imagined possible.

Salter guided the man toward the door.

Murphy joined them. "I've got this. My call, right?"

Salter shook his head. "We'll take him. She hasn't seen jail yet."

Murphy's eyes flicked over Salter's shoulder to Mel. She lowered her hands to her side. The throb in her lip was now punctuated with a sharp pain.

"You sure?" Murphy asked him.

"Will you guys stop fighting over me and figure this out?" Colton complained. "I want to get this bullshit done, get my jail sandwich, and hit the bunk, all right?"

"I'm sure," Salter told Murphy. He handed him his keys. "Put him in my car. I'll finish up in here."

Murphy shrugged. "Come on," he told the man, and led him out the front door.

Once Murphy was gone, Salter turned to the woman. "You can come down now," he said.

The woman glanced down at her feet, as if just realizing where she stood. Then she climbed off the couch. She remained standing, her arms wrapped around herself, seeming unsure of what to do next.

Salter withdrew a light tan card from his breast pocket. He scrawled something on it, then spoke into his radio. "Charlie-411, one in custody for DVOP. Also."

"Copy, at zero-one-fourteen hours. Go ahead your also."

"I need Lincoln-two-oh-five to meet me at jail. Also."

"Copy. Lincoln-two-oh-five?"

Another female voice came across the radio. *"Two-oh-five, copy."*

The dispatcher's voice returned. *"Charlie-four-eleven, your also?"*

"Incident number, please."

The dispatcher dictated a long number that Salter dutifully wrote on the tan card. He copied the transmission, then approached the woman. "Marsha, you've probably received one of these before? It's a crime victim card."

Marsha nodded woodenly.

Salter pointed at the card while he spoke. "This is the incident number. Here is my name and badge number." He flipped the card over, but Marsha wasn't paying attention. She stared at Melody as if seeing her for the first time. "These are some phone numbers for resources available to you," he continued, "including ones for victims of domestic violence. Do you understand?"

When Marsha didn't reply, Salter followed her gaze to Mel. Marsha said, "You're hurt."

As if in answer, Melody's lip twinged in pain.

"What happened?" Salter asked her.

"Nothing," she said automatically. "I'm fine."

"You're hurt," Marsha repeated. "I'll get some ice." She started toward the kitchen.

Mel opened her mouth to object, but Salter cut her off. "When'd you get hurt?"

His gaze was flat and penetrating. Her face tingled with warmth. "When he ran past in the hallway."

She could read Salter's thoughts plainly. His I-told-you-so expression rang out louder than if he'd shouted the words.

In the kitchen, the freezer door opened, and she heard Marsha digging out ice.

"How?" Salter asked her.

Mel swallowed. "He hit me with his hand."

"He *punched* you?"

"More of a shove."

"In the face."

She nodded. "It was open-handed."

Salter stepped closer and peered at her lip. "It's getting puffy. Does it hurt?"

"A little."

"You want to press charges?" he asked. "For assault?"

Mel hesitated. Her first reaction was an emphatic yes. But the images of the swift beating the man had taken, followed by getting choked out, gave her pause.

"I don't know," she said quietly.

Salter's eyebrows went up. "Why not?"

She pointed toward the living room floor. "Seems like maybe that was more than enough."

His eyebrows fell. "Justice administered at the scene, huh?"

"What's that?"

"Nothing. It means you figure it's even."

"Yeah. Maybe. I don't know."

"Well, you don't have to decide right this second."

Marsha returned, holding a beige wash rag. The ice wrapped inside clinked slightly when she handed it to Mel. "Sorry," she whispered.

"It's not your fault."

Marsha didn't answer.

Melody pressed the ice pack to her lip. "Thanks."

Marsha nodded.

Salter spent the next several minutes clarifying facts with Marsha. In reserved but impersonal tones, he established that she hadn't invited Colton to her home that night, that he hadn't assaulted her, and that she understood the process moving forward. She didn't have any questions for Salter. To Mel, Marsha seemed resigned to a fate that included periodic invasions like this, first by her abuser and then by the police.

"All right," Salter announced. "We're finished."

He said good night to Marsha and headed for the door. Mel started to follow, then held out the ice pack.

"Keep it," Marsha said.

Mel nodded her thanks and followed Salter outside.

At the car, Murphy stood next to the front wheel well of Salter's police car. The engine was running. She could see Colton sitting sideways in the back seat.

"Find anything on him?" Salter asked.

"Clean," Murphy answered. He held out a clear plastic bag with a wallet, comb, and a few coins visible in it. "Though we should have searched the bedroom closet while we still could. He probably dropped some dope in there."

Salter shrugged. "Easier if there aren't any drugs involved."

"I suppose."

"I'm going to book him for two counts of third," Salter said.

Murphy eyed him dubiously. "Not resisting?"

"He elbowed me. And he punched you."

Murphy touched his side. "Yeah, he did. There was nothing behind it, though."

"Still an assault."

"Prosecutor will never go on it."

"I don't care. The PC is there to book him."

"Your call."

"No," Salter said. "Technically, it's yours. He assaulted you."

Murphy thought it over. Melody stood at the passenger door of the patrol car and watched the exchange with some interest. She'd wanted to get into the warm car, but the door was locked. Now, she was more than a little fascinated by the officers' discussion.

"If Sarge signs off, I'm okay with it, too," Murphy finally said. "But you know it'll never go anywhere, right?"

"It'll go somewhere tonight," Salter said. He opened the driver's door and popped the lock to Mel's door. "Cut me an additional?"

"Affirm."

Murphy turned away without another word. Salter climbed into the driver's seat, so Mel followed suit. When she got inside, the first thing she noticed was the music. The car's radio was on, and country music was playing. The sounds were faded to the back seat.

Salter typed a few things on the MDC's keyboard, then started driving. Neither spoke for several blocks. Mel kept the ice pack pressed to her lip, grateful for the soothing coolness. Her mind still reeled. The swiftness of events barely allowed her time to process what had happened: Colton striking her, the brutality of the fight in the living room, the empty resignation in Marsha's eyes. All of it swirled around in her head. It was difficult to grab onto any one piece long enough to examine it.

"Hey," Colton called from the back seat.

Salter turned down the music volume. "What?"

"Who called you guys?"

"Why?" Salter responded. "So you can give them trouble?"

Colton scoffed. "Just tell me. I'm going to find out in discovery anyway."

173

"Then that's when you'll find out."

"Come on. It was her, wasn't it? Marsha."

Salter kept driving.

"She played it up while you guys were talking to her, but I could tell she was full of shit."

Salter said nothing.

"She invited me over, you know," Colton said. "The whole thing was a set up."

"If it was, you fell for it."

Colton sighed. "Bitches, man."

Salter didn't reply. They drove in silence for a while. Then he said, "Tell me something."

"Not without a lawyer."

"It's not that kind of question."

"What, then?"

"You were hiding in the closet. When we found you, you gave up. But then you ran."

"You practicing for how you're going to lie in your police report?"

Salter ignored the jibe. "My question is, why? Why give up and then run? If you were going to fight all along, why not wait to see if we found you first?"

"Why should I tell you?"

"Because I asked. If you don't want to say, don't. It just seemed kind of dumb to me."

"It would." Colton sat for a few seconds. Then he shrugged. "You were gonna call a dog."

"You're scared of dogs?"

"I sure as shit don't want to get bit by one." He paused, then shrugged again. "I figured I had a better chance against the two of you than three of you and a dog. So, I played along."

"Fair enough."

"What are you charging me with?"

"Violation of a DV Protection Order."

"No, I know that. What else? Resisting?"

"Assault. Three counts."

"Oh, that's bullshit. I never hit anyone."

"You punched my partner."

"I *pushed* him. To get him off me."

"It was a punch. But a push would still be an assault."

"A chicken shit assault."

"They count the same."

"I didn't touch you."

"I imagined that elbow you threw?"

"Must have. All I did was try to get away. I'll cop to that. But charging me with assault? After you tuned me up like that *and* choked me out? That's some bullshit."

Salter didn't answer. Mel listened to the conversation, transfixed. Focusing on it allowed her to escape the maelstrom of thoughts flashing through her mind. She was strangely reminded of the old Looney Tunes cartoons featuring the coyote and the sheep dog who were natural enemies but only while on duty. Once they punched off the clock, it always seemed like they'd go for a beer together. Salter and Colton weren't at that level, but their exchange seemed less adversarial than she'd have expected.

"Wait," Colton said. "*Three* counts? Is Marsha saying I hit her? I never hit her."

Salter tilted his head toward Mel. "You smacked her in the face when you ran down the hallway."

"What? No way."

"Her fat lip just magically appeared, I guess."

"I didn't hit her."

"Must've been the leprechaun we didn't see that hit her with his shillelagh."

"Very funny. You should take that shit on the road."

"I'm on the road every night."

"Whatever. She musta ran into something. But I didn't hit her."

A ripple of anger went through Mel. Salter told her that pressing charges was up to her. Now he was telling Colton it was already decided. Either he was lying to Colton now or he'd lied to her before. She didn't like either scenario.

Mel opened her mouth to say something, but Colton beat her to it.

"Are you saying I hit you?" He leaned forward and twisted in the backseat to better see her.

"Don't talk to her," Salter said.

"Lady, I didn't hit you."

"Your hand—" Mel began, but Colton interrupted.

"My hand didn't do nothing, you stupid bitch! Maybe you hit the wall trying to get out of my way but don't blame me because you're clumsy."

Mel flashed back to the moment Colton burst from the bedroom. Almost in slow motion, she could see the flat of his palm driving toward her face, forcing her back into the wall.

No. it wasn't an accident and she wasn't clumsy. He hit her on purpose.

She was sure.

"In fact, who the hell *are* you, anyway?" Colton continued in righteous indignation. "You don't look like no cop. What were you even doing in my house?"

"It wasn't your house," Salter said.

"Was I talking to you?" Colton growled.

"Well, you're not talking to her. I think we covered that. So why don't you shut up and sit back, huh?" He reached for the volume knob on the radio.

"Oh, I get it," Colton said, his voice smug. "She's your wife."

"Wrong answer."

"Sure, she is." Colton leaned forward slightly. "It's nice to get a good look at her now. I don't always see a bitch so clear when I'm fucking her in the dark."

A coldness swept down Mel's spine. The casual way Colton spoke made the threat seem very real.

"She tell you about us?" Colton asked.

It was exactly as Salter had said earlier in the night. Certain criminals would look for a weakness in an officer and try to exploit it.

"Say another word to her and I'll stack charges on you like cord wood, Timothy." Salter's tone was even, business-like.

"What is it—bring-your-wife-to-work day?"

"She's not my wife. She's with DOJ."

Colton hesitated. "No lie?"

"No lie."

Another lie, Mel thought. Even though it came easily to Salter, she now knew why he was doing it.

"Hey, DOJ lady," Colton said, "I hope you saw that excessive force back there. Beat the shit out of me *and* choked me out. That's gotta be illegal. I hope you disband this joke of a department. Defund the police, for sure."

Mel didn't answer, keeping her eyes straight ahead.

"And, uh, I'm sorry if I jostled you when I ran by," Colton muttered.

"Okay," Mel said without looking back.

"Still kinda bullshit to press charges over it."

"I'm not—"

Salter cut her off. "You're awful chatty, Timothy. Why don't you sit back and enjoy the ride? Here, I know you love the good old boys." He reached for the knob again.

"Not as much as I'm going to love pounding your wife."

"At least you stay on brand." Salter turned up the country song.

"You think I can't find her?" Colton shouted to be heard over the music. "Huh?" He banged his head hard against the thick plastic divider which caused Mel to jump in her seat. "Huh?"

Salter turned the music back down. Then he lifted his left hand from the steering wheel and held it for Colton to see. "I'm not married," he said, wiggling his ring finger for emphasis.

"Girlfriend, then. I don't care. It'll be just as easy to find her, pig. I'll find her and I'll—"

"No girlfriend, either."

Colton paused. "What? Are you gay or something?"

177

"Don't ask, don't tell."

For several beats, the only sound in the car was the quiet twang of a country guitar and some cowboy singing about drowning in beer. Then Mel heard the thick plastic shift as Colton adjusted his seating position on the bench seat.

"Seriously?" he asked.

Salter drove.

Chapter 17

LEE

At jail, Lee pulled up to the roll-up gate and pressed the call button outside his window. After a harsh buzz, a bored voice came through the speaker.

"Whaddaya got?"

"City booking one," Lee said. "DVOP."

The corrections officer on the other end didn't bother to reply. A moment later, the roll-up door engaged and chains rattled as it rose. Lee waited until he was certain his light bar on the roof would clear, then nudged the patrol car forward. He turned down the country music as he pulled into the narrow sally port.

"Joke's on you, buddy," Colton told him. "I like country."

"So do I," Lee said. But he filed away the information. If he ever came across Colton again, it would be heavy metal all the way to jail.

Lee parked and exited the car. He stowed his gun in the nearby weapons locker, tucking the locker key into his belt. He noticed Weaver still seated in the patrol cruiser. He thought about leaving her there but decided not to. Colton had calmed down for most of the last part of the drive to jail, but you never knew when a suspect might tip over again.

At her door, he tapped the window to get her attention. Then he beckoned her to follow him. Weaver put her makeshift ice pack on the floor and got out, closing the door behind her.

"Stick close to me through the booking process," Lee said. "There are rules where you can and can't go. And jailers are sticklers for the rules."

"All right."

Lee turned and headed into the officer's lobby of the booking area. The glass doors swooshed open as he approached, reminding him of a grocery store. Inside, he got the attention of Mike Tately, a corrections officer better known as Tater. Tall and hulking in a farmhand sort of way, Tater exuded good old boy vibes without even saying a word. Once he opened his mouth, that went double. Even so, the man was as shrewd as any jailer Lee knew.

"Whattaya got, Lee?" Tater asked.

"DVOP violation, for starters. Maybe some assault add-ons. I have to check with my sergeant first."

Tater's brow crinkled. "Doesn't an assault in violation of an order make it a felony?"

"He didn't assault her."

"Oh. Third degree? On you guys?"

"If the sergeant goes for it."

"All right, then. Who is it?"

"Timothy Colton. You know him?"

Tater nodded. "He's not so bad. Got some women issues, but he behaves in here."

Tater motioned for another corrections officer to join him, and the pair left the lobby to retrieve Colton from Lee's patrol vehicle. Lee moved to the officer's work area, which consisted of a long bar-style table without any chairs. The design was smart, as it encouraged officers to hurry up to finish only the most necessary paperwork before departing the booking area.

Lee picked a computer station and pulled up the booking screen. After entering his name and badge number, he minimized the tab and opened the Computer Aided Dispatch (CAD) application. He typed in UNIT STATUS C411 The system brought up the call he was currently assigned to. He cut and pasted the incident number into the booking form. This auto-populated much of the remaining information on the form. He reviewed it, utilizing the option to assign proper roles. He designated Marsha Gold as the victim and Timothy Colton as suspect/defendant. A quick scroll downward verified that the court-assigned number for the protection order hadn't cross-pollinated, so Lee cut and pasted that as well.

A moment later, Colton sauntered in, guided by Tater's hand on his right arm. Colton pointedly ignored Lee but made eye contact with Weaver.

"Remember what you saw," he told her.

"Leave it," Tater said in a low, easy voice. At the same time, he jerked Colton toward the doorway that led to the booking area's in-processing station. The action reminded Lee of a person tugging the leash of a dog barking at another dog while on a walk.

"Tell D.C.!" Colton hollered from the next room.

"Don't worry about him," Lee said to Weaver. "He's a big talker, that's all."

Weaver nodded, but she didn't look so sure.

"You should remember what you saw, though. The sergeant is going to want to talk to you about that."

"What?"

"For the use-of-force report. You're a witness."

"Oh."

He was surprised to see that this hadn't already occurred to her. Maybe she was still getting her head wrapped around what happened. He had to constantly remind himself how things that seemed ordinary to him were extraordinary to civilians.

He glanced back at the booking form, then clicked SAVE PROGRESS. He'd need to get Sergeant Gelabert's approval before adding the two counts of Third-Degree Assault on a Law Enforcement Officer.

And then there was Weaver.

"Did you decide if you want to press charges yet?" he asked her.

Her eyes narrowed. "It sounded to me like you already made that decision for me."

He gave her a confused look. "No, it's up to you. You're the victim."

"In the car, you told him three counts."

"So?" The tickle of frustration that he'd experienced most

181

of the night enveloped him again. "And before you say it, no, I didn't lie to you. And yes, I *did* lie to him."

"Why?"

"Let him sweat it, that's why. Plus, he's a woman beater. He doesn't deserve the truth. People like him use the truth to manipulate people." He motioned to her lip. "Like how he tried to gaslight you about that."

Weaver raised her fingers to touch her swollen lip.

Lee shrugged. "If you have a problem with lying, then you couldn't do this job, because sometimes you need to lie for the greater good."

"Like with that woman? Pretending she didn't call the police?"

"Exactly."

"Was he right when he said he'd find out eventually?"

"Yeah. But the least we can do is give her a head start, if she decides to use it."

Weaver seemed to consider that. Then she said, "I got the sense she might not be able to."

"She can," Lee assured her. "But you're right—she may not." He jerked his head toward the computer screen. "So should I charge him for assaulting you?"

Weaver stared back at him. He waited, letting her work it out. To him, it was a no-brainer, but he had no idea what kind of dissonance she was dealing with. He doubted Weaver had been hit in the mouth before, so this was probably a lot to process.

"No," she said finally.

He cocked his head. "You sure?"

"I'm sure. I don't know what good it'd do."

Lee wanted to say it would do a whole lot of good to make a person pay for smacking some innocent bystander in the mouth. But the pragmatist in him knew she had the right of it. Even if Colton was convicted of the assault, it was a misdemeanor. He was already facing the order violation. His conviction for that was a *fait accompli*, since all the prosecutor had to prove was that the order was valid and that Colton was in the house. No doubt, he'd be found guilty and sentenced. If he got time for the assault on Weaver, it would likely be less because there wasn't a domestic violence element to it. Not only that, the time would run concurrently, anyway. There'd be no extra jail time in it for Colton. Sure, he'd get another conviction on his record, but it was a misdemeanor. After a certain point, those just didn't move the needle when it came to future sentencing.

He said, "Your call."

"Then I want to let it be."

"Done."

Lee turned back to the booking form and scrolled through it again, double-checking details. While he was proofreading, Sergeant Gelabert strode in through the sliding doors.

"Hey Sarge," Lee said. When Gelabert cast a look at Weaver, he introduced the two of them.

Gelabert stepped forward and extended her hand to Weaver. "Nice to meet you, Ms. Weaver."

Weaver took her hand and shook it. "Call me Melody."

"I'm Jamie." Gelabert noticed Weaver's swollen lip. "What happened there?"

Lee opened his mouth to answer but Weaver was quicker.

"The guy they arrested ran into me."

Gelabert raised a brow. "Ran into you?"

Weaver nodded. "His hand hit me as he went by."

The sergeant looked back and forth between Weaver and Lee. "Did you want to press assault charges?"

"No, I'm okay."

"All right. Well, it was nice to meet you, Ms. Weav— I mean, Melody." Gelabert turned to Lee. "Officer, a word, please?"

"Sure." He glanced at Weaver. "I'll be right back."

"Okay."

Lee headed into the sally port. Behind him, Gelabert said, "By the way, I'm sorry we weren't able to pair you with a female officer like you requested."

"It's all right," Weaver answered.

Lee wandered toward his patrol car and waited for Gelabert.

When the sergeant came through the sliding doors, she was straight to business. "Are you all right?"

"Fine. He got in a glancing blow with his elbow, is all."

"And Murph?"

"The guy punched him in the ribs, but Murph said it didn't really hurt."

"What about her?" Gelabert swung a thumb back toward the officer's lobby.

"My guess is she got stiff-armed in the face when Colton ran past her. But I didn't see it, and she's not pressing charges."

Gelabert dropped her hand. "Her choice. So, tell me how it happened."

Lee walked through the call with her, detailing the specific actions he took and the verbal directions he used with Colton. He described the use of force in clinical terms, knowing that was how both he and Gelabert would record it in their respective reports. His report was to chronicle what occurred to serve as the official record of the event, to be used as a resource in Colton's criminal case. Gelabert's report would focus on the use of force—what happened and the reasons for it. Although a determination of whether the conduct was proper rested with the chief's office, Gelabert and his shift lieutenant, Bo Sherman, would make recommendations. So would the patrol commander, Captain Dan Flowers. Flowers had been largely invisible since taking over the position, so Lee didn't know what his take would be.

Still, he wasn't worried. Everything he and Murphy did had been appropriate. Of course, DOJ might decide to look at the report and reach a different conclusion, especially since Lee employed a neck restraint. The feds hated that technique with a passion that bordered on irrational, at least in Lee's opinion.

The sergeant glanced over her shoulder to the booking lobby. When her attention returned to him, she asked, "When did you decide to apply the LVNR?"

"After he became assaultive."

"Level one?"

The Lateral Vascular Neck Restraint technique was broken into two distinct levels. Level one consisted of the officer getting into position with an arm fully around the suspect's neck and applying pressure. The technique became a level two when the officer rendered the suspect unconscious.

"I started to go straight to level two," Lee told her. "Then he tapped out, so I let up and went back to level one. But it was a ploy. Guy tried to get free as soon as I stopped, so I applied pressure again."

"And rendered him unconscious." She sounded disappointed.

"That's the purpose of the technique, Sarge."

"Don't get wise," she admonished him, but there was little force behind it. "How long was Colton out?"

Lee thought back to the scuffle. "Five or six seconds. Turned out it wasn't long enough to get him cuffed, though."

"How about the knee strikes? Did you see Murphy throw them?"

"Yeah. I was on top of the guy, trying to pin him down, but he just got his arms under him and did a pushup with me on his back." Lee shook his head. "Dude was strong."

"He works cement," Gelabert said.

"Yeah? How'd you know that?"

"Power shift picked him up four, maybe five weeks ago, on the DV that probably resulted in your protection order. He fought with them, too. I interviewed him after."

Colton was a serial fighter. That didn't surprise Lee.

He studied her eyes. "You see a problem with this?"

Gelabert shook her head. "*I* don't. Neither will the El-Tee. Flowers, I don't know. He's already a little too cozy with city hall, and the recent promotion makes him a wild card. But I don't see the chief's office balking at anything you did."

"That might depend on if it's the big chief or the little chief," Lee said, referring to Baumgartner and Hatcher, respectively.

"Don't let Dana hear you call her little," Gelabert warned. "She's carrying a lot of the load since getting promoted."

Lee had long suspected that Assistant Chief Dana Hatcher had taken Gelabert under her wing. It was an old practice on the department, as senior commanders identified capable leaders in the junior ranks and mentored them. This didn't ensure those mentees made rank, but it certainly gave them an advantage. Lee had seen it happen even before he came on the job, as his father became rabbi to a few different officers, including Baumgartner himself.

The entire tradition was something more than simple mentorship and maybe a little less than a good-old-boys network. Lee wasn't sure if it was a good thing or a bad thing, but it seemed right that if Hatcher was going to play the same game, she chose another woman, one who deserved it.

"I'll remember that," Lee said. "Especially since she's all but assured of taking the big chair when Chief B leaves."

"If Mayor Patterson is still on the seventh floor when that happens, I'd say you're probably right." Then Gelabert frowned. "Tell me about the ride so far."

He shrugged. "You know."

Gelabert looked at him carefully. "No, I don't."

Lee glanced into the booking lobby. Weaver's attention was on her cell phone. He lowered his voice. "We're not exactly getting along."

"How so?"

His attention returned to Gelabert. "She finds fault in everything I do and explaining things doesn't seem to matter."

"Asking questions is why she's here."

Lee shuffled his feet slightly. "It is," he admitted. "but it's been more than that. Constant criticism."

"Constant?"

He shrugged again. "Maybe not constant but it sure as hell feels close to that."

"Okay. What do you want to do?"

"I'd like to drop her off and be done with it, you want the truth."

Gelabert watched him without answering.

Lee realized how he sounded and smiled apologetically. "I'll finish out the shift, but don't be surprised if it goes to shit."

"We can't control what she says or does after she goes home, but the one thing she can't say is that we terminated the ride."

Lee didn't imagine that would provide much shelter for Assistant Chief Hatcher—Dana —when she stood in front of the city council or the PRI. But he kept his opinion to himself.

"Anything else for me?" Gelabert asked.

"I need booking approval for two counts of third assault."

"Third? On law enforcement?"

Lee nodded.

Gelabert pursed her lips. "The prosecutor will never go on it."

"I know."

"Then why waste the paper?"

"Because there's PC and if he goes before the right judge, maybe his bail gets jacked up. Might keep him away from the DV victim for a little while longer. Maybe give her a chance to make some changes."

"That's it? That's the only reason?"

Lee shrugged. "The only one that matters."

Gelabert thought it over. "All right, it's approved."

"Thanks, Sarge."

"I'm glad no one was seriously hurt." Gelabert turned to go, then stopped. "And thanks for your effort with your rider. I won't forget it."

"No problem."

"For what it's worth, she seems decent enough to me."

"She is decent," Lee agreed. "She's just a pain in the ass, too."

"Just so you know, you can be a pain in the ass yourself." Gelabert chuckled and motioned toward the lobby. "I've got to go interview Ms. Weaver for the use of force. You want to wait here?"

"How about if I jet over to property? You could drop her there when you're done."

"You've got evidence?"

"The victim wrote me a note, remember?"

"Ah. All right. You want a picture of Melody's lip, too, even though she isn't pressing charges?"

"That'd be great."

"You got it."

Gelabert walked back through the sliding doors and disappeared around the corner into the officer's lobby.

Lee retrieved his gun from the weapons locker and holstered it. Then he pulled out of the sally port and headed over to the property room. The emptiness of his patrol car felt like freedom.

Chapter 18

MEL

Jamie Gelabert was easy to talk to.

She asked questions of Melody in a way that was both open-ended but still steered the conversation forward. She took diligent notes on a steno pad. After Melody described what she'd seen during the arrest, Jamie circled back to when Colton struck her in the hallway.

"Do you think that was intentional?"

Mel thought about it. "I think pushing me aside was on purpose. Actually hitting me in the face? I don't think it was."

"You know why there was an order in place, don't you?"

"I assume the woman asked for it."

"No," Jamie said. "About a month or so ago, he beat her up. We arrested him and as part of being charged with domestic violence assault, the judge issued a protection order."

"Why are you telling me this?"

"In case you are having any feelings of misplaced sympathy for Timothy Colton. He's a criminal and a domestic abuser."

"I don't feel sorry for him," Mel said. "I just don't want to press charges."

"That's your choice, and I respect that."

"Then why are you bringing it up?"

Jamie smiled tightly. "How are things otherwise?"

"What do you mean?"

"Your ride-along? Anything I can do to help?"

Mel took a deep breath and let it out. "I don't know what you can do. Officer Salter said—"

"Lee."

"What?"

"His name's Lee. What did he say?"

"He said that he thought our frames of reference were too different to have a meaningful conversation."

"Are they?"

"I don't know. Maybe. But isn't that the whole reason I'm here?"

"Good point. Any other issues?"

Mel gave her a questioning look. "What do you mean?"

"I've been on the job for a long time," the sergeant said. "The department's about twenty percent female now, and that's a far sight more than when I came on. In all that time, I've learned that the male/female dynamic can be challenging in all sorts of ways."

"Oh," Mel said. She thought about it. "No, that's not the problem. Nothing out of the ordinary, anyway."

"Good." Jamie flipped her notebook shut. "Sometimes being able to hear each other takes a little while, you know?"

"Maybe so."

"Come on. I'll drop you off at the property room."

The ride took less than two minutes. Jamie parked the car and led Mel to the square, non-descript building. She used her ID card to gain access at the secure door and held it open for Mel.

Inside, the musky odor of marijuana permeated the air. The small lobby with several workstations was empty except for Salter, who sat typing at a terminal.

Not Salter, Mel corrected. *Lee.*

"That was fast," he said, without looking back.

"Pretty straightforward," Jamie answered him.

"I need just a few minutes to finish knocking out this report." He pointed through a doorway into another, smaller lobby. "Soda machine is in there, if you want."

"Sounds good," Mel said. "I could go for something caffeine-free."

"I've got it." Jamie headed that way. Mel tried to protest, but Jamie waved away her attempt. "My pleasure."

Mel found a seat and sat. Lee continued to type, the rattle and tap of the keyboard filling the room. She opened an app on her phone to see if she had any messages but found none.

That only made sense. David would be somewhere over the Pacific Ocean right then.

Jamie returned with a can of soda. "This one okay?"

"Of course. Thanks." The crisp, carbonated soda was refreshing. She took several swallows before putting it on the table in front of her.

"I have to head out," Jamie said. She slid a business card across the tabletop to Mel. "But call me if you need anything." She turned toward the typing officer. "And Lee?"

"Sarge?"

"You take care of Melody here, all right?"

"Copy that."

Jamie smiled and nodded to Mel before heading out the door.

Mel let some time pass without any conversation. While Lee typed, she scrolled through Facebook on her phone. The few minutes of escape was nice, even if the posts on social media were as polarized as ever.

"I was thinking about something," Lee said, not looking away from the computer screen.

"What's that?" She continued scrolling.

"You said you never used the college scholarship, the one in your dad's name. Why not?"

She lowered her phone. "Why do you ask?"

"I'm just curious. I mean, the whole reason the police union started the scholarship was initially to help his kids, so..."

"I didn't need it," she said, but even to her, the words sounded limp.

"Huh."

They were quiet for a moment. The room was silent except for the clacking of the keyboard as Lee wrote his report. The air was thick with tension and with the pervasive smell of marijuana.

"We weren't close," Melody finally said.

Lee paused in his typing but didn't turn in his seat.

"The truth is," she continued, "I stopped being proud of him by the time I was twelve or thirteen. He had one face for the rest of the world and another one for us at home. I didn't like the dissonance in the masks he wore."

She paused, remembering how angry he'd been when she coined the term 'resting cop face.' "It went on like that for years—one mask for the family, a mask for his friends, and another for the rest of the world. By the time my dad died, I was seventeen and in full-on rebel mode. I'm sure I was a major disappointment to him."

Lee glanced at her. The mask he'd worn most of the night slipped. "I'm sorry."

She couldn't read what was going on in his eyes. Had they been friends, she might have asked. Instead, she shrugged. "It's the past."

Lee swiveled fully in his chair to face her. "If it's any consolation, my dad's disappointed in me, too."

She cocked her head. "Why? You followed in his footsteps."

"Only to the job. I haven't promoted up at all. He's on my case about that every chance he gets. Thanksgiving is particularly brutal."

"I can only imagine." She sipped the soda, wondering how the holidays would have been if her father was still around. Would he have mellowed? She didn't think so. Probably gotten harder, and more distant. "What about your grandfather?"

"He wanted me to promote, too. But he also told me to stay in patrol for ten years first so that I didn't lose touch with the line. That's what happened with dad. Or so some people say."

"What people?"

"My granddad, for one. He and my father never got along that great when both were on the department." Salter turned back to the computer. He rested his fingers on the keyboard but didn't type. "Granddad died when I was just hitting the ten-year mark. He didn't get the chance to be disappointed."

"You think he would have been?"

Lee stared at the computer screen before finally shrugging a single shoulder.

"I'm sorry," she said.

"No, *I'm* sorry." Lee eyed her. "I didn't mean to lay all that on you. I was just curious about the thing with your dad."

He resumed typing.

Melody sat for a few moments, the weight of the conversation hanging thick in the air. Then she decided to try to lighten the mood a little. "You know what I'm curious about?" she said. "Is that marijuana I'm smelling?"

"Can confirm."

"Why is it here?"

"It's evidence."

"Of what? Pot's been legal for years."

"Some of it is still here from before it was legal. Those cases are still valid because it was illegal at the time. And the rest is here because it's still illegal to grow without a permit. Unlawful grow operations get taken down all the time."

"There's that much in here, though? For it to smell like this?"

"This is nothing," he said. "There's one hell of a ventilation system back there now and it vents out most of the odor. Our old property room barely had any ventilation. That place stunk to high heaven."

The thought made Mel grin.

"What?" Lee asked.

"I'm just imagining a bunch of cops getting a contact high from turning in evidence."

"Weed doesn't work that way."

"I know that. But it's still funny."

Lee turned his head toward her, a trace of smile lighting on his mouth. "Well, if that were the case, the drive-thru lane at Taco Bell would constantly be six deep with police cruisers."

"Exactly."

They sat still for a moment, as if both were testing out the shared levity, to see if it took. Then Lee said, "Sure would make the job easier."

Mel's grin twitched upward. "Could be that we found the answer to police reform," she joked. "Instead of defunding the police, maybe we should approve a line item in the budget for some weed."

"Get some for the judges and prosecutors, too, and I'm on board."

"I'll see what I can do."

"Hell, everyone else is getting stoned," Lee said as he typed. "We might as well, too."

Chapter 19

LEE

Once the report was finished and Marsha Gold's note placed on evidence, Lee announced that he was ready to go. Melody followed him out to the car.

They'd remained quiet after the exchange regarding marijuana. For his part, Lee was content to let a slightly positive moment linger while he finished writing the Colton arrest report. Just to be safe, he saved it as a draft rather than submitting it. He'd review it again in the late hours of the shift when things were slow. Once he hit send, the report was his official account of the event. Many officers became blasé about so-called routine reports, but Lee had learned early on to treat every report like it was going to be pored over by a dozen different people. It was a lesson that had been pounded into him by his father, his FTOs, and Sergeant Gelabert, among others.

In the car, he started the heater and checked calls. There were several holding but most were low priority. Another report of possible vehicle prowlers in East Central was in the queue. He scanned the text. The descriptions were the same as before but were also general enough to fit that entire subspecies of criminal.

Still, it was his assigned neighborhood, so he should check it out. Besides, it irked him that these little bastards were out preying on people who worked for a living.

His stomach grumbled in protest. He thought about his lunch bag in the trunk. If nothing turned up on the search for vehicle prowlers, there was a substation in that area as well. He could take a quick lunch break there.

"You didn't bring a lunch, did you?" he asked Melody.

"No. I ate dinner with David before he dropped me off."

"I'm thinking about taking a short break in a bit to eat my

lunch. If you're hungry, there's usually some things at the substation that the volunteers bring in. Or I can hit a drive-thru for you."

"Taco Bell?" she asked lightly.

"Whatever you want."

"No. I meant... after the pot smell at the property place?"

"Oh." He forced a small smile. "I get it. But seriously, anywhere you want that's open."

"I'm fine for now."

Lee started to dispatch himself on the vehicle prowling call, then stopped. A new call had appeared while they were talking, labeled ABAND CHILD. He pulled it up and read the text.

"What's that?" Melody asked.

"Looks like a neighbor is reporting a four-year-old kid who has been left alone in the house next door," he said.

"Four-years-old?"

Lee nodded absently. Then he picked up his phone and dialed dispatch. Jackie Reynolds answered on the second ring.

"Police communications."

"Jackie, Lee."

"Hey. I'm glad you called. There's an abandoned child call I was about to send you to on the edge of downtown."

"I'm looking at it now. Do we know who the kid is?"

"No. The neighbor, Kathy Lindblom, said that a woman and her kid moved in a couple of weeks ago. I did a CAD search but there's been no calls to that address in the last thirty days. There was a burglary there about six weeks ago, so I could try to contact the listed tenant then but..."

"But it's two in the morning and they don't live there anymore."

"Exactly."

"All right. I'll head over. Maybe mom is crashed out, and the neighbor isn't aware she's home."

"Could be but she said she saw the woman leave the house about six-thirty."

"Still could have missed her coming back," he said.

"Maybe."

"Go ahead and put me on it."

"Done," Jackie replied.

A half-second later, his MDC beeped.

"*Adios*," Lee said.

"Happy trails." Jackie clicked off.

He glanced at Melody. "You catch all of that?"

"I think so, but how's the neighbor know the kid is there?"

Lee scrolled down the call while he drove. "Says here that she got up to go to the bathroom and noticed the lights were still on. Then there was movement on the porch, which turned out to be the kid. She went out to check on him and then called us."

"Is that typical?"

"What, negligent parents or nosy neighbors?"

"The lack of details. Or missing ones, at least."

Lee shrugged. "It's an imperfect world. We'll find out the rest when we get there. That's one thing I learned a long time ago. The information you get on a call is a starting point and not always an accurate one. You've got to be adaptable because when you get on scene, things are frequently different than what you expected them to be."

"I get that. I have to adapt my lesson plans when the kids react differently than I expected. It's not the same thing but it's similar."

Lee shrugged. He supposed it was close enough.

"I want to ask you something," Melody said.

"Go ahead."

"That fight, from before."

"With Colton."

"Yes."

"What about it?"

"Your sergeant—Jamie—she asked me some questions. I told her what I saw, but there was one thing she didn't ask me."

"She missed a fact?"

"No. She didn't ask me what I thought about what happened."

"Your opinion, you mean?"

"Yes. I thought it was curious that she didn't ask."

"There was no reason to. Opinions don't matter. All they do is muddy the waters." He glanced over at her while he drove. "What's your point? You had a problem with what happened?"

"Honestly, I don't know. But I think so, yes."

Lee looked back out at the road. "What was the issue?"

"A couple of things. For one, why did Murphy knee him like that? I know he was trying to get away but—"

"He kneed Colton twice after the guy threw a punch. We were trying to force him into a prone position so he could be handcuffed."

"I didn't see a punch."

"I did. And Murph felt it."

"Okay."

Lee cocked his head. "Things happen fast in a fight. If you're not used to being in one or even seeing it, it's easy to miss."

"I can accept that. But the whole thing seemed... brutal."

"It is. Violence is ugly. But I find it interesting how people always seem to blame the police for that violence when it is the suspect who drives the situation."

"How?"

"He could give up at any time."

Melody scoffed. "He was in flight mode."

"He knew exactly what he was doing. And at any moment, he could have surrendered." Lee turned onto Monroe and headed downtown. "Not only that but his actions dictated our response. We escalate our force to match and overcome whatever he's doing. If all he's doing is lying there, non-compliant like a dead fish, he's not going to get a knee in the side. But when he's punching cops, that raises things. We need to employ techniques that will defeat his actions. And the sooner we do it, the safer for everyone."

"You know earlier, when you said I was quoting something out of the PRI handbook?"

"Yeah?" He glanced over again.

Melody spread her hands in a *there-you-go* gesture.

Lee looked away. "I'm giving you the reality of the situation. Fights look bad, but the suspect is the one driving the bus."

"There's been a lot of instances captured on video in the past few years where you'd be hard pressed to argue that."

"I can't be responsible for what happens at other agencies, or what other officers do. I can only control what I do."

"Well, that's actually the other thing I'm struggling with."

"Me?"

"The chokehold you used is illegal."

"No, it's not. The LVNR is an approved technique."

"The state legislature just signed a bill outlawing its use. It's sitting on the governor's desk."

"Which means it isn't a law yet," Lee said. "And until that bill is signed, it is an entirely legal technique."

"That's technically true, but why use it at this point?"

"At what point? When a suspect who is stronger than I am is being assaultive? Or when the winds of political correctness are blowing a certain way?"

"It's not about political correctness. It's about making things safer."

"*Safer?* How does taking away a valuable tool from law enforcement make anything safer?"

"The chokehold has long been abused by police. You can't argue that isn't true."

"It's not a chokehold, it's a neck restraint. They are two entirely different things. And every single technique used to subdue a suspect has been abused by some police officer somewhere at some point. Instead of taking away the technique as an option, why don't we focus on those few instances where there is actual abuse? How about that?"

"Like George Floyd?"

"Perfect example. That cop is in prison now."

"If kneeling on someone's neck was an illegal tactic, he wouldn't be. And more importantly, George Floyd would be alive."

Lee shook his head. "The problem there wasn't that he used a particular technique. It was that he didn't stop using it once he had control of the subject."

"So, you agree with the verdict?"

"Do you remember what I said earlier about my reaction to these kinds of cases?"

"That you weren't there?"

"That's right. And neither were you. You don't know all the facts. But a fact I do know is that pinning a suspect to the ground with a knee across the upper back or neck is an effective way to get him handcuffed. Staying in that position for an extended period is another matter."

"You feel the same way about the chokehold, then?"

"The LVNR," he corrected again. "And yeah, I do. It's one of the most effective tools we have out here for ending a fight. You can go back through our use-of-force records and see. Injuries are rare. Compliance is almost one hundred percent. Suspects give up, sometimes even before you put on the pressure. So why would you take that away? It saves lives."

"That's quite an endorsement."

"It's a fact."

"What about people who have died from it?"

"Show me where that's happened."

"It's happened," Mel said. "I've seen the studies."

"So have I. What those studies fail to point out is that the rate of injury or fatality is extremely low. You're in more danger now, riding in a car, than a suspect is of being hurt or killed from an LVNR application. And when it does happen, the reason is almost always either an underlying medical issue on the part of the suspect or a misapplication of the technique by the officer, getting the windpipe in front instead of compressing the blood flow on the side."

"Even if that's true—"

"It's true. You just don't want it to be."

"Even if it is, why take the chance? You can't know if someone has one of those medical issues. Anyone could. And there's always a chance the officer will make a mistake or purposefully use the technique wrong."

Lee sniffed and shook his head, looking straight ahead. "This is the same kind of thinking that results in people asking why we can't just shoot someone in the leg or shoot the gun out of their hand."

"No, it's *not*," Melody said, her tone sharp. "I'm not asking police to do ridiculous movie or TV stunts. I understand the real world is different and so do most people who want police reform. Why are you so resistive?"

"Because it's unrealistic and uninformed."

"One thing I can assure you is that the PRI is not uninformed. We have reams of information, much of it provided by your own department."

"Maybe so, but the way you look at it is unrealistic." He drove under the Hamilton Street underpass, changing lanes to the middle one. "Most of these opinions come from people who have never been in a fight before, who don't understand the dynamics of physical conflict, and have no idea what goes into use-of-force decision-making. They think it's easy for some reason. Fighting is not easy at all. It's hard. And you know what's even harder? Trying to get someone under control without hurting them."

"That's the job," Melody said.

"I know it's the job. I've got no problem with it. My problem is with people who don't know my job trying to tell me how to do it."

"You know, you keep insulting my intelligence. It's getting old."

"I'm not insulting your intelligence. I'm pointing out where your thinking is wrong."

"What about yours?"

"Mine is based on hard-earned experience."

"That's why you used a technique that is universally criticized as dangerous and racist?"

"I used it because it's effective and safe. Experience has shown me that. To your point, everything out here is dangerous, and there's nothing racist about a technique. Only a person can be racist."

"Now you're being pedantic. The chokehold has been disproportionately utilized against people of color for decades."

"Not here."

Melody paused, as if considering the point. Finally, she said, "I'm going to withhold judgment on that one. I'd need to see the statistics. But that doesn't change the fact that it's about to be banned by state law."

"You keep hitting on that. I don't care. It *isn't* law yet. It is still legal and within policy. And the results speak for themselves. I ended the fight with Colton. No one got hurt. You take away the LVNR in that situation and what does that leave me? Arm bars? Wrist locks? Great techniques, but he had all the leverage and was strong as an ox. So then what?"

"I don't know."

"That's my point. I'll tell you what comes next if we're going to get him into custody. Knee strikes, elbow strikes, Tasers, or pepper spray. All of which are either less effective or more violent. And I'm sure any of those would register a protest from the PRI as well."

"I'm not advocating taking away all of your options. Just the most dangerous ones. The ones that get misused the most."

"If the governor signs that bill into law and the LVNR is banned, you're going to see an uptick in injuries during use-of-force incidents. I'm talking cops and suspects both. Hell, you'll probably see some kind of high-profile bad event that could have been avoided. And when it does, instead of blaming the loss of a valuable technique as an option, groups like yours will decide it's because the cops are bad."

"Some cops are. You can't deny that."

He thought about that. "I'm not. Cops are people, so it's going to happen. But bad cops are rare."

Melody was quiet. After a few moments, he glanced over. Her expression was one of disbelief.

"What?" Lee asked. "Now you think bad cops are a dime a dozen?"

"No. But calling them rare isn't accurate, either."

"I've worked this job for fourteen years. Trust me, most cops are hard-working, dedicated people who care. The occasional bad cop—"

"What about Tyler Garrett?"

Lee stopped. He looked away again, taking a deep breath and letting it out. "Garrett was a bad cop," he admitted.

"Did you know he was bad?"

"No!" The ferocity of his denial surprised even himself. He swallowed before continuing. "No. I don't think anyone did, not until the very end."

"The Norris Commission's investigation said otherwise."

"You mean Detective Clint and Captain Farrell."

"Exactly. From what the report said, they knew for two years."

"I read it."

"And?"

"Seemed like they knew, yeah. But that only proves what I'm saying. They spent those two years trying to take him down. And what'd they get for it? Farrell was forced into retirement and Clint got suspended."

"It's interesting to me that you characterize them as good cops taking down a bad cop. They conducted a secret investigation for two years while allowing a drug-dealing murderer to remain as a police officer. That sounds dirty to me."

"Their cause was noble, even if they went about it wrong."

"And all along, no one else knew about Garrett?"

203

"No. The guy was a master at hiding who he really was."

"Did you know him?"

"Not really. Mostly by reputation. He worked south on power shift. I mostly worked north on graveyard. Plus, our schedules were opposite. I ran into him once or twice a year on the street. Even less often at some kind of training."

"Aren't we south right now?"

Lee nodded. "I followed Sergeant Gelabert when she got moved. Anyway, I'm not going to argue with you about Garrett. The guy was a piece of shit. He betrayed the badge. All I'm saying is that he's the exception, not the rule."

"He's an outlier, I agree." Melody shifted in her seat. "But only in terms of extreme. There are other cops we're worried about."

"Not me, I hope."

She shook her head. "No. Of course, not."

"Who, then?"

"Ray Zielinski."

"Not worth arguing. He was wrong, but again, he did it for the right reason. And you can't say the system didn't work in that situation. He's in prison for his actions."

"What about Mark Asham?"

Lee leaned back in this seat, letting the back of his head hit the headrest. "What about him?"

"Asham has shot and killed four people, two of them persons of color."

"Believe me, he's not a racist."

"I didn't say he was."

"His wife is Mexican."

"And that doesn't mean anything. Racism is more complicated than that."

"Mark is a warrior," Lee said. "And this job needs warriors."

"I thought you were sheep dogs. That sounds more like the guardian model to me."

"I'm fully on board with the guardian model," Lee said. "I

think it's the correct way to look at the role of law enforcement. But you still need warriors. Sometimes it gets ugly out here, and that is a gear every cop has to have."

"It seems like it might be the only one Asham has."

"You're wrong."

"Four shootings in eleven years," Melody said. "You've been on fourteen, you said. How many shootings have you been involved in?"

"As the shooter? None."

"You see my point."

"What, that I've been lucky? Or that Mark has been unlucky?"

"I don't think he was unlucky. I think the people he shot were."

"I'm familiar with every one of those shootings," Lee told her. "Each one was a good shoot."

Melody winced. "That's such a terrible term."

"Every one of them was fully investigated. And each was deemed a justified use of force. The independent investigators said so, and the prosecutors agreed. He did nothing wrong."

"I'm not saying he's Tyler Garrett two-point-oh. But four times in eleven years? Those are startling numbers."

"They are. But his odds are way up there, too."

"Those are some lottery-level odds."

"Not really. Police shootings are going to occur. It is an inevitable tragedy of life in the real world. There are three hundred police officers on this department. So, he has a one in three hundred chance of being the officer involved right off the bat. Factor in he works patrol, and most shootings stem from a patrol situation, and now he's down to one in a hundred forty. He works power shift, which is the most active shift. That bumps his odds, too."

Lee slowed as he reached the edges of downtown.

"Mark's on the SWAT team and has been for a long time. If I remember, two of the four shootings you're talking about involved a SWAT callout. So now he's down to one in twenty-four to be the SWAT officer involved. Higher, actually, because of his role on the team. Throw in that his primary duty is as a K-9 officer who ends up on all kinds of high-risk calls, and the odds of him being involved in a shooting in any given month aren't that long at all."

"You've given this some thought."

"I've had this discussion before. People like to act like Mark is some kind of bloodthirsty killer. He's not. He's a guy who takes on some of the most dangerous parts of this job because he's got the skill set to do it. He's a warrior."

"You've said that. Still, four shootings in eleven years…"

"Who would you rather have in those situations? A patrol officer who has never been in a critical incident before? Or someone like Mark, with all the abilities and experience to bring to bear?"

Melody was silent for a block. Lee turned off Second Avenue and pulled up to the target address. He pushed the on-scene button on the MDC and put the car into park. As he silenced the engine, Melody spoke again.

"What about him?" she asked quietly.

Lee turned to her, waiting for her to explain.

"All those shootings," Melody said. "That has to weigh on him."

"Yeah, well, nobody seems to worry about that," Lee said. "They just call him a monster."

"I never said he's a monster."

Lee hesitated. "I know." He opened the door and got out of the car. "Come on. Let's figure out what's going on with this kid."

Chapter 20

MEL

Melody sat in the car for a moment. Aside from the short respite at the property building, things had been coming at her in a torrent. First the violent arrest, then the interview with Jamie, and now this most recent conversation with Lee.

There was no time to process.

That didn't play to her strengths. She was a processor, someone who mulled things over and examined them before forming an opinion or acting on it. Tonight's barrage of events and ideas hadn't allowed her much time for that.

There was something more, too—masks.

Watching Lee exchange one mask for another all evening was disconcerting. Perhaps it was her father's memory that made it more pronounced, but that didn't change the impact. She sat rooted to the passenger seat, unsure if she wanted to see more.

Has he heard me at all? she wondered. Sometimes it seemed like he listened. Other times, like he only waited for his turn to speak, to convince her. Were they having a conversation or a verbal war?

She didn't know.

Mel reached for the door handle and got out. Lee was already waiting on the sidewalk. As soon as she started to swing the door shut, he stopped her.

"Wait," he said.

She paused with the door hanging open. "What?"

He stepped in her direction and took control of the door from her. "In patrol, we do it this way," he said. Then he brought the door almost to the latch before stopping. The door latch caught, and Lee gave it an additional shove, snugging it.

"Silent and invisible deployment," he said. "This way, the bad guys don't know we're coming, or at least when." He turned and headed toward the house.

She looked at the door and then at his retreating form. "Hunh," she muttered.

Lee was already yards away, so she followed, quickening her step to catch up with him.

As she went up the walkway leading to the small porch, an older woman looked out at them from the front window. She disappeared and a few moments later, the front door opened.

"Are you Mrs. Lindblom?" Lee asked.

She nodded. "Come in."

Lee stepped inside, and Melody followed him. When Lindblom had closed the door, Lee said, "Where's the child?"

Lindblom pointed to the living room. "In there. I've got the cartoon channel on for him."

"Good idea. And you're sure his mother isn't here?"

"I called out for her. Really loud. But I haven't gone looking for her."

"Why not?"

Lindblom frowned. "It isn't my house. It's one thing to come into the front rooms here to make sure he's okay, but to go snooping through bedrooms…?"

"I understand. What's the boy's name?"

"He said it was Casey."

"Will you stay with Casey while I check the rest of the house?"

"Of course."

Lee nodded tersely, then strode away. Lindblom watched him go. Then she looked at Melody. Melody gave her what she hoped was a reassuring smile.

"Are you his supervisor?" Lindblom asked.

"No. Just an observer."

"Oh." Lindblom seemed to mull that over, then nodded approvingly. "I've always said we had a wonderful police department in this town, but the truth is that lately… well, I'm glad you folks are fixing things."

Further explanation seemed like it would take too long, so

Melody simply said, "Thank you." Then she pointed into the living room. "He's in there?"

"Yes."

Melody poked her head around the corner. A dark-haired boy sat on the couch, sucking his thumb, and staring at a flickering TV screen. He wore a Spider-man T-shirt that looked like it might hang to his knees. In his left arm, he clutched a tattered, yellow stuffed dog.

"It's a shame, isn't it?" Lindblom said. "He seems like a sweet boy."

Melody made a vague sound of acknowledgment. She glanced at the boy. Despite the late hour, he didn't seem sleepy.

Lee returned to the living room. He met her eyes and shook his head.

The boy noticed Lee and stared at him. Lee grinned and walked closer to him. Casey didn't shrink away but pulled his thumb from his mouth, his eyes widening a little.

"Hey, fella," Lee said. He squatted onto his haunches, causing the leather on his equipment belt to groan in protest. "Would you like a sticker?"

Casey's eyes widened further. He nodded.

"I thought so," Lee said. He opened his breast pocket and withdrew a sticker that was almost the size of a playing card. Melody couldn't see what it was but Casey could. He smiled and reached for it. Lee let him take it and waited for a couple of seconds while the boy admired his prize.

"You want me to put it on you?" Lee asked.

Casey nodded again and held it out to him. Lee took it and peeled off the backing. He applied the sticker to Casey's chest, smoothing it onto his shirt with a circular motion. When he pulled his hand away, he said, "There you go. Now you're officially a junior police officer."

Melody could see the gold badge on Casey's shirt, directly to the left of Spidey's head.

"Maybe you can help me, Officer Casey," Lee said. "I'm

trying to find your mommy so I can talk to her. Do you know where she is?"

Casey shook his head slowly.

"That's okay. How about this—do you know your mommy's name?"

Casey nodded. "Mommy."

Lee smiled. "Good job."

Casey smiled back.

"Hey, are you hungry?" Lee asked.

"No."

"I made him a sandwich while we waited," Lindblom offered from just behind Melody.

"Oh, I see. Was it a good sandwich?"

Casey nodded. "Peanut buttah 'n jelwee."

"That's the best," Lee said. He kept his voice soft. Melody had never taught elementary school, but she knew enough to see that he'd hit that perfect pitch with a younger kid. Soft enough to be non-threatening but not condescending. Most kids could smoke out condescension as if it were a bad smell.

"How old are you, Casey?" Lee asked.

Casey held up three fingers. Then he added, "And a half."

"And a half?"

The boy nodded.

"You know how many years I am?" Lee asked.

"No."

Lee held up his hands and flicked his fingers out several times. Casey giggled at that

"And a half," Lee added. Then he looked down at the tattered stuffed dog Casey clutched to his side. "What's his name?"

Casey followed Lee's gaze, then looked back up at him. "Arfie."

Lee patted the toy on the head. "Good boy, Arfie. Listen, Casey, you want to stay here and watch this show while I check on a few things? Can you do that?"

"Yeah."

"Okay." Lee patted him on the shoulder and stood. He moved toward Melody, walking past her into the kitchen. Once there, he began searching through the room, lifting papers on the counter and examining them.

Melody turned back to Casey, but the boy was already engrossed in the cartoon he was watching, his thumb back in his mouth.

"What are you looking for?" Lindblom asked Lee.

"Mail," he said. "Something to tell me who his mom is."

"I wish I could help, but they only moved in a few weeks ago."

"Have you seen a dad around during that time?"

"No. No men at all."

"Other women?"

Lindblom considered. "Maybe one or two. But not very often. They've actually been good neighbors up to this point. Really quiet."

Lee stopped and stared at the refrigerator. Melody followed his gaze. A small white board was attached to the top freezer. The word "Cheryl" with a phone number scrawled beneath it was all that was written there.

He pulled out his cell phone. All three of them waited while he dialed. In the quiet of the house, Melody could hear the rings from the phone's earpiece, mixed in with the music and sound effects from the cartoon. Then the ringing stopped, and a woman's voice came on.

Lee frowned. "Voicemail." When the message ended with a tone, he said, "This is Officer Lee Salter, Spokane Police. I'm here with Casey and we're trying to locate his mother. Call me back at this number or call the non-emergency line to Police Dispatch." He rattled off the number, thanked her, and severed the connection.

"Now what?" Melody asked.

But Lee was already dialing again. "Hey Jackie," he said. "I've got a number that was on the fridge. Maybe a friend or something. I called it but got voicemail. Can you keep trying it to see if she answers?" He recited the number, then was silent for a moment, listening. Then he said, "Okay, thanks," and hung up.

He looked at Melody. "I'm going to keep searching for something to identify her. Would you be comfortable sitting with Casey while I do that?"

"Sure."

"Good." Lee started to look around the kitchen again.

"What about me?" Lindblom asked.

Lee thought for a moment. Then he said, "I think you've done everything you can do, Mrs. Lindblom. Thanks for your help."

"What will happen to him?" Lindblom motioned toward Casey sitting on the couch.

"I'm going to try to find his mother."

"What if you can't?"

"I'll have to bring in Child Protective Services."

Lindblom frowned. "That might be for the best. You know, if she's going to leave him alone like this. A lot could happen. It's a good thing I saw him when I did."

"It was a good thing," Lee agreed. "Thank you again, Mrs. Lindblom."

Lindblom hovered for a few moments, as if she didn't want to miss any new developments. Then, reluctantly, she made her way toward the door. "You'll let me know?" she asked hopefully. "What happens with him?"

"Do we have your number?"

"Yes. I gave it to the lady on the phone."

"Your mobile phone?"

"That, too."

"I'll send you a text, then, once it is all resolved."

Lindblom seemed satisfied with that. She left, pulling the front door shut behind her.

Once she was gone, Mel made her way into the living room. She approached Casey slowly, a slight smile on her face. When the boy looked up, she said, "Hey, can I sit and watch cartoons with you?"

Casey nodded while still sucking his thumb.

Mel sat down lightly, leaving a few inches of space between them. "My name is Melody. What's your name?"

Casey pulled out his thumb. "Caythee."

"Hi, Casey." She pointed to the sticker on his shirt. "I see you got a badge sticker. How cool is that?"

He glanced down at the sticker on his chest. With his free hand, he stroked it a couple of times. Then he looked back at the television.

She glanced toward the screen. "Is this your favorite cartoon?"

Casey hesitated, then shook his head.

Melody paused, not wanting to overwhelm him. Then she said, "It looks like you're feeling like being quiet right now. Is it okay if I just sit here and watch cartoons with you?"

Casey nodded.

Melody looked at the TV. She wasn't familiar with the cartoon, which seemed to revolve around a dog whose imagination became reality. Out of the corner of her eye, she kept tabs on Casey. The boy stared ahead, fully engrossed in the show. He sucked his thumb absently, his eyes alert.

She could hear Lee searching throughout the house, opening and closing drawers and cupboards. When he was close enough, she heard the leather of his equipment belt squeak as he moved. The sound was a familiar one, one she'd long forgotten. Like stumbling across an ancient scent, the sound brought back memories of her father in his uniform. Him at the kitchen table, home from lunch, shifting in his seat. The creaking sound his belt made when he stood to leave. The extra bulk she always felt whenever she hugged him, due to the vest he wore beneath his uniform shirt. The smell of wool and gun oil.

Casey said something around his thumb that she couldn't decipher.

"What's that?" she asked, meeting his gaze. "I couldn't

understand you."

Patiently, he removed his thumb. "Big thitty gween."

It took her a moment to translate it in her head. "Big City Green?"

He nodded.

"That's your favorite?"

He nodded again.

She knew that one. Her youngest, Hattie, watched it occasionally and Isaac sometimes joined her, even though he wanted her to think he was too big for "baby shows."

"It's a good show," she told Casey.

Casey nodded and turned back to the TV.

Mel did the same. She thought of her kids, right now sleeping over at her sister-in-law's. They were safe, and she didn't have to worry about them. That was something she'd always taken for granted. It was never a question. The thought of what it would be like for a child not to have that basic level of security made her heart hurt.

In another room, Lee made a triumphant sound. Before she could wonder what he found, Casey shifted in his seat. The boy moved closer to her, snuggling up to her arm, all the while staring ahead. Automatically, Mel lifted her arm. Casey leaned further into her. After a moment, he shifted again, laying his head onto her lap.

A pang flared in her chest.

Melody let her hand rest on his leg, then patted him gently while they watched the cartoon.

Chapter 21

LEE

Score! Lee thought. In the top drawer of a bedroom dresser, he found an envelope poking out from underneath an open jewelry box. He spotted the familiar Irish green of official state letters on the nearest corner as he pulled it out. The letter was addressed to Angela Kemp.

Lee's lip curled.

He knew her. It'd been at least six months since he'd seen her last, maybe longer. But the call sprang to mind immediately. She'd been assaulted by a john out on the East Sprague corridor, which was one of the high crime areas that he and Melody had argued about earlier. This was a perfect example of the point he tried to make about that. People paid for sex or drugs in that area regardless of police presence. The only difference the cops made was tempering how prevalent the activity was.

But she never mentioned anything about a kid. And he hadn't asked when they talked. Why would he?

Lee removed the folded document from the jagged opening of the envelope. The letter inside approved Kemp's application for food stamps.

He clenched his jaw and walked out of the bedroom. In the living room, Casey lay in Melody's lap, watching TV. She looked over at him as he approached.

"I figured out who she is." Lee held up the envelope. "Angela Kemp."

Mel stared at him vacantly. "It sounds like you know her."

"She's a..." he paused, glancing at Casey. The boy sucked his thumb, transfixed by the television. Lee looked to Melody, then mimed injecting a needle into his arm. "I've stopped her working out on East Sprague," he added, knowing even a civilian would grasp the area's reputation.

"Oh," Melody whispered. "Do you think she's out getting...?"

"Probably," he gritted. It angered him to think that finding a fix was more important to someone than caring for a child. He'd seen plenty of neglect over his career, but he never grew accustomed to it. "I've got to make a couple of calls."

She nodded that she understood.

Lee moved into the kitchen. As he reached for his phone, it buzzed in his hand. The number seemed familiar. Then he realized it was one he'd dialed a short while ago.

"Hello?"

"Hello? This is Cheryl Ward. A police dispatcher told me to call you. She wouldn't tell me what it was about."

"This is Officer Lee Salter, SPD."

The line was quiet for a second. Then Cheryl spoke, her tone guarded. "Yeah, okay. What do you want?"

"Do you know Angela Kemp?"

"Why?"

"Do you know her?"

"Maybe. Why?"

"Look, Ms. Ward. I'm trying to find out where she is so I can talk to her. If you know anything—"

"She's not home?"

"No."

"Wait, where are you calling from?"

"Her house."

"And she's not there?"

"No. Just her son, Casey."

"Oh, shit. Really?" A moment passed. Then she added, "It's not my fault. She was supposed to be back in five minutes."

"Let's back up a little. How do you know Angela?"

"We met in rehab."

"How long ago?"

"Three, four months, maybe."

"In-patient?"

"Yeah. And then the transition home."

"So Casey wasn't with her then?"

"No, he was with Angie's mother."

"Do you know her mother's name?"

"Not really. I might be able to find it. But that won't help you."

"Why not?"

"She died. It was while we were in the transition home, right at the end. Angela had to get permission to leave a few days early, and I remember we were talking about how hard it was going to be. How she might relapse."

"Did she?"

"Not that I could tell."

"Do you know where Angela is now?"

"I have no idea."

"When did you see her last?"

"I came over there a little before two so I could watch Casey while she worked a half shift at her job."

"Where's that?"

"She helps with intake down at the women's shelter. The one downtown?"

Lee knew it. The building was only ten or twelve blocks away. "When did she get home?"

Cheryl fell silent.

He waited a few moments before pressing her. "Cheryl? When'd Angela get home?"

"I... I assume about six-thirty."

"You're not sure?"

"No. I—" She stopped again. "I had to leave."

"What do you mean?"

Cheryl let out a long, exasperated sigh. "Look, my daughter was at gymnastics up on the northside. My ex was supposed to stay through practice and then drop her off with me. But he's a goddamn flake, so he just brought her to practice and bailed. Halfway through, Sidney twisted her ankle on a landing. Nothing that needed a trip to emergency, but they wanted me to come and get her. She was crying and was pretty

---

217

hysterical."

Heat built on Lee's neck and face. "So you just left Casey?"

"No! I mean, not really."

"Explain.

"I called Angie and told her I had to go get Sidney."

"When was this?"

"A little after six."

"You couldn't wait? Or get someone else to pick up your daughter?"

"I tried her dad, but he didn't pick up, which is typical for him, the asshole. And I told Angie I could bring Casey along and then drop him off again after. The thing was, he was asleep. The kid doesn't sleep enough as it is, and I managed to get him to crash out. I didn't want to wake him up, but I didn't want to leave him, either."

"But you did."

"Only because Angie said it was okay. She was already walking home when I called her. She said she'd be home in five minutes, tops."

"It's a ten-minute walk from the women's shelter to here."

"Maybe she was already halfway home. What do I know? All I know is my little girl was bawling, I didn't know for sure if the gymnastics instructor was right about it only being a twisted ankle, and Casey was zonked out."

"You left him."

"Angie said it was all right," she whined. "She told me to go get my daughter."

"You left a three-year-old alone." His tone was cold.

"He was going to be alone for five minutes!" Cheryl protested.

"Well, it looks like he's been alone for over eight hours."

Silence.

Lee let it sit, grinding his teeth. He wanted to drive over to wherever Cheryl was and arrest her for child endangerment. But he knew it would never get past Sergeant Gelabert, much less a prosecutor.

When he was sure he could speak again without rancor, he broke the silence. "Do you have any idea where Angela could be right now?"

"No." Cheryl's voice was subdued.

"Has she been using again?"

"No. She's been doing good. I swear. Getting hours at the shelter, going to meetings, taking care of her son..."

"Why would she leave him alone, then?"

"It was only supposed to be five minutes. It wasn't supposed to be a big deal."

Lee rubbed the bridge of his nose. "Does she have other friends or family you know of?"

"Not since her mom died."

"Casey's dad?"

"Not in the picture. I don't even know who he is. And I don't know about other friends, but I don't think so. Everyone she knew was into using, and if you wanna stay clean, you gotta stay away from people in the life."

Lee frowned. He wasn't going to get anything further out of Cheryl. He quickly took down her biographical information for his report and broke the connection. Then he dialed Dispatch.

"Police Radio, this is Jackie."

"Hey, Jackie, Lee. The so-called friend got back to me."

"So-called?"

Lee recounted his conversation with Cheryl.

"Great parenting," Jackie murmured when he'd finished.

"No kidding. Look, I'm going to need you to start CPS for a placement. If this isn't neglect, I don't know what is."

"I'll call them as soon as we hang up. Anything else?"

"Yeah, a couple of things. Would you message Sergeant Gelabert to call me or come by so I can let her know what's happening?"

He heard the clatter of a keyboard in the background. "Done. What else?"

"Run up Angela Kemp for me. She's a white female, about

thirty. Should be in pretty extensive."

"Wait," Jackie said, "are you serious?"

"Yeah. She's the mom. I found a food stamps letter with her name on it, and the friend I talked to confirmed. Why?"

"Kemp's DOA."

Lee blinked. "What? When?"

"Earlier tonight. She was the auto-ped victim—the one downtown on Monroe."

He remembered the call. He'd dodged perimeter duty thanks to Melody's presence, and Murph got stuck with it. He wiped his lip, thinking. "What time did that happen?"

Jackie typed at the keyboard, the keys rattling. "It came in at eighteen-twenty-nine. Delay of about five."

"Oh, man." Lee shook his head. "She really was walking home."

"I talked with Corporal Bradford, who was called out for the collision. He tried to run down her address but we didn't have anything current."

"She was in rehab for a while and then in a transition home," he explained. "She's only been at this address a few weeks."

"Makes sense. Both rehab clinics and those homes are private and don't share records."

"Neither does DSHS?"

"Only if we ask specifically. Our computer systems aren't linked so it takes a direct phone call during business hours. If it's a major emergency, then we can wake someone up. We did it for that Amber Alert a few months ago."

Lee didn't answer. He imagined Corporal Bradford making all the reasonable efforts he could do in order to find out where Angela Kemp lived. After a certain point, especially given the lifestyle her criminal record portrayed, he probably would have given up for the night. Bradford was a good investigator, so Lee knew he'd eventually find the information. But without knowing about Casey, there wasn't as much urgency to it.

"What do you want to do, Lee?"

"Exactly what we're doing," he said woodenly. "Call CPS. Let them know they have to come pick up an orphan."

Jackie tapped feverishly on her keyboard. Then she said, "I'll take care of it."

Lee thanked her and hung up.

He looked through the entryway into the living room where Casey sat snuggled in tight to Melody. She was looking at him with an odd expression. No doubt, she heard his end of the conversation. He'd have to explain it to her, but he didn't have the heart to do it within earshot of Casey. Even though he knew the boy wouldn't understand the words, it still felt wrong.

His daughter was seven now. But he could remember her being Casey's age as if it were yesterday. He tried to imagine the pain she'd feel if she lost her mother. Or him, for that matter. Sparing Olivia that grief was part of what motivated him to be so safe on the job.

Lee met Mel's gaze, realizing that she'd gone through something very similar when her dad died. How old did she say she was? Sixteen, seventeen? He imagined it was still hard.

Before he could follow that thought any further, his phone buzzed in his hand. He glanced at the display. Robotically, he pressed the ACCEPT button and raised the phone to his ear.

"Hey, Sarge."

Chapter 22

MEL

She listened to Lee's half of the phone conversation, trying to discern what was going on. The first call must have been with the friend whose name and number he'd found on the refrigerator white board. That conversation went poorly. It wasn't difficult to gather the gist of what had happened. Whoever had been watching Casey had left him alone. Lee's tone with her was cold and accusatory. She didn't blame him one bit.

The next call was obviously with the dispatcher he'd spoken with before. Her heart sank as she overheard further details. She was no stranger to stories of child neglect. To varying degrees, she faced repercussions from it every day in the classroom. But leaving a three-and-a-half-year-old alone? She wasn't sure whom to be angrier at—the friend who left or the mother who told her it was okay to do so.

Beside her, Casey nestled in a little closer, watching the television. She patted his leg again.

Then came the bombshell.

"Hey, Sarge," Lee said into the phone. His voice was a bit lower than before. He was quiet for a while, listening.

Melody stared at him, unabashed in her eavesdropping. Lee glanced up and noticed but didn't seem to mind.

"Yeah," he said. "I've got CPS coming. Did Jackie update the call in CAD yet?"

He waited for a reply.

"Well, she's probably on the phone with CPS. Anyway, I figured out who mom is."

Another pause.

"I'd love to. But here's the thing—she's DOA."

Melody cocked her head.

"No, not here," said Lee. "She was the victim in that auto-ped on Monroe earlier tonight."

Melody shook her head in denial. Casey's mom was dead? She remembered something Lee had mentioned about a crash near the beginning of the shift, but that seemed like forever ago. All she could recall was how callous he seemed about it at the time.

"She's only been here for a few weeks," Lee explained. "Most databases hadn't caught up with her yet."

A dull ache grew in her chest.

"By some mail from the state for her food stamps," he continued.

Melody looked down at the top of Casey's head. Tears stung her eyes.

This poor boy, she thought. He woke up to an empty house, and now his mother is gone. He won't understand how, or why—

"If you'd call him," Lee said, "I'd appreciate it. I don't know that it matters much now, but he'll want the information for his investigative file."

She marveled at how evenly Lee spoke. Wasn't he affected at all? For all the bad situations she encountered at school, the emotional impact never lessened for her. It was always devastating when something happened to one of her kids. How could he be so robotic about it?

Melody stroked Casey's hair. Even though she knew it was impossible, all she wanted to do right now was take him home with her. Take care of him.

"All right. Thanks, Sarge."

Lee tucked his phone into his shirt pocket. Then he wandered into the living room. "Did you get most of that?"

"Enough of it." Melody brushed her tears away.

"CPS is on the way."

"What happens to him?"

"Foster care, for now." Lee glanced down at Casey. "At his age, probably adoption."

Melody nodded stiffly. She wondered how it would all

appear to Casey. Strangers sitting with him now. More strangers would appear and take him away from his home, his things. He'd never see his mother again and wouldn't understand why until he was older.

How much damage would that do to him?

She saw the answer on a weekly basis in the classroom. The so-called hard kids, the ones a lot of teachers didn't like. Sometimes she didn't either if she were being honest. They could be a pain. But she knew that each one of them had a story like Casey's, and that made her heart break.

"So, it's going to be a while," Lee said. "CPS is never fast."

"Do they have people on call or something?"

"Yes, but they're not standing by. They're getting woken up and coming from wherever they live, so… we wait."

"All right."

"I'm going to grab my lunch from the trunk."

"Okay."

Lee pointed at Casey. "He said he wasn't hungry, but…"

"I'll ask him again at the next commercial."

Lee left the house. Casey didn't look up when the door opened or closed again, although he did shift against her to get more comfortable. Melody squeezed his arm. She wanted to make this moment of calm and safety go on for as long as it could. She knew a storm lay ahead for him.

When Lee returned, he opened the refrigerator. A few moments later, he came into the living room. He held a soft lunch box in one hand and a cheese stick in the other.

"Look what I found," he said. He held out the cheese stick toward Casey. "You hungry, pal?"

The boy glanced away from the TV. When he saw the cheese stick, he nodded and held out his hand. Lee peeled the wrapper back before leaning down and handing him the snack. Casey sat up, turned his attention back to the television, and started eating. In the crook of his left arm, he held onto his stuffed dog.

Lee unzipped his lunch bag. "I've got a meatloaf sandwich,

if you want half."

"I'm good."

"Wendy makes killer meatloaf."

"I'm actually not that hungry." She glanced at her watch. It was after three. She hadn't eaten since seven-thirty. By rights, she should be hungry. But the emotion of Casey's plight and the odd hours conspired to dampen her appetite.

Lee held up a mandarin. He raised his eyebrows questioningly.

She almost refused the gesture. Instead, she nodded. "Thanks."

Lee handed her the fruit. Then he set his lunch bag on the opposite arm of the couch and dug out his sandwich. He turned toward the TV and began eating it while standing in the living room. Melody suggested he sit on the couch, but he shook his head. "I sit in the car all shift long. It's nice to stand sometimes."

The three of them were silent for a long stretch, each eating their food. The citrus sweetness of the orange hit her tongue and was refreshing. Sitting next to Casey, watching TV, she was surprised she hadn't started to feel sleepy. She'd napped earlier in the day, but it had been a fitful sleep. The lateness of the hour should have weighed on her. But the emotion associated with discovering Casey's situation had spiked her energy, and the bite of the orange only added to that. The shift was scheduled until seven, but the PIO had informed her that graveyard units were frequently relieved earlier as day shift units checked into service around six-fifteen. She wondered if her energy would crash before then or if she'd remain wired when she got home.

Either way, when it came to staying awake, she could make it another three hours.

The emotional rollercoaster, though? That was another question.

They ate and watched cartoons in near silence. When Casey finished his cheese stick, Melody took the wrapper from his hands out of sheer mom-habit. Just as automatically, it seemed, Lee held out his empty sandwich baggie to her and she put the cheese wrapper and her orange peels into it. He tucked it away in his lunch bag. Was that how he was as a father?

One cartoon spilled into another. They were on their third episode since Gelabert's call when someone knocked at the front door.

Lee went to answer it. She heard a terse greeting from a female voice. A moment later, he escorted a woman in her late fifties into the living room. Her stocky frame and dark business clothes gave Melody the impression of someone's elderly aunt. She had an empty gym bag dangling from her arm.

"This is the little guy?" the woman asked.

"That's him," Lee answered.

The woman turned her attention to Melody. "I'm Elizabeth Young with CPS. Are you family?" Her tone sounded somehow both accusatory and hopeful at the same time.

"No."

Young's eyes narrowed in confusion.

"She's with me," Lee said. "Ride-along."

"Oh." Young pursed her lips. "Well, let's see about getting him some clothes. What's your name, son?"

Casey pressed closer to Melody.

"It's Casey," she told Young.

Young frowned at her. "I know." Then she looked back at Casey. "Casey, you want to show me your room?"

Casey shook his head.

"Come on, it'll be fun."

He turned his head and buried his face into Melody's side.

"Great," Young muttered. She stood and looked at Lee expectantly.

"It's back here," he said.

While Young followed Lee into the bedroom, Melody sat with Casey, stroking his hair. "It's going to be all right," she whispered to him. "This nice woman is going to take you somewhere safe, okay?"

Casey didn't answer.

A few minutes later, Young emerged from the rear of the house. The bag was now weighed down with some clothing. "I didn't see any diapers." She spoke over her shoulder to Lee. "Is he toilet-trained?"

"I don't know."

Young peered at Casey. "Do you go pee-pee in the potty, son?"

Casey didn't move.

"He's not wearing a diaper," Melody said.

"Good." Young squatted, her knees crackling as she did so. She leaned closer to Casey. "Do you have to go to the toilet before we go?"

Casey didn't respond. He kept his face pressed into Melody's chest.

"Let's hope that's a no," said Young. She held out her free hand. "C'mon, honey."

Casey clutched at Melody tighter. When Young's hand took hold of his forearm, his fingers dug sharply into Melody's back.

"Wait," she said.

"Waiting doesn't help," Young said, continuing to pull him toward her. "Trust me. I've done this a hundred times. It's better to just take care of business."

Better for him or for her, Melody wondered, but she held her tongue. Instead, she leaned down and tried to whisper to Casey in a soothing tone, but her voice broke. "It's going to be okay," she said thickly.

Young gave a steady, insistent tug on Casey's arm. A low sound started in the boy's throat, rising up as she pulled him away from Melody. By the time his body broke contact from hers, it became a cry of protest. He dropped his stuffed dog and wrapped his free arm around Melody's neck.

"Nooooo!" Casey wailed. He pulled frantically at the arm

Young still held, trying to free it.

"Stop," Melody said again, this time in a firm tone.

Young let go of Casey's arm. The boy wrapped it around Melody and buried his face in her neck.

"Can't you see he's upset?" Melody asked.

"They're all upset. It's the nature of the situation. But I've got to take him, and we need to get going."

"I understand that, but—"

"But nothing. I know how to do my job. You're not helping matters. You're making it harder."

"What if I carry him out the car?" Melody offered.

"That's not policy. Maybe if you were family, but—"

"Isn't policy more of a guideline?" Lee asked. "Not a hard and fast rule?"

Young frowned. "That's a loosey-goosey view of things."

"I'm just saying, maybe this is a reasonable deviation." His tone was conciliatory but firm. "For the well-being of a child."

She considered for a few moments. Then she sighed. "All right. Let's go."

Young stood, knees popping on the way up. She slung the bag over her shoulder and turned around. Without looking back, she headed toward the front door.

Melody struggled up to her feet. Casey clung to her as if it were life or death. She kept her arms wrapped around him. "It'll be all right," she whispered, rocking and swaying with him for a few moments. "You're going to be all right."

Tears stung at her eyes again.

"You're going to be all right," she repeated.

Then she followed Young, brushing past Lee, who stood nearby, his face a flat mask.

Out front, she found the CPS worker waiting next to a silver minivan. She'd already started the engine. The side door stood open.

"Put him in this one," Young said, motioning to the nearest seat. "That way I can keep a better eye on him while I drive."

Melody leaned into the minivan. The funk of sweaty kids

and feet filled her nostrils. She leaned in through the door opening, lowering Casey into the car seat. His grip remained steadfast. She had to reach up and peel his little hands away from her.

"No, no, no, no," he murmured.

"You'll be okay," she told him.

When she pulled away, Casey yelped and lunged for her. Melody caught him and lowered him back into the car seat.

"Put the clasp on," Young instructed. "I'll take care of snugging him in."

Almost from muscle memory, Melody slid the main clasp over Casey's head and fastened it into the slot at the base of the car seat. The resounding click rang out like an accusation. She pulled away to an arm's length. Casey reached out for her, tears streaming down his cheeks. "I doan wanna," he yelled. "I doan wanna!"

She stroked his head. "It'll be okay." His cries muffled her words.

Young shouldered her way into the opening. With brisk, precise motions, she adjusted and tightened the straps, securing Casey in the car seat. Melody looked on, transfixed, before slowly backing away.

When Young finished, she stood back and reached for the door handle.

"Wait," Lee said.

Melody didn't know when he had arrived at the van. She hadn't been aware he'd even left the house with them. But now he stood just a few inches behind her. He stepped past both women, leaning in closer to Casey. In his hand, he held the stuffed yellow dog.

"Can't forget Arfie," Lee said, holding it out to him.

Casey ignored him and the toy. His eyes were locked on Melody, his arms outstretched toward her as he strained against the car seat. "No, no, no," he kept repeating, his voice something between a cry and a wail.

"Hey, Casey." Lee waggled the dog to get the boy's

attention.

It didn't work.

He tried a couple times more. Casey continued to ignore him and focus on Melody.

"All right," Lee said. He wedged the tattered yellow dog behind one of the straps. "We'll put him here for later, okay?"

He stepped back.

Young slid the door shut, muffling Casey's cries. "He'll settle down," she assured them. "You'll copy me on your report?"

Lee nodded. "Affirm."

"Good, then."

Without saying a word to Melody, Young made her way around the front of the van. The pitiful sounds of Casey's protests rose momentarily as she got into the driver's seat, then were again muffled. Young put on her seatbelt, gave Casey a quick look, then pulled away.

Melody stood on the curb and watched the van go. She stared after it, her chest aching, until the red taillights flashed, turned right, and disappeared.

Chapter 23

LEE

After CPS left with the child, Lee secured the house.

Melody waited for him near the patrol car. He could tell she was shaken by the placement. As he double-checked the backdoor locks and ensured the windows were all closed, it started to make a sort of sense to him.

Teachers no doubt heard about or directly encountered instances of abuse and neglect. But what they saw were symptoms or the aftereffects of an event. Tonight, she experienced up close the ugly reality of what happened to kids and the sometimes shitty world they inhabited. He likened the difference to seeing something firsthand versus hearing about it from someone who was there. Both have impact, but one experience was far more visceral.

He was sorry she had to see it. At her core, she seemed like a decent person. Beyond that, he believed the bubble most of the world got to live in was a blessing. It was part of what kept him doing this job. Watching it burst for anyone wasn't something he took any joy in seeing.

When he'd secured the home, he jotted a note on the back of one of his business cards, letting Kathy Lindblom know what had become of Casey. Her house was dark, so he slid the card into the crack of her door, just above the knob. Then Lee headed toward the patrol cruiser. Melody stood with her arms folded near the passenger door.

"Sorry about that," he said. "I should've started the cruiser and got the heater going for you."

Melody gave a small shrug. "It's not too bad."

She was right. It was brisk, cooler than when the shift started, but there was no wind. Lee opened the door and popped the locks. Wordlessly, they both got inside. He fired up the engine. As the MDC booted up, he put the car in gear and started driving. The engine would heat up quicker that way.

"Are they always like that?" she asked.

"Who?"

"CPS."

"You've never dealt with them? I figured you would have since you're a mandatory reporter."

Mel shook her head. "I've only ever interacted with them on the phone. I've had to make a few reports or be interviewed when other teachers reported something."

Lee shrugged. "Most of the case workers are a little... softer. This one was ..."

"Harsh."

"I was going to say businesslike."

"That's a convenient euphemism."

"It's a polite one." He drove in silence. The MDC beeped its readiness. He glanced down while he drove and punched in his clearance code for the call and hit SEND. Then he said, "It's like any other job, I guess. The daily grind of it, the details, they all get to be commonplace. You take care of business and let the results speak for themselves."

She seemed to think about his words for a moment. "I'm not sure I agree with that. And I don't think you entirely believe what you're saying, either. The process matters. It's important."

"Not saying it doesn't matter. But this is a country where results speak the loudest."

"Maybe that's the problem."

"Why?" He glanced at her. "Results definitely matter."

"Maybe we're focused on the wrong results."

"Like making sure little Casey is safe?"

She waved her hand. "No, that's obviously important. But so is making him feel safe. And cared for. If you don't do that, you won't like the results later on. I see it every day."

"So do I." Lee checked the calls for service holding. One caught his eye immediately. "Son of a bitch," he muttered.

"What?"

"Those vehicle prowlers are at it again." He swung a U-turn and headed east. He put himself on the call with quick fingers, only glancing briefly at the MDC to perform the task.

"The same ones from before?" she asked.

"Description's the same."

"They've been at it for hours."

"At least," he said. "Or more likely, they're making multiple passes."

They rode quietly for several seconds. Finally, Lee broke the silence. "And you're right," he said.

"About?"

"Making Casey feel safe. It matters."

"I know."

"He seemed like a sweet kid."

"Most kids are."

"For a while." A large apartment building flitted by. "You seemed upset by the whole thing."

"Weren't you?"

He thought about it. "I was mad when I found out who his mom was. Heroin addict and a prostitute. I figured she was out doing one or the other instead of taking care of her kid."

Melody was quiet. Then she said, "I wondered the same thing."

"But she wasn't," Lee said. "It sounds like she got her act together. I mean, it's stupid to leave a kid that age alone at all, even for five minutes, but he was asleep and she…"

"She couldn't have predicted getting hit by a car," Melody finished.

"No. She couldn't." Lee slowed for the traffic light at Altamont. "I passed judgment on her, why she wasn't with her kid, and the whole time I was doing that, she was on a slab down at the morgue."

"You didn't know."

"I sure thought I did."

Melody didn't answer.

"I guess the truth isn't always what we think it is," Lee said, turning right and accelerating. "I'm out here fourteen years, and still I get surprised like this."

"The truth can be difficult to pin down. My father-in-law likes to say that there's three sides to every situation. Your side, my side, and the truth."

"Yeah, but whose truth?"

Melody paused at the callback to their earlier discussion. Then she said, "That's a good question."

"I know." Lee didn't have an answer, either. He turned onto Hartson Avenue.

A flash of gray dropped behind a car on the south side of the street, halfway up the block.

He gunned the engine.

Melody yelped with surprise as she slammed backward in her seat. He ignored her, keeping his eyes trained on the spot where the suspect ducked. A moment after his engine roared, the prowler broke from his hiding spot and scuttled south through a yard and between two houses.

Lee screeched to a halt. He jammed the car into park.

"Stay here!" he bellowed as he reached across to grab his flashlight.

Melody didn't argue or attempt to get out.

He jumped out of the car and raced after the suspect. His legs were tight and awkward for the first several steps as he tried to shake out the stiffness from sitting. Before he caught his stride, he reached up to his shoulder mic and depressed the transmit button.

"Charlie-411, foot pursuit!"

He didn't transmit further to allow the dispatcher a moment to prepare and to signal other units to hold any non-emergency traffic. Then he hit the button again.

"Two thousand block of Hartson," he said. His pace accelerated even though it was an awkward gait with one hand grasping the microphone attached to his epaulet. "Southbound through the houses."

"Copy, four-eleven."

The dispatcher immediately sent backup units toward his location. Unless they were close by, Lee knew they wouldn't arrive soon enough to do much good if he lost the suspect.

Lost him? He had to *find* him again before he could worry about losing him.

Lee sprinted through the space between the houses and scrambled to a hard stop in the alley. He shot glances in both directions, scanning for movement. There was none. He stared at the ground, straining his ears for sound.

There!

The light slap of rubber on concrete echoed back at him from behind the next row of houses. He bolted in that direction, stretching out his long legs and eating up as much ground as he could with each step.

When he broke out onto the sidewalk, he realized where he was. This block abutted to an undeveloped patch of forest that separated East Central from the ritzier parts of southeast Spokane. The Ben Burr Walking and Biking Trail snaked through the unofficial park, but no other roads or houses were present.

If his suspect cut back north into the residential area, he had a chance of catching him. If he opted for the woods to the south...

Lee started down the sidewalk at a trot. A couple of seconds later, he spotted a streak of light gray shoot across the street, southbound.

He accelerated into a sprint again.

"Stop, police!"

The suspect ignored the order and kept running. A few strides later, he disappeared into the brush on the south side of the street.

Lee shined his flashlight after the suspect as he ran. The circle of light bobbed and bounced with each stride. He kept it trained near the area where the suspect disappeared, sweeping it left and right, then deeper into the wooded area. The mag light always seemed so powerful indoors, but the trees and bushes soaked in the brightness and washed it out.

Deeper in the woods, there was another flash of gray, like the quick flip of a whitetail. It was gone again a moment later.

Lee pulled up at the tree line. In vain, he probed the woods with his flashlight beam. A distant crack and snap of someone moving through the forest filtered back to him.

If it had been a serious crime, he would have plunged in after the suspect. Or called for the dog. Mark Asham was probably drifting this way already without being dispatched. The K-9 officer always headed in the direction of calls that he thought might need his services.

Then Lee realized that *everyone* was coming.

He depressed his mic button. "Charlie-411, code four."

"Copy, four-eleven is code four. Disregard units?"

"Affirm," Lee said. "It was just one, and I lost him."

"Perimeter?" Mark's voice came over the radio, right on cue.

"Negative. No PC for a track." There was no need for a perimeter. The reality was that he didn't actually have a crime, just suspicious circumstances. Even if he hadn't lost the kid into the woods, he couldn't have justified a search with the K-9.

Mark clicked his mic in response. Lee imagined he could hear the disappointment in that brief squelch. Mark loved to chase criminals. He also hated to lose.

So did Lee.

He shut off his flashlight and turned to head back to his car. As he crossed the street to the sidewalk, a man in his late twenties watched him, leaning against the porch railing of the nearest house. His front door stood open behind him. The porch reflected off his dark skin.

"'Fraid to go in the woods?" he asked.

"No," Lee answered reflexively.

The man held up his hands in a peaceful gesture. "Hey, I don't blame you, man. They got bears up in that shit. No lie.

236

It's *Wild Kingdom* out here, right in the middle of the damn city."

Lee grinned in spite of the sting of losing his suspect. "I was chasing a vehicle prowler."

"I heard. Not catching one, though."

"You know what they say: some days you eat the bear…"

"Some days the bear eats you. That ain't no lie."

"Has your car been broken into?"

"No. But those little punks know I'll bust 'em right upside the head they even look at my ride."

He knew his official role was to discourage that kind of response, but Lee only grinned a little wider. "Maybe hang onto them for me after that?"

"No can do. That's double jeopardy. Take the beating or go to jail but never both." He was quiet for a second. When he spoke again, his voice was cooler, more distant. "I know you know that rule, Officer."

Lee said the only thing he could say to that.

Nothing.

He trudged back the way he came. As he walked between the houses again, he powered on his flashlight. He swept the ground, searching in case the suspect had dropped anything while he was out of sight. He was always surprised at what he'd find this way.

In this case, though, nothing out of the ordinary caught his eye. He clicked off his mag as he emerged back onto Hartson Avenue. The dull yellow glow from the streetlights illuminated the way now. He stopped next to the car he'd seen the suspect hide behind. The window was intact, and the door still locked. Inside, a pile of silver coins filled up the driver's cup holder.

This one had definitely not been hit.

Lee looked down near his feet, searching the ground.

Nothing.

Lee squatted and shined his light beneath the car. A few inches underneath lay a stubby screwdriver with a standard tip.

He reached out and recovered it. Then he stood and returned to the patrol car.

Even though he was certain he prevented a vehicle prowling, frustration stung in his gut. His hunter's instinct may not have burned as intensely as someone like Mark's, but he hated to lose, too. Not only would this little shit be back, but now he could tell all his pals how he eluded the police. He had a great story.

What did Lee have?

A goddamn screwdriver.

He got into the car, a little relieved to see Melody still in the passenger seat. He tossed the screwdriver onto the dashboard. It rattled and rolled until it came to rest in the corner, against the windshield.

"You didn't catch him?" she asked.

Lee glanced over at her.

Everyone's a critic, he thought.

Chapter 24

MEL

As soon as he opened the door, she could tell he was angry. He flung something onto the dashboard. The short screwdriver clattered into the corner, against the windshield.

"You didn't catch him?" Melody asked.

He smirked. "He ran into the woods."

Is that some kind of no-fly zone? She wondered but didn't ask. Instead, she waited to see what he would say next.

"The only way I was catching him in there was with a dog." He put the car into gear, and it lurched forward. "But using the K-9 requires a felony crime, except for DVs. I didn't have PC for a felony, so there you go."

"But you chased him."

He glanced over again, his jaw set. "Yeah, of course I did." He pointed toward the stubby screwdriver on the dash. "He was one of those prowlers we've been looking for since the start of shift."

In silence, they cruised through the neighborhood, crisscrossing the blocks. Lee scanned outside the patrol car. He was obviously looking for other accomplices and becoming more frustrated as time passed and he found nothing.

A pair of headlights appeared at the end of the block. When they drew closer, Melody saw it was another patrol car. Lee glided to a stop and rolled down his window. Cool air spilled inside the interior. The other car rolled up next to them. The letters "K-9" and "Police dog—do not approach" were emblazoned on the side.

The other officer's window was already down. He sat tall in the driver's seat. His sandy blond hair was closely cropped in a military style cut. His face and shoulders gave her the sense of a wiry, muscular build. When he glanced over at them, it was with a flinty gaze.

"Same ones?" he asked. His voice sounded like crushed gravel.

"That's my bet." Lee held up the stubby screwdriver. "But all I saw was him ducking down behind the car, so…"

"No PC." The other officer frowned. "Shit. I'm getting tired of these little thieving bastards out here. They've been at it all week."

"Yeah."

The other officer shook his head in disgust. Then his eyes flicked toward Melody, his gaze appraising her.

Lee noticed, too. "This is Melody Weaver. She's from the PRI."

The narrowing of the officer's eyes was barely perceptible. She wondered if she'd imagined it.

Lee turned her way. He made a casual wave, pointing to the other officer. "This is the world-famous Mark Asham."

"Infamous, you mean," Asham said. He nodded to her. "Ma'am."

"Nice to meet you," she said, purely out of habit.

"You, too," Asham said, his tone cold, distilled politeness. He turned his attention back to Lee. "I've been all over the neighborhood. Nothing else showing."

As if in answer, a low growl followed by a light yip sounded from behind Asham. "Hush," he said, but instead of complying, the dog barked twice. Asham looked over his shoulder. "Gunny, phooey! Be quiet."

The dog whined but fell silent.

Asham looked back to them. "He got a little wound up when your foot pursuit came over the radio and then I punched it to get here. Thought he was going to get to chase some bad guys."

"Sorry," Lee said.

"It is what it is." Asham glanced at his watch. "I'm going to head home. I'm already over by half an hour."

"All right. Thanks for coming by."

"Always." Asham glanced over to Melody and gave her a short nod. "Ma'am."

Before she could respond, he pulled away.

Lee rolled up his window and started driving again. After a few blocks, he said, "Not quite the monster you all paint him to be, is he?"

"I never said he was a monster."

"Maybe not you personally, but your people."

"My people?"

"The PRI, the media, the defund the police crowd. Your people."

Melody drew in a deep breath before responding. "The media is completely separate from our work in the PRI."

"Separate but aligned."

"We don't coordinate."

"You might as well." He was quiet for a moment. Then he said, "Here's what I don't understand. If you cut our budget, you lay off cops. But crime doesn't go away. What's the endgame? It seems more like a tantrum to me than a true plan."

"The concept of Defund the Police doesn't mean abolishing law enforcement," Melody said. "At least, not to most people. It's about reform. Will we have fewer officers? Probably. But the idea is to bring on other subject matter experts to supplement the remaining police. Like mental health professionals."

"I'm all for that. But we're already operating at minimum staffing. We don't have enough cops, so get the money elsewhere."

"Baumgartner has been beating that same tired drum for a decade."

Lee's jaw tightened. "Because it's true."

"Have you studied the budget?"

Lee shifted in his seat. "No."

"I have and so have other people who know more than I do about municipal finances. And most people agree that there is room to cut the police budget to pay for other services instead."

"You do that, you lose cops. You lose cops, and this thin grasp on civilization we've got won't last long."

"That's fear-mongering."

"That's reality-seeing." He drove in silence for a few seconds. Then he said, "If you're going to take away resources, you have to revamp what we do."

"That's the idea."

"It won't work. Every time something falls through the cracks, everyone expects the police to handle it. That won't change. We'll be expected to pick up the slack, only with fewer resources."

"That's pessimistic."

"It's what's happened historically."

"Maybe that's why we need to make a more radical change. Take away responsibilities from the police and give them to qualified experts. Narrow the scope of the police mission."

"I'm all for that. But it won't happen. We'll get a bunch of social programs funded at our expense, and when all is said and done, we'll still end up holding the shit end of the stick."

"I don't see it like that."

"Ride around with me for a few weeks and you will." He seemed to realize what he said and faced her. "I'm serious. Come back and do this again."

"Maybe I will." She couldn't let his challenge go unmet.

They fell silent after that. Melody looked out the window at the houses that rolled by. She was tired of arguing, even if it was low key. Her eyes had begun to feel sandy. Bed called out to her. A glance at the dash clock told her she didn't have long to wait.

Lee seemed to sense her thoughts. "Look, I know you wanted to ride the whole shift, but—"

"I do," she asserted.

"I know. But the reality is, hardly anything ever happens in the last part of the shift. It's dead. And I'm going to find someplace to write up the rest of my paperwork, so it'll be even more boring for you."

"I'll stay."

"I'm not trying to get rid of you."

"Sounds like it."

"I'm just saying. It's going to be a big nothing. And if you're already tired…"

She wanted to take him up on it, but she couldn't. "I finish what I start."

He raised his hands off the wheel slightly in surrender. "Okay, it's your call."

"Thank you."

They drove for a while further without speaking. Melody could feel her eyelids getting heavy atop her already scratchy eyes. She glanced at the clock again.

Just a couple more hours.

Chapter 25

LEE

He spent a half hour patrolling through his neighborhoods. As he predicted to Melody, there was nothing happening. He came across the newspaper delivery folks, rolling slowly down the street with the flashers on. The same husband and wife team had been delivering in this area for years. He'd discovered this when he stopped to chat with them early in the year. It had been the same in his old sector, although in that case, it was a mother and daughter who teamed up to make the deliveries.

Beside him, Melody remained quiet, staring out of the passenger window. The silence was an easy one as it lacked the tension they'd encountered earlier in the evening. She seemed resigned to riding out the last couple of dead hours of the shift.

After the sting of losing the vehicle prowling suspect faded, Lee let his thoughts drift. They kept coming back to his rider. More accurately, to Sergeant Gelabert. Had he done everything she asked? What she needed him to do?

Probably not, he realized.

Yeah, they'd stopped fighting and actually started talking. But when he told Melody earlier in the night that their respective frames of reference were just too different, he'd meant it. Best as he could see, that was the problem across the board. One night in a police car wasn't going to change that. A thousand nights might not.

Even so, he felt a little guilty. He could have done better.

Melody adjusted her position in her seat.

She could have, too, he thought. Then he cringed inwardly at how whiny that sentiment sounded to him. He'd long ago learned that he couldn't control what others did. He couldn't count on it, either. He could only control his own actions. That had to be enough.

What could he say to salvage things at this point?

Lee cleared his throat. Melody didn't react to the sound. She was looking out the windshield with a slightly foggy expression. She was probably about to pass out. Graveyard shift will get anyone if they're not used to it.

Should he thank her for coming out? For actually discussing some things instead of just chanting slogans at him? Given his initial expectations for the evening, he was grateful for both of those outcomes.

It should be something simple like that, he realized. Just an honest, human sentiment. Maybe it wouldn't change a thing, but that didn't mean it wouldn't make a difference.

He opened his mouth to speak.

Before he could, the radio chirped. *"Charlie-411, K-9-3?"*

Lee reached for the mic. "Four-eleven."

"K-9-3," answered Mark Asham. *"I'm short north, en route to secure."*

"Copy, are you available to respond to a domestic with four-eleven?"

"K-9-3, affirm, go ahead."

"Charlie-411, K-9-3, an ongoing domestic," the dispatcher intoned. She followed with the address, then added, *"Neighbor to the east reports a loud argument for the past thirty. Now hearing banging noises and more yelling. Address comes back to Rosetta Jefferson. She's in with several entries as a DV victim. Currently the petitioner on a no-contact order. The respondent is Tamik Osmund."*

Lee copied the call and turned the car around to head toward the address. Mark copied as well. Immediately afterward, Murph answered up. *"Charlie-409, I can go for the K-9 if he's headed home."*

"Copy, four-oh-nine. K-9-3, you can disregard."

Mark came back on. *"I'll keep heading that way until they're code four."*

"Copy," the dispatcher said. *"Continuing, Osmund is a*

black male, five-seven, one-forty-five. He's listed as a caution subject. He has two outstanding warrants for DV assault and failure to appear on a drug charge."

Lee copied, then asked, "Does the complainant know if that's who's in the house now?"

"*Negative. But both of those charges show happening at that address.*"

"Copy." Lee replaced the mic. He glanced over at Melody. "I guess I was wrong about the rest of the night being quiet."

She didn't answer, but her eyes looked sharp again.

The drive was swift. He sped but kept his emergency lights off. The roads were almost empty. Melody grabbed onto the door handle as he took one particularly hard turn, but she didn't object. He accelerated down Altamont, then braked for another turn, extinguishing his headlights right before. His car cut onto the side street like a shark cruising through dark waters. Halfway up the block, he pulled to the curb while he reached for the mic.

"Charlie-411, on scene to the east."

"*Copy, four-eleven.*"

Lee twisted the keys and shut everything off. He reached for his flashlight, muttering a quick "excuse me." Melody angled her knees toward the door. As he tugged on the heavy black mag, he met her eyes.

"It might be best for you to wait here," he said.

She shook her head. "I want to see everything."

He shrugged. This wasn't any more or less dangerous than the previous DVOP with Colton. Of course, that had resulted in her getting smacked in the face. "Your call."

Without waiting for her reply, he popped open the door and got out.

Melody quickly followed. Lee locked the cruiser and eased the door shut. He saw Melody do the same. Both doors closed with a muted metallic click. He almost grinned at that.

Lee slid his flashlight into his thigh pocket and headed up the sidewalk. Melody scrambled along behind him, trying to keep up. One house away, he cut into the unfenced front yard to make a tactical approach. When he drew close to the target address, he heard raised voices, slightly muffled inside the house.

He keyed his mic and spoke in a low voice. "Four-eleven, they're still arguing."

"*Copy.*" He could hear the clatter of keys as Jackie updated the entry in the computer.

Murphy quickly responded. "*Four-oh-nine, about thirty seconds off.*"

Mark also updated his status. "*Kay-nine-three, one mike out.*"

Lee didn't bother to respond. The house had a narrow set of concrete steps, barely wider than the doorway itself. There was no screen door. He stood next to the house, at the edge of the steps. Melody pressed in behind him, her shoulder brushing the siding of the house. He would rather have been to the side of the door, but there wasn't enough room on the porch, and there was no way he was going to stand in the fatal funnel—that position directly in front of the door.

The sounds of argument were slightly unclear, almost fuzzy, but he could make out two distinct voices. One male and one female. The intensity seemed to be steadily climbing.

Wait, he told himself. In less than thirty seconds, Murph would be there. Another thirty after that and Mark—

A terrible, primal scream erupted from the front of the house.

Instinctively, Lee moved. He hopped onto the steps.

"NO!" The desperate yell from a woman was just on the other side of the door.

As soon as he had his footing, he reached for his shoulder mic.

"I'm going in," he transmitted.

Then Lee took a heavy step forward and drove his foot into the door. His thrust struck to the left of the knob. He was rewarded with the sound of crackling wood as the doorjamb shattered, and the door swung violently open.

"Police!" he bellowed.

He took in the scene in a micro-second. A mid-thirties woman sat on the couch, pressed against the back of it as she leaned away from the man in front of her. Her eyes were fearful, even as they whipped away from the man towering over her with his fist raised. They lighted onto Lee without comprehension.

The man was no bigger than the woman he menaced. His wiry frame was punctuated with defined musculature, much of it visible in the undersized tank top he wore. The man's gaze snapped to Lee as well. He saw no fear or surprise in his eyes, only cunning anger.

Almost before Lee had finished identifying himself, the man bolted in the opposite direction, deeper into the house. He plunged through a large opening into what Lee was pretty certain was the kitchen.

Lee chased him, running past the woman on the couch. The sound of a door banging open made him swing in a wide arc as he approached the entryway. The sound might have been the back door, but it could also be a cupboard or a drawer, where a weapon might be stashed.

When he reached the entryway, he realized what it had been. The backdoor to the house remained closed, the deadbolt still twisted horizontally. However, a different door across the kitchen stood halfway open. Lee approached swiftly but cautiously. He stood to the side. With the toe of his boot, he nudged the door wider. The light from the kitchen illuminated the first few steps down into a basement. Beyond that, darkness. The musty smell of still air and earth wafted up to him.

A cellar.

Lee had a sudden vision of a Rudyard Kipling story he'd read to Olivia only last week about a mongoose named Rikki Tikki Tavi. Near the end of the tale, Rikki pursued a cobra down into her den. The mongoose survived but the lesson was clear.

He wasn't going down there.

With his left hand, he fumbled along the wall for a light switch but didn't find one. He shuffled back slightly and pressed his mic button. "Four-eleven, suspect has fled into a dark basement. I need the first two units to secure the perimeter of the house. Start at least one more unit to relieve the K-9. Mark, come in here with me, and we'll call him out."

Jackie acknowledged, followed by a clipped copy from Murph, and a hurried click from Mark. Jackie immediately dispatched two more officers to the call, but Lee didn't pay attention. Instead, he looked over his shoulder so he could see the woman on the couch. Both she and Melody were staring at him.

"Is there a door in the basement?" he asked the woman.

Her only response was a dazed expression. He noticed a trickle of blood flowing from her nose.

"Can he get out of the basement?" he asked, changing the question to jar her.

She shook her head. "No door. And the windows are all too small."

Lee had seen enough people get into or through small spaces to doubt it, but he still wasn't going to plunge into a dark basement by himself. The best bet was to use the K-9, if the suspect didn't slip out a window first.

"No doors in the basement," he transmitted. "Small windows."

Jackie copied.

Lee shuffled back to the open doorway. He withdrew his flashlight and snapped it on. Then he shined it down the dark stairway, illuminating it.

He glanced over his shoulder again. Now the woman stood in the entryway next to Melody, watching him. She'd wiped the blood from her face, but her expression remained confused.

"Are you Rosetta?" he asked her.

She nodded.

Lee jerked his head toward the basement. "And that's Tamik?"

She nodded again but stopped halfway through. "Don't hurt him," she pleaded, her face twisted with concern. "Please, we was just having a bad night on account his mama died, and—"

"Okay," Lee interrupted. He didn't need to know anything more at the moment. There'd be time later to sort out all the minor details. Right now, he had probable cause that an order for protection had been violated. The assault on Rosetta made it a felony. Plus, Tamik had warrants. All of that was more than enough to make the arrest and secure the situation. He could interview her and get the rest after.

"Please," the woman repeated.

Lee didn't reply. Instead, he turned his head back to the basement. Then he did a double take.

Tamik Osmund stood at the base of the stairs, glaring up at him.

Chapter 26

MEL

Melody stopped in the kitchen entry way. In the dim light, she saw Lee standing across the room near an open door. He was looking over his shoulder at the woman next to her.

In a sharp voice, he demanded, "Are you Rosetta?"

Melody stared past him into the basement doorway. Darkness gaped downward.

"And that's Tamik?" Lee asked.

"Please don't hurt him," she begged.

Something in the woman's voice made Melody turn to her. She was holding her hands out beseechingly toward Lee. "It was just a bad night. His mama died, and—"

"Okay." Lee's tone was curt and rang with finality.

Tears sprang to Rosetta's eyes. "Please," she said, both more quietly and more urgently at the same time. She clutched her hands to her chest anxiously.

Melody started to reach out to her, to comfort her.

"Show me your hands!" boomed Lee's voice.

She swung her head back toward the sound.

Lee had his gun in his hand, pointed down the stairway.

Cold adrenaline surged through her. Her skin prickled.

"No, no, no, NO!" Lee yelled.

An impossibly bright flash erupted in front of the officer, illuminating the darkness beyond. A milli-second later, a sharp crack assaulted her ears.

She jumped at the sudden loudness of the sound. Instinctively, her hands flew to cover her ears, dropping into a crouch and squeezing her eyes shut.

Two more barking shots rang out.

Sounds became muffled, as if she were hearing everything through layers of cotton. She forced her eyes open.

Everything moved slowly, as if at three-quarter speed.

Lee reached for his shoulder. He kept his gun leveled down the stairway, his eyes locked forward as he tipped his head to speak into the mic.

"Charlie-411 shots fired. Suspect down. I need medics here."

The words hung in front of her, almost visible, while she processed them. Then something bumped her shoulder, shunting her aside. Murphy brushed past her with his gun out as he moved toward Lee.

A guttural yell of agonized grief erupted next to her. Rosetta cried out, "No!" and another word that she couldn't decipher. After a few moments, she realized it was the man's name.

Tamik.

"Stay there!" Murphy commanded, and she didn't know if he was telling her or Rosetta.

"You killed him!" Rosetta screamed. "Oh my God! You killed him!"

Melody wanted to reach for her, to comfort her, but she couldn't make her arms move. She turned her eyes back to the kitchen. Lee stood at the open basement doorway. In front of him, the darkness had returned. He held his gun steady, unmoving. Melody was frozen in place as well.

Neither of them moved for a long time.

Part II: Aftermath

"The country is changing, the city is changing, and this police department is making every effort to change right along with it."

- Spokane Police Chief Robert Baumgartner

"The police lecture us about change and meanwhile, the band plays on."

- Spokane City Council President Cody Lofton

Chapter 27

DAVID WEAVER

David eased the door open to check on a sleeping Melody. She lay curled up on the bed atop the covers, her back to him. He waited a moment, then started to close the door again.

"You don't have to go," she said, her voice flat.

He reversed the door and went into the bedroom. Carefully, he climbed onto the bed and over to her still form. He lay facing her, propping himself up on an elbow. "I thought you might get some sleep."

"I feel like all I do is sleep these days."

"You do a lot more than that."

"Not well." She shook her head. "I feel like I've been in a fog. I don't remember teaching a single lesson all week. Or a single dinner we've had. It's like those memories have been erased. Or never stored in the first place."

"You're dealing with some shock, that's all."

"I want it to end."

He reached out and stroked her arm. "It will, baby. You just need some time."

Melody's eyes glistened. "It's hard to believe I was there. I was five steps away when he killed that man. And now it's all on TV and..." She shook her head in frustration and wiped at her eyes. "Everyone wants to know what I saw."

"I know."

He'd seen the barrage of interview requests that came at her over the past week. News outlets of every persuasion wanted her to talk. TV, radio, newspapers, podcasts. Left and right, moderate and crazy. Everyone had a different angle, but all had the same goal: get a quote from Melody Weaver.

"I want to be honest," she said, "but the detective and the prosecutor are both saying I shouldn't talk to anyone until the case is over."

"Maybe that'd be for the best."

His only experience with investigations came from the flight world, but he supposed that the same principles still held. Keeping witness or participant information contained ensured their recollections weren't influenced by others. Memory was tricky. The natural human tendency to conform was powerful. Most of all, the echo chambers that existed today seemed especially virulent to him.

Besides, his concern for the police investigation took a distant second to his wife's mental well-being. If putting off talking about her experience was better for her, that's what she should do. Having the police directive provided a ready-made reason for demurring when the interview requests came.

Only it wasn't that easy. Everything was political these days. He'd become the gatekeeper for Mel as she struggled to come to terms with what she experienced. It was the one thing having to do with the event that he could take off her plate. He took it on without hesitation and was immediately rewarded with a reporter from the local weekly magazine accusing him of being manipulated by the police for adhering to the no-interview mandate.

"You of all people should know better," the reporter told him.

"Why should I know better?" he demanded.

The reporter hesitated, then doubled down. "How any black man in this country can cooperate with police at this point is beyond me."

David hung up on him.

He grew up with very traditional parents who taught him very traditional values. Authority was to be respected. Institutions were there for a reason. It wasn't until he was a teenager that he started to see the cracks in that philosophy. Those cracks slowly widened over time but never quite to the point of breaking.

That was the contradiction of his life, he'd come to realize.

His career in the Air Force did little to change his outlook.

He still encountered racism in uniform. How could he not? That pernicious song was everywhere. But the notes and melody were muted in the service and its impact blunted. It was one of the few things that he believed the military did better than the society it served.

It didn't hurt that he was a pilot. Elite status further cushioned the impact of institutional racism, something his wife rightfully pointed out to him while they were dating. By the time he retired and started flying planes for Alaska, that was his norm. The surprise that came with the frequency of his encounters with police in Spokane and the flimsy reasons for them was genuine, but looking back, he should have known it was coming.

"I don't know what's best," Melody said to him now. "My mind is going a million miles an hour in a million different directions."

"That's to be expected."

"Ellen wants me to speak out right away. The police don't want me to say a word. All the news people want their piece of me…"

"What do you want?"

"I want things to be normal again. I want you and the kids."

"You've got us." He squeezed her arm affectionately. "And things will get there. It just might take a while."

Melody nodded. "I wish I had listened to you."

"What do you mean?"

"When you said I didn't have to go that night. That I could just go home. I should have listened."

"You don't mean that."

She didn't answer right away. Her eyes took on a faraway look. Eventually, she said, "I went on a ride-along I didn't want to go on with a cop who didn't want me there. I thought I could learn, that I'd see things that would help change the way things are. Instead, I stood a few feet away from another police shooting. I bore witness to another black man getting killed by the police."

David didn't reply but resumed stroking her arm, comforting her.

"Everyone thinks they know what happened. They're all so sure. Ellen knows the cop was wrong. She just can't decide how wrong. Meanwhile that police union president is confident that Lee's actions were justified. All of the media outlets are just as sure of their own take. And yet, it feels like everyone is still looking to me for the final word. Like I'm the one who is supposed to pass judgment on the whole thing." She shook her head, tears filling her eyes again. "And all I can keep thinking is, what if that was you? Or Isaac?"

"Aw, come on."

"I mean it."

"Neither one of us would be hitting you."

"It's not that easy," she said. "And you know it."

"Maybe not. But I guarantee neither of us would charge at a police officer while holding a hatchet either."

Her eyes bore into his. "You're so... even. I still don't understand why. How many times have you been stopped? And for shit excuses, too, so you know the real reason why."

David didn't shy away from her gaze. This was a conversation they'd had before. "What can I say? I've worn the uniform. Some of the things people say about cops, they say about the military, too."

"I'm not talking about what people say. I'm talking about things you know. How you've been treated."

"I'm not blind to that. The world is a messed-up place. Racism is a very real part of that. Maybe I haven't had it as bad as some, but I've seen my share."

"That's why I don't get—"

"I wish you'd worry more about yourself and how you're feeling right now," he interrupted softly. "That's way more important."

"This is a part of it," she insisted. "We've both seen George Floyd, and how many others? I've seen how you've been treated by store owners, by cops, by the airlines. It's wrong."

"'Course it is. And when I watched that Floyd video, it turned my stomach. Broke my heart, too. That was flat out murder by purposeful apathy. But if you want me to say that every cop is like that...? Baby, I just can't. I've seen too many people of all kinds to believe something that sweeping."

She shook her head in wonder. "You're amazing."

"Do tell."

"It amazes me how you can know what you know and yet you don't hate. You're not angry."

"There's already enough hate in this world. Don't need me adding to it." He shifted his shoulder in a slight shrug. "And I get plenty angry. Sometimes it boils up to the point I feel like I might burst. But then I remember something my pops said to me."

"Good old Pops," she joked. "Full of wisdom."

"Full of something anyway." The thought of his father brought a bittersweet twinge with it. He passed three years ago, but it seemed like yesterday to David.

"What'd he say?" she asked.

"That anger is only any good if it jumpstarts you to doing something worthwhile. It's no good for dwelling on."

She thought about it for a moment. "Sounds wise enough."

"The way I see it here, getting mad about how things are is a good thing if it spurs you to action, makes you want to change how things are. But outside of that, all it does is eat away at you. Like acid. Makes a person bitter."

"Did you add that last bit? Or was that part of Pops's original message?"

"More likely my takeaway from what he said."

She made an impressed face. "Pretty good."

"Point is, Mel, I *know* how messed up things are. Yeah, it makes me angry, but after a while that anger does me no good. Starts to become like being mad at the winter for being cold. First step is, I put on a coat, you know?"

"We're mixing metaphors now, but yes."

"What you're doing on the PRI board is good work. I think

it'll change things, in a positive way. But I just can't believe every cop is bad. Some say the same about every airman and soldier, and that isn't true, either."

"No, it's not."

"And from what you said, this cop you rode with wasn't all bad."

She considered. "He had his good points," she allowed. "More so than I expected."

"There you go."

"But the system is still fucked."

"Fucked, it is. And it needs to change. Long overdue. Like, yesterday."

She was quiet for a few seconds. Then she said, "If all I knew about this was the news coverage, I wonder if I'd be right there with Ellen on this, thinking the worst."

"But you were there."

She nodded. "It wasn't just those moments in the kitchen. It was the whole night." She glanced up at him. "Even before the shooting, it made me think."

"Think how?"

She let out a long, billowing sigh. "That things aren't nearly as simple as everyone would like them to be."

David didn't answer.

She watched him in silence for a while. Then she said, "You know what I just realized?"

"What's that?"

"You haven't asked me."

"Asked you what?"

"You're the only one who hasn't asked me what I think happened on that basement stairway."

"Nope."

"Why haven't you?"

He shifted his position, wriggling closer to her. "I already know he shot that man."

"Tamik Osmund was his name."

"I know."

"It's important that we remember his name, no matter how it happened." She paused. "We have to remember all of the names."

"I agree. But it doesn't matter to me as much as you matter to me. You being okay is the most important thing in my book."

"Do you want to know?"

"When you're ready to tell me. Are you?"

She hesitated. Then, slowly, she shook her head. "No," she said. "No, I guess I'm not."

Chapter 28

WENDY SALTER

Once Olivia was off to school, Wendy Salter turned her attention to Lee. He was still in his bathrobe, drinking coffee on the back deck off their second-story bedroom. She wrapped up in a quilt before joining him with her own cup. They sat in the Adirondack chairs, looking out over their residential neighborhood. Liberty Lake was less than a ten-minute drive down I-90 from Spokane, but at times, it had seemed half a continent away. The bedroom community was a great place to raise a family. Most of the time, being insulated somewhat from the goings-on in the nearby city was a blessing. But at other times, the world was too small and interconnected for it to seem very far away.

Especially when something like this happened.

They kept an easy silence for a while. They stared out at the intermittent activity in the neighborhood. Much of it was still and quiet, save for a smattering of traffic. Subarus and Fords rolled through streets lined with garbage containers. Small clusters of kids walked down the sidewalk, headed for the nearby middle school.

Lee didn't say a word. He sipped and stared, his face carved into a stoic mask.

Wendy waited almost five minutes. When it was clear he wasn't going to say anything on his own, she asked, "Any word from Murph?"

He sipped his coffee and shrugged. "He called last night."

"Oh? Why didn't you tell me?"

"You were reading to Olivia."

"You could have told me after."

"I forgot."

He didn't forget, she knew. It was his age-old habit of trying to protect her. That was the reason for the mask he wore, too. The tendency both endeared her to him and frustrated her at the same time. She loved him for the desire to keep her and their family safe. That was part of his nature, something that was inseparable from the rest of his being. He was a protector.

But it was frustrating, too. She didn't always need to be protected. Most of the time, she didn't, in fact. In those times, she had to remind herself not to see condescension in the behavior, to remember what motivated it.

It was even harder at times like these, when *he* needed *her*, when she wanted to be there for him. His protective nature got in the way. Instead of protecting her, it worked like a wall, keeping her at a distance. Or like a shell he wrapped himself up in.

She pushed past the frustration. "What did he say?"

"That I'm still on admin leave," Lee said flatly.

"Any idea how long?"

"Dale says probably until they rule on it."

She crinkled her nose. She didn't much care for Dale Thomas, the union president. He seemed far too much a lawyer for her liking. Lee always told her that was his role, though, and that the other side had lawyers, so they should, too. She didn't have an answer to that, but it didn't make her like Thomas any better.

"Maybe the time away is a good thing," she offered.

Lee frowned. "Babe, I'm going to worry about this no matter what. Sitting around here doing it is a lot harder than being at work. At least I'm distracted by calls there."

"You want distraction?" she teased. "You could clean out the garage."

Lee grunted and sipped his coffee.

"Besides, didn't you always say being distracted is what gets cops hurt?"

"My dad said that, but yeah, it's true."

"So, it seems like being home while you're distracted might be for the best."

His eyes flicked over to her and away again. "Point taken.

Doesn't make it easier, though."

It was anything but easy, she knew. She also knew about distraction. She worried to distraction. Worried about how this was impacting Lee. About what people were saying about him, about the other officers. Or how this tragic event might affect Olivia. What she might have to endure at school, simply because of who her father was.

She worried in circles and then back again. And all the while, she tried to pierce Lee's protective shell. She'd always thought it was there to protect her, but lately she'd started to wonder if it wasn't also there to protect him.

Of course, it is, she thought.

"Hon?"

"Huh?"

"Look at me."

Lee turned slowly to look at her. "Yeah?"

"You're a good cop," she said.

"I know."

"And a good man."

He grunted again and looked away.

"I mean it," she said. "I know you did the absolute best job you possibly could that night. That man—"

"Tamik Osmund," Lee said, enunciating each syllable clearly.

"He had a hatchet, Lee. He was going to hurt you. And after what you went through when that other man cut you with a knife..." She shook her head. "You did what you had to do."

"That's not what people are saying."

"They were already saying plenty before this happened," Wendy reminded him. "Don't listen to them."

Lee took in a deep breath and blew it out. "If you'd asked me the night it happened, I would have told you I had no choice. That I did the right thing. He hit that woman. There was a no-contact order. He had warrants. He had to go to jail. No discretion, it's a mandatory arrest. Then he comes at me with that hatchet. I shot him. Done and done."

"That's what I'm saying."

"I don't know," he whispered.

"I do." She reached out and grabbed hold of his forearm. "You're a good man."

"You said that."

"It bears repeating because it's true." She slid her hand down to take his. "And the truth of this will come out, and people will see what I already know."

He squeezed her hand, then let go. "Thanks." He turned his gaze out to the neighborhood again, his face still a frozen mask.

She watched his eyes for a bit. The mournful, contemplative set to them managed to pierce through the implacable veil of his expression. If she waited long enough, the rest of the mask would eventually slip.

Still, it was easy to sense that what she said to him wasn't enough. She wanted to ask him why, ask him what he needed from her. But would he tell her? Did he even know? What small bits he'd shared with her since that night almost two weeks ago was riddled with uncertainty, something she'd seen little of from him throughout his career. When he'd been attacked by the knife wielder, there'd certainly been physical damage and some emotional trauma, but he'd worked through it. He'd shared more of the experience with her that time, too. Once he realized she could handle it, he detailed every moment of the event to her.

This time was different. He'd told her less about the actual event itself. All she knew was the barest details. As for how he felt about it, he'd been tight-lipped about that as well. It didn't take a psychologist to guess what that meant.

"Don't second-guess yourself," she said quietly.

He glanced at her, then away again. "It's hard not to. I've been thinking… wondering about certain things."

"Like what?"

"People are saying I only shot him because he's black."

"That's ridiculous. He had an axe. He—"

"I know," Lee interrupted. "But that's not what I wonder about."

"Then what?"

He drew in a wavering breath. "I told you about the woman who rode with me that night, right?"

"What about her?"

"She said some things that made me think, that's all. And I can't seem to stop thinking about them."

"Lee, she's part of the anti-police crowd. She's on that committee, too. You can't listen to people like that."

He lifted his hands, as if to shrug. Then he reached for his cup again. Wendy waited while he sipped some coffee and gathered his thoughts.

"Some of what she said was typical bullshit," he said. "Especially early on in the night. But there were a couple of things that maybe weren't."

"Like what?"

"Like how we're all biased, and don't even recognize it in ourselves."

Wendy frowned. "What, like we're all closet racists and don't know it?"

"Not exactly. But maybe we're biased in ways we don't realize. Then when we take action, those biases influence our decisions."

She gave it some careful thought. Then she said, "Whether that's true or not, I think our deliberate selves would overpower anything like what you describe."

"That's the thing, though. You wouldn't even realize it."

"Lee, honey, even if that is one hundred percent true, it doesn't change one thing."

He turned to her, questioning.

She met his gaze firmly. "That man came at you with a hatchet in his hand, meaning to do you harm."

"Tamik Osmund," he reminded her.

"I don't care who he is," she said forcefully, struggling to limit the frustration in her voice. "He tried to kill my husband."

The slightest of wry grins tugged at the corners of Lee's mouth. "You're always on my side."

"Of course, I am."

"Thank you for that."

She leaned over and kissed him. "I told you before, you're a good man."

He nodded but said nothing. Then he looked away again. She thought they might be in for another long silence but after a minute or so, Lee spoke.

"Those things she mentioned, about being biased? I don't think it made a difference one way or another when it came to deciding whether or not to shoot."

"What, then?"

He turned back to her. "Here's the thing I can't shake. It's the when of it all."

"When?" She shook her head. "I don't understand."

He swallowed. "*When* did I make the decision to shoot? Was it really the last possible second?"

"Oh, Lee..."

"Even more than that, did I decide when to shoot at least partly based on him being black?" He blinked and swallowed again. "Could that be a piece of it?"

"You're not a racist."

"That's not what I'm saying."

"This woman, this activist, she planted doubts for the sake of it. That's what's happening here."

"That doesn't change the question. If he's a white man, do I wait a little longer? Just one more stair step?"

"Does it matter?"

Lee turned his head to look back out over the neighborhood. "Yes," he whispered. "I think it matters a lot."

Chapter 29

DETECTIVE CASSIDY HARRIS

"I think I'm cursed."

Sheriff's Detective Cassidy Harris leaned back in her barstool and looked at her partner, Detective Shawn McNutt. She let the statement sit for a few seconds. The idea took up valuable mental space in her mind, shunting aside the details that had been pounding at her for the past several weeks now. Once tasked with investigating the officer-involved shooting of Tamik Osmund, her professional life was subsumed by the case. Her personal life, too, for that matter, though there was little enough of that.

"Cursed?" McNutt frowned dubiously. "Who believes in that shit?"

She motioned toward one of the several televisions hanging from the walls of the bar, a different sport playing on each. "Every athlete I ever heard of."

"That's different."

"Different how?"

"With athletes, you're talking about superstition," McNutt explained. "That's about getting into the right place psychologically in order to perform, to win. But curses? Voodoo or whatever? Come on."

Harris lifted her shot glass and threw her head back, draining it. As the fiery liquid slid down her throat, she chased it with some beer. Next to her, McNutt followed suit. Once he'd clapped the empty glass back down onto the bar, she said, "Let's look at the facts."

"Okay, let's."

She heard the slight slur in his voice, and her own. Getting bombed on a Thursday night when she still had to work the next day wasn't the best idea she'd ever had. Then again, it wasn't the worst.

Harris held up a finger. "This is my third officer-involved."

"Mine, too."

"First Trotter, then Stone. Now this one. Osmund." She sipped her beer. "All three have sucked."

"They all do. Always."

"I mean that they're not just another investigation. They're political." She said the word as if it had no place in a homicide case. Which, to her mind, it didn't.

"Come on, Cass—everything's political. Where have you been?"

There was a time when she didn't like him calling her that. No one did, not even her family. At first, she found it presumptuous of him. She resented the tone of forced intimacy. But over time, he'd worn her down.

"God, I hate officer-involveds," she said, raising her hand to the bartender for another round.

"Me, too," McNutt agreed. "Still, the protocol is a good idea. Better to have an outside agency investigate a shooting than to keep it in-house. At least, as far as the public is concerned."

"As far as the public is concerned," Harris said, "one cop is the same as another."

"You're starting to sound like me."

"God forbid."

"Good to know I'm rubbing off on you."

She didn't bite at the innuendo. Instead, she stayed silent until Margie set up two shots for them. She tipped the woman, then lifted the glass. "Third time's the charm, right?"

McNutt clinked her glass. "Nothing wrong with the first two, but sure."

They drank.

A country song came on the radio. Harris found herself tapping her foot, remembering when it had been a big hit, years ago. Crossed over onto the pop charts, too. Whenever she'd gone dancing with friends that year, it was one that got them all out onto the floor.

"You think this shooting is like those other two?" McNutt asked, his voice a notch lower. She wasn't sure if he was trying to be confidential or seductive.

"Like them, how?"

"Clean up front but dirty underneath."

She thought about it. Was that it? Or did she just get the heebie jeebies every time she had to investigate a PD shooting? She didn't like investigating other cops, that was for sure. Let Internal Affairs do that. She became a detective to investigate criminals.

Of course, that was exactly what the cop behind the first two officer-involved shootings she'd been assigned turned out to be.

A criminal.

Tyler fucking Garrett..

"Cass?" McNutt prompted. "That what you think?"

"No," she said, only realizing the answer as she spoke it. "The opposite."

McNutt squinted. "Dirty up front but clean underneath?"

"Not exactly that, either."

"Then what?"

"You know Salter?"

"Lee?" McNutt shrugged. "Sure. He's solid enough. Gets a little more mileage from his dad and granddad than he probably deserves, but I'd go to war with him."

"Any chance he could be dirty?"

"Nah."

"That's what you said about Garrett."

"He's no Garrett."

Harris shrugged. He was probably right. Garrett was one in a million but not in a good way. "At the end of the day, I don't think Salter's dirty, either," she said. "But up front, I see possible issues with this case."

McNutt leaned back in affected surprise. "Seriously? Guy charged him with a hatchet." He mimed holding one in his right hand, then swung it at her a couple of times.

Harris pushed his hand away. "That's what he said."

Her partner's surprise turned genuine. He glanced around. The Maxwell House was no longer a cop bar, per se, though a lot of old school cops still frequented it. The few patrons didn't appear to hear either of them over the music. Even so, McNutt lowered his voice further.

"You think he's *lying*? Come *on*."

"I didn't say that."

"It sounded like you did."

"Then clean out your ears."

"How about you speak more clearly instead?"

"Okay, how's this? There are two people in this entire world who know for sure what happened on that basement staircase. And one of them's dead."

"Because he charged a cop with a hatchet."

"See, that's part of the problem. Where'd we find that hatchet?"

McNutt sighed, exasperated. "So what?"

"It doesn't bother you that it was wedged underneath the dryer?"

"Not at all."

"It does me."

"Look," McNutt said, holding up his imaginary hatchet again. "Guy is running up the stairs with the hatchet, right?" He pumped his arms like he was running.

"You're a dork."

He ignored the insult. "Lee smokes the guy." He lowered his hand to form a gun with his thumb and forefinger. "And justifiably so." He dropped the thumb. Then he tapped his chest, his fingers stabbing into his thick pecs three times for emphasis. "Bam, bam, and bam." He continued his mime of the physics of his description. "Guy falls over backward. Hatchet goes flying. Lands on the floor and goes skidding along until it slides under the dryer blade-first and gets wedged there." McNutt finished and grabbed his beer. He took a swig. "Which is where we found it."

"You sound like you're describing the magic bullet theory in some JFK conspiracy."

"No crazier than some of the other stuff I've seen out there. People are calling this a murder?" He shook his head in disgust. "This keeps up and pretty soon, no one will want to do this job."

"Except you."

"Except me. Last man standing." He grinned at her. "Which means I'll be sheriff."

"Get over yourself."

His grin didn't waver. "When the world gets over me, I'll think about it."

Harris turned her beer glass in front of her. "The fact that no one else saw Osmund with the hatchet in his hand is only one problem."

"It shouldn't be a problem at all. Lee said he did, and Osmund's prints were on it."

"Those prints could've come at any time. He lived there."

"He wasn't supposed to be."

"That's not the point."

"So, what? You think that's where he stored his hatchet, then? Wedged underneath the dryer?"

"Maybe it stabilized the thing, like a coaster underneath the leg of a rickety table or something. I don't know."

McNutt scoffed. "You're starting to sound like a defense attorney. I should start calling you Little Pamela Wei."

"I'm bigger than her."

"Fine, Bigger Pamela Wei."

"Shut up." Harris spun the glass another quarter turn. "How about the fact that he's charging uphill at him. I mean, when do you shoot in that scenario?"

"Whenever you want. Guy has a hatchet, remember? And he's charging." He gave her an exasperated look. "Jeez. Twenty-one-foot rule, Cass, huh?"

She shook her head. "Doesn't apply."

"Hatchet is an edged weapon."

"Yeah, but the whole premise is based upon the officer's weapon being holstered. Not drawn."

McNutt paused, then reluctantly nodded. "You're right. He said he was already at the low ready when the guy charged."

"So, no twenty-one-foot rule," Harris said.

"No." McNutt smirked. "Just the guy-charging-with-an-edged-weapon rule. Which is even more cut and dried, you ask me."

He had a point, she admitted. She raised her beer to acknowledge it. They both drank.

There probably wasn't anything wrong with Salter's actions. She didn't like to reach any conclusions before all the data was in, but things were close to being wrapped up when it came to evidence collection. They'd just interviewed Salter two days ago, and that was usually the last task. There were still a few supplementary interviews but only minor witnesses, people Salter interacted with during his shift that night. Those interviews were purely for background information, and she doubted the prosecutor would use any of them.

"You know the biggest difference in this third one?" she said.

"No Garrett?"

"Thank God, no. It's the suspect."

"That he's black?"

"No, not that. I mean, that's true, but that's not what I'm getting at."

"What, then?"

"The guys Garrett shot—"

"Trotter and Strayer."

"—were both big-time shitheads. Extensive criminal records. Active bad guys. But Tamik Osmund—"

"Only beat up his girlfriend? Repeatedly?"

Harris scowled. "You know, you interrupt a lot."

He scowled back at her, then broke into a rakish grin. "It's not interrupting. It's banter. All good partners have it."

"You're an idiot."

275

"See?"

Harris shook her head and polished off her beer. She thought about calling it a night but instead waved at Margie standing at the other end of the bar. Rather than yelling over the music, which had transitioned into an old Steely Dan tune, Margie mimed back a shot questioningly. Harris considered, then decided against it. She signaled a larger drink instead. Margie nodded and set about pulling two beers from the tap.

"You two are psychic sisters or something," McNutt mused.

"Don't be impressed. It's basic communication."

"Where you're concerned, I'm always impressed."

She ignored his foray. "To your point about Osmund," she said. "Yes, he was a domestic abuser. But outside of that, nothing else worth talking about."

"You're being pretty casual about a woman getting her ass kicked."

"I'm not being casual. I'm only pointing out that he might be an asshole, but he's a particular kind of asshole. And that it's not the kind that usually gets shot by police."

"Dude charged a cop with a hatchet," McNutt said, in a sing-song voice.

"I am aware of that. Repeating that fact doesn't answer every question, you know?"

"It actually does answer most of them, if you're not looking for ninjas hiding in every bush." He snickered a little at the description.

"It seems a little odd, that's all." She shrugged. "I don't know. Maybe I'm listening to all the shit bouncing around the airwaves too much."

"The echo chamber is powerful stuff," McNutt agreed. "But look, it's not surprising. Guy is already a known woman-beater. His mom passes, so he's upset. He smacks his girl around—"

"Rosetta Jefferson says he didn't."

McNutt raised his eyebrows. "See? That's banter, not

interrupting."

"It's correcting your information, to make it accurate."

"It's not up for debate. He obviously hit her that night."

"We can't prove that."

"Maybe not enough to charge his corpse with domestic assault, but come on, Cass. He's got a history of it. They were arguing. And Salter said that she was bleeding from her nose when he went in."

"Which Melody Weaver didn't see."

McNutt held up a finger, signaling her to wait. Then he took a long swig of his beer, finishing it. When he put the glass down, he exaggeratedly wiped his mouth with the back of his hand, including his upper lip and nose. Then he gave her a knowing look. "Maybe that's why the rider didn't notice it—because she wiped it off before Murph got there. Point is, he smacked the woman. Let's be for real here."

"But we can't prove it."

"We don't need to. But whatever. They're arguing, right? And probably he hits her, too. He's still amped up when Lee shows up. He runs downstairs, maybe to get away, but he's still pissed. And now he's trapped. So, he grabs the hatchet. It's a heat of the moment thing, like a crime of passion or whatever. You know how those people are."

She turned slowly to face him. "Those people?"

"Yeah. Blacks. They're emotional."

It was her turn to look around to see if anyone was listening. Margie approached and plunked down their beers. Harris wondered if she'd overheard what McNutt said.

He at least had the good sense to wait until she was back out of earshot. Then he started to open his mouth to speak, but Harris held up her hand. The Steely Dan song faded out. She kept her hand in place until the next song, this one by The Rolling Stones, kicked in and rose to full volume. Then she lowered it.

"You can't say things like that," she said.

"What? It's true."

"It's racist."

"It's cultural. I don't mean it hateful."

"It's racist," she repeated.

"Come on. I didn't, you know, put a value statement on it. It's just a fact. This guy was all wound up, and Lee came along at the wrong time. Then the guy makes a bad choice. An emotional choice." McNutt shrugged. "And he got shot because of the action he chose."

"You can't say things like that, Shawn? Okay?"

"Why?"

"I already told you why."

"So I have to stay quiet about an objective truth because someone doesn't like it?"

"Are all cops macho assholes?"

"What? No."

"Some are."

"Some maybe, but—"

"Maybe even a lot."

"Okay, I see what you're doing."

"Do you?"

He rolled his eyes. In a slight falsetto, he said, "You wouldn't want people to make those same generalizations about cops, would you? It's no different" He looked at her pointedly.

"I'm so transparent, I guess."

"What people are saying about cops is a lot worse than that. And way less true."

"Whatever. I don't want to argue about it. I just wanted to have a couple of drinks and go to bed."

McNutt's grin returned. Somehow, he resisted stating the obvious.

Small favors, she thought.

"You know what I think?" he asked her.

Then again, maybe she was wrong about his ability to resist.

"What?"

"Despite everything we did on this investigation, most of it will come down to two things."

His focus on the shooting surprised her in a pleasant way. She shifted on her barstool and looked at him expectantly. "What two things?"

"Well, one thing, really. The grand jury."

Hearing those words was still an adjustment for Harris. The grand jury system had never been in place in Spokane before. But the DOJ consent decree brought with it a number of reforms. One of them had been to institute a grand jury system for police shootings. Instead of the prosecutor deciding whether an officer was criminally liable in those instances, the question was put to civilian jurors. If the grand jury chose to indict, the case went forward as a criminal matter.

"You're right," she said, and clinked McNutt's glass with her own. "It's all up to them." She drank.

McNutt didn't. Instead, he held up a finger. "The two things about the grand jury, though? One, whether the jurors believe Lee's statement or not."

"And two?"

McNutt flicked out his second finger. "What does that ride-along say when she testifies?"

Harris nodded slowly. Melody Weaver had told them she didn't see anything Tamik Osmund did. She only witnessed Salter's actions. Harris had no doubt that was what the teacher would tell the grand jury. The woman seemed honest to her. Painfully so, in fact. But she also knew what McNutt was getting at. How she painted Salter, both him and his actions, would go a long way toward informing the grand jury's verdict.

McNutt tapped his temple with his two fingers. "See? Not just a muscle head."

Harris stopped nodding. Then she spread her hands in acknowledgment. "You have your moments," she admitted.

They drank in near silence for a while. She tapped her foot to the music. McNutt hummed along with the song, then started singing, too.

"Just a shot away," he sang, off-key. "Just a shot away."

"Who sings this?" Harris asked innocently.

"The Stones, baby!" McNutt bellowed back with enthusiasm.

"Yeah? How about we keep it that way?"

It was an old joke, and he fell for it every time.

Chapter 30

OFFICER COLM MURPHY

Union President Dale Thomas waved both of them into the tiny conference room next to his small office. Murph always wondered how the guy couldn't afford better office space. As a union rep, he was painfully aware of the lawyer's retainer fee. It was forty percent of the union budget. Every year, it seemed like they ended up going over the billable hours that the retainer covered by a healthy margin, adding to the cost.

And some years have been worse than others, he mused.

Truthfully, though, the specter of the DOJ consent decree made the most news, day in and day out. That was, until Lee's shooting.

Don't call it that, Murphy thought.

He'd been chided often enough by Thomas to know better. Calling it Lee's shooting carried with it a form of responsibility that wasn't accurate. Lee hadn't driven events that night; Tamik Osmund did. So, the incident should carry his name.

But old police habits died hard, and he still thought of each incident in the terms he'd learned years ago.

He and Lee settled into a chair. Thomas made no effort to see if they wanted coffee or water. He finished up his phone call, then bustled in importantly.

"I'll get right to it," he said. "We are positioned well."

"What does *that* mean?" Lee asked.

Thomas narrowed his eyes. "It means that we are positioned well. According to discovery, the evidence that the prosecutor will present to the grand jury is mostly favorable."

"Mostly? That's not what I want to hear."

Murph raised his hand slightly. Not enough for Thomas to notice, but Lee did. The habit of simple police observation was part of the reason, but their long history of working together added to it. Lee scowled, but Murph could see he got the message to cool it.

Thomas rolled on, unaware. "I'm not paid to tell you what you want to hear, only the truth. And the truth is that much of what the grand jury will hear is favorable to you."

"But some isn't."

Thomas raised his eyebrows. "You shot and killed a man, Officer. That man gave you—"

"Tamik Osmund," Lee interrupted. His jaw muscles worked while he stared down at his hands.

Thomas paused.

"Okay," he said. "But my point—*our* point—is that he gave you no choice. He charged at you with a hatchet in his hand, a deadly weapon." Thomas turned up his hands. "What else were you supposed to do?"

Lee shrugged. "I've seen plenty of suggestions out there."

"You know better than to watch the news."

"Not just the news. Facebook, too. All of social media, actually."

Thomas looked at Murph beseechingly.

Murph cleared his throat. "You shouldn't be looking at that. It's a giant echo chamber."

"Yeah, well, a lot of shit is echoing around in that chamber," Lee said. "Like how maybe he didn't have the hatchet in his hand."

"But he *did*," Murph said.

"They wonder if he didn't. Then they say he didn't."

"But he did."

Lee waved a hand in the air. "They say that even if he did, I should have done something besides shoot him."

"Like what? Use harsh language?"

"Pepper spray."

Murph snorted at that.

"Or Tase him," Lee said.

"And if that fails," Murph said, "you get chopped in the face with an axe." He shook his head. "When you're faced with deadly force, you reply with lethal force. It's a simple equation, and the suspect is the one who chooses it."

"That's not what they're saying."

"You're not listening to that, are you? These shoot-him-in-the-leg-or-just-wing-him people? Lee, they have no concept of reality."

"They think I'm a racist," Lee said softly. "They think I shot him because he's black."

"Now, that's a different crowd. Just as wrong, but different."

Lee didn't answer. His frown said everything.

Murph understood why Lee struggled so much. The system sucked, and it was even worse now that DOJ hovered over the department like a vulture. In the past, waiting for the prosecutor to rule on a shooting was bad enough, but at least everyone involved knew and understood the law intimately. It wasn't an unreasonable hope to believe that the prosecutor's finding would represent that. But now, a grand jury full of civilians? That was dangerous. Most civilians learned that something was ruled a homicide and equated it to murder, rather than understanding that the term simply meant one person causing the death of another. A homicide could be ruled as justified or accidental. Neither was murder. Only criminal homicide was, but the distinction was lost on most civilians.

And those people were the ones deciding whether Lee's case went to trial or not.

"I know it's hard," Murph said, "but let's focus on what matters in this moment. And all that matters right now is the investigation—"

"Which has concluded," Thomas interjected.

"—and the grand jury."

"Which is empaneled," Thomas added. "And which you'll be testifying at soon."

"Soon," Lee repeated. "Everything is *soon* and *later*. No one has any direct information, any timeline. Meanwhile, I'm sitting at home, and all I see or hear is how I murdered this guy, how I'm a racist, how—"

"Echo chamber," Thomas reminded him.

Lee stopped short and looked away. "Shit," he muttered.

Murph wanted to reach out and pat his friend's shoulder. It tore him up to see a good cop like Lee get put through the ringer. And over what? Some wife beater who charged at him with a hatchet?

It wasn't fair.

Captain Salter, Lee's father, once told Murph that *fair* is where people go to eat cotton candy and ride the ponies. He knew life wasn't fair, but those words wouldn't do Lee any good right now, especially given their source. He decided to redirect slightly.

"What can he expect at the grand jury?" he asked Thomas.

The attorney seemed glad to get back on point. "You might be a little uncomfortable with the proceedings. Usually, when a police officer testifies, the prosecutor could be viewed as a friendly. That's what you're probably used to. In this case, though, it might feel more akin to being cross-examined by a defense attorney."

"Great," Lee muttered.

"Though there will be some familiarity with the process," Thomas continued. "He'll walk you through events in much the same way."

"Any traps he should look out for?" Murph asked.

"Not really. That was my point before." He turned to Lee. "Most of the questions should reflect favorably upon you. So answer truthfully. And, of course, all the standard rules of testimony apply. Only answer what you're asked. Stay calm and polite. All of that."

"Got it," Lee said.

"What's your take on the whole thing?" Murph asked, hoping it wasn't a mistake to ask, and fully expecting Thomas to equivocate.

"I think that unless a certain witness goes against him, it'll be fine."

Murph didn't have to ask which witness. They all knew that Rosetta Jefferson was critical of what happened, placing the blame for what occurred squarely onto Lee's shoulders. She'd no doubt do that when she testified, too. But Melody Weaver was considered a more objective witness. Her testimony would have weight.

"As long as she tells the truth," Thomas said, "and doesn't bleat out some liberal bullshit to bury him, it's a slam dunk no-indict."

"Will she tell the truth, do you think?" Murph directed his question to Thomas, but the lawyer didn't answer. Instead, he turned his attention to Lee.

Lee glanced up at both of them. He had an odd look on his face before answering.

"The truth is the truth," he said.

"You know what he means," the lawyer said.

"I do, but my answer remains the same."

Chapter 31

SECRETARY-TREASURER ELLEN MICHAELS, PRI

"The board meeting is Thursday," Ellen Michaels said into the phone. "Wait, hold on a second." She pressed the speaker button, then hung up the receiver. "Okay, go ahead."

"I know when the meeting is," Melody answered. Her voice rung out through the office. "I'll be there."

"But will you *speak*?"

There was momentary silence on the other end. Ellen waited her out. Patience was one of her strengths.

Finally, Melody sighed. "I can't. I don't testify for another two weeks. After that, the prosecutor said I could talk about it to whoever I want. Unless there's an indictment."

"He has no authority to abridge your first amendment rights," Ellen said firmly, "now or later."

"He said he does, and my lawyer agrees."

Ellen waved her hand even though Melody couldn't see the action. "Lawyers are always overly cautious."

"She's the lawyer you hired for me."

"Money well spent, but let's not deify Ms. Wei just yet. She has an opinion, and I disagree with it. Your story should be shared with the people of this city."

"I'll talk, Ellen. I *want* to talk. But I need to obey the rules, too."

Rules put in place by powerful white men, she almost said. Rules meant to keep those powerful white men in power.

But she resisted saying those words aloud. Instead, she stood and walked around the front of her desk. She paced while she spoke. "You've got to do what's best for you. I understand."

"Don't sound so disappointed."

"Anytime truth is muffled, I feel disappointed."

"Truth?" The sarcasm in Melody's voice was apparent. "Is

that what people want?"

"It's what I want." She touched her hands to her chest.

"What's the truth, Ellen? Because I only know what *I* saw. And even that isn't entirely clear to me these days."

Ellen took a moment to answer. At best, the killing of Tamik Osmund was an overzealous application of force by the police. At worst, it was outright murder. But she sensed that wouldn't play well with Melody.

She put her hands on her desktop and leaned toward the phone. "The truth is that the police had no business being in that house."

"They were called there," Melody said.

"By racist neighbors, I don't doubt. And instead of getting more information, they see a black couple lives there, so off they go, no questions asked."

"That's not what happened."

"Did this officer you were with ever talk to whoever called the police in the first place?"

"No, but—"

"Well, there you go."

"I think... I think the detectives did later."

Ellen didn't know if that was true or not. Since the shooting was being investigated by the County Sheriff's Office, which wasn't subject to the consent decree the police department was under, they were subject to far less pressure to cooperate with the PRI. This limited her access to the finer points in their ongoing cases.

She forged ahead. "Then he kicked down their door like he owned the place." Ellen mimicked the kick, her foot snapping in the air just shy of the desk front. "That's a Fourth Amendment violation, clear as day."

"I heard the scream," Melody said. "It made the hair on my neck stand up."

"No law against screaming, especially in one's own home."

Melody didn't answer.

Ellen shrugged, even though she knew Melody couldn't see

her. Despite what she'd just said, she was willing to concede that a woman screaming should be considered exigent circumstances, and thus the police officer was allowed to intervene. In fact, she'd probably have condemned him if he hadn't. But she also knew the system was rigged, so she swung at it with everything she could.

Justice wasn't clean.

She resumed pacing. "They're saying Rosetta Jefferson was assaulted. You're saying it sounded like it?"

"It certainly sounded like something."

"She says Tamik never hit her that night."

"I know."

"And yet, the officer says she had a bloody nose or lip or whatever. Which you never saw."

Melody hesitated. "I probably shouldn't be talking about this, even with you."

"All of this comes from the newspaper. You're not breaking any confidences here."

"Yeah, but where'd they get their information?"

"Who knows? Some crusading soul leaked it, trying to get the truth out there. If it's accurate, what does it matter?"

It took a few moments for Melody to answer. Then she said, "I guess it makes me trust the system a little less, that's all."

"You can't trust the system." Ellen stopped and waved her hand demonstratively toward the phone. "*That's* the point."

"I know. You're right."

"You bet I'm right. So, we've got the missing blood, which makes a person wonder about this officer. This same officer who says Tamik had a hatchet? That doesn't hold water. You know where they found that hatchet? Wedged under a dryer in the basement." She shook her head knowingly. "No. That hatchet bit was some slapped-together story they came up with after the fact. *After* he straight up murdered that man."

Melody didn't answer.

Ellen leaned forward and continued to press. "That's why your story is so important, Melody. People need to hear what you saw. They need to know the truth of what happened." When there was no immediate reply, she added, "If we don't tell the truth first, how are we going to change things?"

"You don't have to convince me of that."

"We have a momentous opportunity with DOJ here. This consent decree is busting up the old boys' club, forcing changes. But we must do our part. We have to tell the truth."

"The truth?" Melody asked her. "You keep saying *the truth*. Everyone's so sure what that is. They've got me spinning around over it."

"I *told* you the truth," Ellen said quietly.

"You weren't there."

"Then tell me. Tell me and everyone else how that cop murdered Tamik Osmund."

Another silence. Then, "I don't know that he did, Ellen. I just... I don't know."

"You rode around with him all night. What kind of man was he?"

Ellen stood, listening to the open line for as long as she could stand. Then she forced herself to wait longer. She knew patience won in situations like this.

"I don't know for sure," Melody whispered. Then, louder, she said, "There were moments I thought Lee was a decent guy. He really seemed like it. But there were times I wondered. And he seemed to be able to slip between masks so easily..."

"Masks are the devil's greatest tool," Ellen said. "Outside of human failing, of course."

"It's the masks that worry me." Melody's voice sounded pained. "I mean, who was the real person, and which ones were masks?"

"We are what we repeatedly do," Ellen told her.

"Aristotle."

"An old white man, to be sure, but he had a point, don't you think?" She returned to her chair, settling back into the seat. "The police can talk about service, pride, and dedication all day long. But when what happened to Tamik happens time and time again, how should we judge them? By what they repeatedly say, or what they repeatedly do?"

Melody let out a short sigh. "Believe someone when they show you who they are? That's what you're saying?"

"Yes. Sister Angelou had that one right, no doubt. Only she said, the *first* time. Yet we have people who keep on believing in the words of the police instead of their actions."

"It wasn't just words that night," Melody answered. "There were other actions he took, too. Some good ones."

"Yet, at the end of the night, what happened?"

Melody was quiet for a long time. Then she said, "That's what I'm trying to figure out."

Chapter 32

ASSISTANT CHIEF OF POLICE DANA HATCHER

Assistant Chief Dana Hatcher stood at the lectern in front of the city council. She'd just finished presenting the monthly crime statistics summary. The numbers were good this month, which made her job easier. Regardless, the report always resulted in responses from councilmembers. In the past, commentary disguised as questions came from all points on the spectrum. Police supporters and detractors alike used the moment to get their positions across to everyone in the chamber, and more importantly, for posterity. Council meetings were aired live on the community access channel and then replayed several times throughout the week. Any messages the councilors delivered were guaranteed to be on repeat until the next meeting.

In the past, when Chief Baumgartner delivered this report, there'd been no shortage of police supporters on the council. There'd been detractors, too, but at least the questions that came his way were largely balanced. Some councilors threw hardballs at the chief, some threw softballs. Since Baumgartner was adept at hitting even the hardballs, the end result, on balance, was positive.

Now, though? Not so much.

The cynical part of her wondered if that's why Baumgartner transitioned to her delivering the report. At first, she was eased into it every few months. But in less than a year, she did them all. Baumgartner no longer answered any of the hard questions on the first Monday of each month.

Except, she knew it wasn't true. There were two very good reasons for her to be standing here and not him. One was that everyone on that dais knew she had the full confidence of Mayor Margaret Patterson. Some may even have known how close the two of them were. They were certainly aware that she was the mayor's obvious choice for the big chair when Baumgartner retired.

And that was the second reason she knew this wasn't the chief ducking an uncomfortable political duty. All of this was part of a planned succession. They were preparing everyone— the council, the department, and the public—for her to take over. Baumgartner was going to retire, everyone knew. But what they didn't know was that it would happen sooner rather than later. The chief was old school, and he wanted to go out on his terms.

Actually, what he said to her was that he wanted to retire still wearing the championship belt, not have it taken from him by a knockout. "I don't want my last fight to be a loss," he'd said.

She respected that. Hell, she respected him, even though she thought his time had passed, right along with some of his old school ideas. Policing had to change, and not just due to the practical reality of external pressures. It had to change for the good of the officer and the community. The current model was unsustainable.

The questions tonight started with veiled innocuity. Clarifications and explanations. Feigned misunderstandings that were gently backpedaled from. Nothing too direct. That was usually how it started. She knew more was coming though. Council President Cody Lofton was writing notes on his legal pad. That only meant one thing.

She wished things had remained quiet regarding the department. They'd been that way for a while. After the Garrett fiasco and the Department of Justice putting them under a consent decree, the sound and fury in the media had subsided briefly. There was a sense of anticipation, and even their critics took a step back to wait and see. Then a slew of events happened at the national level that took up much of the same bandwidth that local issues had resided in previously. So, instead of focusing on Tyler Garrett and SPD, people focused on George Floyd and public demonstrations and Covid-19.

Things still bubbled up locally. There were protests for and against masks, and for and against the police. Thanks to a white supremacist group arriving uninvited to "patrol" the downtown streets, a near-riot erupted. There were plenty of political diatribes about that, but the police reaction was generally lauded, her leadership in particular. Some of that praise was deserved for actions she took and decisions she made. But some of it also came from Chief Baumgartner redirecting credit to her for much of what he did.

The last part didn't sit well with her. She'd always carried her own water and never asked for any special treatment. But Baumgartner had assured her that it was smart politics, and when she objected further, he reminded her that the two of them were a team. "The Office of the Chief" got the credit for what they did as that team, and right now, their goal was to make her the face of that office.

She relented but didn't like the duplicitous taste of it.

All in all, it had been a trying time for the department and for the country, not to mention the difficulty her people had when it came to doing their jobs. But thankfully, most of what got people angry at the police happened elsewhere. There were no local flashpoints.

Until now.

She realized that Councilor Owens was waiting for her to answer his ridiculously contrived question. She took a strategic sip of water. Then she said, "I'm not sure I understand what information you're looking for, sir. Can you clarify?"

Owens looked put out, but Hatcher knew he was secretly happy to get more time on the microphone. He blathered a bit but streamlined his question. The new version even turned out to be a little more sympathetic toward the department.

She answered his question succinctly and waited patiently for the next one. But Owens ceded the floor. That left Cody Lofton.

Lofton was ostensibly an ally of the mayor, but Hatcher

didn't trust him. When she'd told Patterson this, she'd only laughed. "I don't trust him either," the mayor said. "But I know what he wants, so I know what to expect from him. And for now, our interests align."

"Assistant Chief," Lofton began. "Thank you for all of the information you shared tonight. I'm wondering, any news on the shooting death of Tamik Osmund?"

Hatcher was convinced that Lofton's political strategy was to out-do the mayor at hating the police, which was kind of funny because Dana knew for a fact the mayor didn't hate cops. She despised Baumgartner—a fact that made for some uncomfortable moments for both of the two women. Mayor Patterson was critical of the police, but that was different than hate.

"I have no new information to report on that case, sir."

"None?"

"No, sir."

"There's a rumor that the grand jury was finally empaneled to determine the question of Officer Salter's criminality in that situation. Is that true?"

Hatcher avoided clenching her jaw. That information was supposed to remain confidential until the grand jury rendered its determination. But someone in the prosecutor's officer leaked it to the media, along with a lot more, and the press was going wild with it. For their part, the local politicians knew a political football when they saw one.

"As per municipal code and department regulations, I can't comment on whether that information is accurate or not." She cringed at her own words, as they reminded her of someone pleading the Fifth. Which in a way, she supposed she was.

"You can't confirm?" Lofton asked. "Don't the people deserve to know?"

"They do. And if there is anything to know, sir, then they will know as soon as it can be legally shared."

"Come on, Chief. It was in the newspaper."

Hatcher gave him a tight smile. "So was the horoscope, sir."

This brought a titter of laughter from the assembled crowd in the chamber.

Lofton mirrored her expression. His eyes danced a little. He seemed to like all of this. It was apparent in everything he did as if the whole thing was a game to him. That was part of why she didn't trust him. It wasn't about people for him. It was about pieces on a board.

"How goes the work with the DOJ recommendations?" Lofton asked, pivoting.

"We've worked hard to incorporate all of them as quickly as feasible," she said, reciting the party line. Baumgartner said it all the time, and it seemed to suffice. But Lofton wasn't put off so easily.

"Do you think these reforms go far enough, Chief?"

She noticed he'd dropped the 'assistant' part of her title twice now. It wasn't an uncommon usage. Most people called her 'chief', reserving her full title for formal, ceremonial use. But never Lofton. He seemed to revel in reminding her of her subordinate status to Baumgartner. Dropping it here and now meant something. Probably something dangerous.

"I think our end state is a moving target," she said, cautiously. "Each reform has to be evaluated before it is implemented and then assessed afterward for effectiveness. Then we can better understand what else needs to change."

"Don't you think the entire culture of SPD needs to change?"

She saw the trap he was setting for her. "The *entire* culture? No."

"Some parts of it, then?"

"Every organization needs to strive continually to improve."

Lofton smiled humorlessly. "That's the chalk answer. I'm looking for the real one."

"That is a real answer."

"It's a little light, though, isn't it, Chief?"

"I wasn't expecting to speak to this tonight," she said, "so if you are asking for a deeper examination, I wouldn't be doing justice to you or the council if I didn't prepare. But I will say that the men and women of your Spokane Police Department are hard-working, dedicated people who are doing this job—this very difficult job—for the right reasons. That's our culture."

"Service, Pride, Dedication?" Lofton asked, reciting the department motto.

"Yes, sir. It's more than just a slogan."

"So, what are you doing to make sure there isn't another Tamik Osmund tragedy? Or, given some of the questions that event has raised, another Tyler Garrett betrayal?"

Hatcher stared at him. With a struggle, she kept her face as impassive as she could. His play was obvious now, and it was exactly what she'd always suspected. He knew that when Baumgartner left and she became Chief, the mayor's stance toward the department would soften. That left him poised to be the number one police-basher. Or, as she was sure he'd characterize it, the number one proponent for reform.

As if reform were easy, she thought. Just deciding *what* to reform was a monumental task. *How* to reform it was exponentially more difficult. There were always unintended consequences. And even if the right decisions were made and the will to implement them was present, it still took *time*. In a world that demanded instant satisfaction, the last fact especially didn't sit well.

Hatcher believed changes were on the way. She wanted to usher them in. They'd been a long time coming. But Lofton using the slow, difficult process for his own political gain irked her.

Some things were worth fighting over. She refused to back down or let the moment hang for longer than a beat. She stared hard at Lofton and answered him.

"Sir, I can promise you, the council, the mayor, and every citizen in Spokane this: what am I doing?" She tapped the podium with her finger, near the microphone. The heavy thud echoed loudly throughout the chamber. It was a trick she'd picked up from Baumgartner.

"I am doing absolutely everything within my power," she said. "Everything, and then some more."

"But is that enough?" Lofton asked.

Before she could answer, he said, "Thank you for your time, Assistant Chief. Now to new business."

Hatcher lowered her head and ignored whatever Lofton was talking about now—something about the Parks Department. She closed her notebook and left the podium.

Chapter 33

REPORTER KELLY DAVIS, SPOKESMAN REVIEW

Kelly Davis scrolled through the text of her article, noting the revisions Brendan, her editor, had made. Most of them were good, she conceded. A couple were stylistic, and those she resented. But he had told her that a newspaper's style should be consistent from article to article, so she let her own stylistic preferences be slaughtered at that altar. Only when she wrote an opinion piece did she insist on a lighter hand with the editing. To his credit, Brendan acquiesced.

Of course, that didn't stop him from imposing his own click bait of a headline, but she had long ago learned to pick her battles.

The Tamik Osmund shooting was the biggest local story since Tyler Garrett. The near riot in response to the white militia patrols was the only thing to come close. She'd covered aspects of the disturbance, but almost all the Garrett coverage in the newspaper was hers. In addition to all the articles she wrote, Davis still had a slew of notes that she intended to include in the book she was quietly working on about the Garrett affair. She wasn't one hundred percent set on the title yet, but knew she wanted to make some sort of a play on the saying of a wolf in sheep's clothing. Given the popular police-as-sheepdog metaphor she'd heard more than once, her current working title was *A Sheepdog in Wolf's Clothing*. However, the shorthand she'd been using of *In Wolf's Clothing* might end up being what she went with. Of course, depending on the publisher, it might get changed altogether. If nothing else, working for the paper had taught her who gets to write the headlines.

Ultimately, it didn't matter what went on the cover, at least not nearly as much as what was between those covers.

Lee Salter didn't seem to be cut from the same mold as

Garrett, though she didn't imagine many were. As much as Garrett had long been the department's poster boy—quite literally, she had several pieces of marketing material she hoped to include in her book—Salter could have qualified for the same role. The son and grandson of well-known police officers, he was considered by some to be SPD royalty.

Davis didn't buy that. She didn't care who someone's parents were, only what that person did in this life. But she didn't see anything in Salter's history that seemed fishy to her.

Most cops, she knew, never fired their weapon, much less shot or killed anyone. But Salter had joined the exclusive club of those who had. It was still a far cry from Mark Asham, who she had some serious reservations about, but even one was still substantial. Was he on his way to becoming an Asham? Or even a Garrett?

She didn't think so. But then again, this was a news story, not an opinion piece, so what she thought didn't quite matter.

She read some of the text Brendan had tweaked. It detailed that a grand jury was underway to determine whether to indict Salter for criminal homicide. The information was solid, coming from a source in the prosecutor's office. Brendan had pressed her to identify her informant, but she steadfastly refused. He was irritated by this, but never reached the point of threatening not to run it. She'd assured him it was legit. Luckily, she had the track record for her word to mean something.

The grand jury was only part of the story. She'd written a separate piece on the DOJ-mandated reforms, but Brendan had decided to fold those into the Salter piece and make it a feature. She didn't argue. Column inches, after all, were column inches, whether on dead trees or pixels on a screen.

She'd done wide-ranging interviews and managed to get some great quotes. Chief Baumgartner was his typical blustering self. After trying to shunt her off on the assistant chief, he finally held forth on things in his typical fashion.

"If today, people suddenly truly understood policing," he

told her, "tomorrow there would be twice as many cops on the street and three times as many people volunteering to help them."

"Okay, boomer," she muttered as she re-read the quote.

The mayor had a similar reaction when Davis shared the chief's comment with her. Her first reply was off the record and unprintable anyway, at least according to the newspaper's standards. But she got in a zinger on her second take, anyway.

"If people truly understood policing today," Patterson had said, "they would defund the police tomorrow."

It was a brazen statement, especially for a mayor to make. Most mayors lived or died by the success of their police departments. Patterson's strategy seemed to be to beat on the PD until Baumgartner retired and then position his chosen successor, almost certainly to be Assistant Chief Hatcher, as the reformer, the savior.

Davis wondered if the two of them could pull it off. Police reform was going to happen in some fashion or another. "Defund the Police" was a code word for a massive version of that reform. As an individual, Davis was there for it. As a reporter, the whole thing was pure news gold.

Speaking of gold, Chief Baumgartner served up some more when she went back to him for a second interview. He bristled at some of the statements others made about him overseeing the biggest corruption scandal in department history and his perceived lack of desire to change. He told her, "The country is changing, the city is changing, and this police department is making every effort to change right along with it."

It was a good line, she had to admit. Baumgartner supporters—and there were still quite a few, make no mistake, which was why he still had a job—ate it up when he delivered lines like this one.

It took a well-placed reply from Cody Lofton to deflate his words a little. "The police lecture us about change," the council president told her wryly, "and meanwhile, the band plays on."

The cynics in Spokane had their spirit animal at city hall, she supposed.

The story closed out with some predictable blathering from Union President Dale Thomas, a no comment from Officer Salter (relayed by Thomas) and circled back to where it started with a mention of the approximate completion of the grand jury process.

Of course, she couldn't cite an exact time, as no one had any idea how long the jurors would deliberate. But she didn't think it would take long. Sometime soon, Spokane would have its answer as to whether Officer Salter was going on trial for murdering Tamik Osmund, or if the shooting was ruled as justified.

Davis wondered how crazy things might get no matter which way the ruling broke. A justified shooting decision in these circumstances and in this current political environment might lead to demonstrations. In the popular conversation, Tamik Osmund's death had begun to become conflated with other police shootings or in-custody deaths. That alone could cause social unrest, regardless of the merits of the case. If people truly believed Osmund was murdered on top of that? Riots, she didn't doubt.

Of course, an indictment would only enrage the other end of the spectrum, she realized. Political unrest didn't reside only on one side of the aisle. National and local events had proven that over the past few years.

She envisioned a scenario where things got dicey either way. It wasn't unrealistic to think she might have to put aside working on her Garrett book for a while just to focus on the here and now, to cover it accurately.

Davis finished her review of the copy and sent it back to Brendan, ready for publication. Then she got ready for the next story, whatever it may be. She didn't necessarily wish for it to be chaotic, but she would damn well cover it anyway.

Chapter 34

WITNESS LONNIE MARTIN

Lonnie shifted uncomfortably on the wooden bench where he sat. Sitting anywhere for an extended period aggravated his old injuries, something for which he didn't lack. Airplanes were brutal, but this hard bench outside the courtroom was running a close second.

He tugged at his collar. The tie he wore today was a real one, unlike the clip-on he usually sported at work. The extra material around his neck was suffocating, and he'd be glad when he was able to pull it off at home.

For now, though, he sat and waited. The prosecutor said it would only be a little while, and that was damn near an hour ago. He'd remained on the bench as requested but ended up needing to go to the restroom after forty-five minutes. He figured it would be his luck that the lawyers would come out for him during those two minutes he was taking care of business. Actually, he realized that still could have been what happened. He just wouldn't know about it until the next time they bothered to exit the courtroom.

When he'd returned from the restroom, a woman was sitting in his spot. He didn't mind. The bench was big enough for half a dozen people, even people his size. He sat a respectful distance away from her and set about minding his own business.

"I know you," the woman said, after a bit.

Lonnie turned to her. "Maybe," he said. "I work at a grocery store. Where do you shop?"

"Pac 'n Save," she said. "But I remember you from the store where you work."

He looked more closely at her. Then he thought about where he was, and it clicked. "You were with him that night."

She nodded. "I was."

"You all came on that shoplifter."

"We did."

He didn't know what else to say, so he offered his hand. "Nice to see you again. I'm Lonnie."

"Melody," she replied, shaking his hand.

They fell into an awkward silence, both looking off in different directions. He wondered how much longer the lawyer was going to be.

After a while, she spoke again. "Can I ask you something?"

"Sure."

"Why are you here?"

"I got a subpoena."

Melody smiled. "Me, too. But why?"

He shrugged. "From what I gather, they're looking to fill in the events of the night before... you know."

She nodded absently. Lonnie responded with a perfunctory smile and looked away again. He had mixed feelings about being there, truth be told. When they asked, he'd wondered about the reasons behind it, too.

"Why me?" he'd asked the lawyer who called him, who turned out to be a thin, arrogant whelp with a beak nose and thinning hair named Allen Wesley.

"Because you know him."

Lonnie figured that lots of people knew Lee. There was more, and he pushed to get at it. "That's all, then?"

"No," Wesley admitted but his annoyance showed. Lonnie could tell he was a junior attorney in the office, obviously given the gopher tasks. Probably put up with crap from senior attorneys all day, so he wasn't keen on getting any from civilians. "You interacted with him that night. You can help set the stage."

"Interacted, huh?"

"Yes." The lawyer's answer was precise and self-important.

Lonnie was no fool. Sure, he played football, and no one got out of that game unscathed. Sitting on this bench outside the courtroom, he had the aches in his knees, back, and shoulders to prove it. But he'd managed to escape without having his brains rattled. He knew the score.

"How much of it is that I *interacted*, and how much of it is because I'm a black man?"

Wesley had the audacity to act surprised. Then he doubled down and got indignant about it. But Lonnie knew his suspicion was right. He'd double-checked with a college teammate, a punter who went on to law school at Gonzaga. He'd told Lonnie that the prosecutor's job before a grand jury was to present the objective facts, but none of them did. Most times, they gave the jurors only what they needed to decide to indict. In this case, though, they were more likely to stack the information the other direction, so that Lee Salter *wasn't* indicted.

Lonnie thought Lee was a good guy, and the truth was, he was happy to help him out if he could. He didn't believe what some people were saying, that he gunned down Tamik Osmund and then made up some bullshit about the hatchet afterward. Lee wouldn't do such a thing. So, if the lawyers asked if he'd come down and say exactly that, he was more than willing, even if part of the reason why had to do with his race. He could live with that. But them dressing it up as something it wasn't irked him.

When he glanced back at Melody, he could see she'd arrived at the same conclusion regarding the reason for his presence. He also saw that she wasn't going to pursue it any further.

Good, he thought. It wasn't his fault that lawyers lied. They couldn't help themselves.

That was a good example of the reason why his loyalties didn't lie much beyond Lee and a couple of the other cops that came into the store. Beyond them, Lonnie knew the system was stacked. There were racists up and down that system, too. He'd dealt with more than a few, though his size mitigated things.

If he had a chance to take a swing at the system, he would. But right now, he had a chance to help a decent guy, and that was what he intended to do. If he didn't, based strictly on the principle that Lee was white and he was black, then he didn't figure he was much better than those supremacist idiots who'd come to town to patrol around with their guns last summer.

"Are you nervous?" Melody asked, breaking his reverie.

He smiled weakly. "I guess I am. I played football in front of thousands of people, but the idea of sitting on that witness stand in front of a dozen or so? It's a little unnerving." He adjusted the tie at his neck. "How about you?"

"Terrified."

"Yeah?"

"Definitely. And I stand in front of thirty different kids every hour, all day long."

"You teach?"

She nodded. "Middle school."

"This is different, that's for sure."

"Very."

He started to say something else, but then stopped himself.

"What?" she asked.

He hesitated, but her open expression convinced him to continue. "I was just going to say that you being here is probably a lot more important than me."

She gave him an odd look.

"Just in terms of what you can offer," he added. "I mean, you saw a lot more. You were there the whole night, right?"

"I was." She looked sad for a moment. "Yeah, I suppose I've got a lot to say."

Critical things, he almost added, but didn't. It was obvious she was uncomfortable with her role. He didn't envy her one bit. He could tell himself he was here to be honest about Lee and how he knew him. The lawyers were looking to get mileage out of his race, no doubt. But his truth wasn't going to convict Lee or set him free. Lonnie had a feeling Weaver's might.

He opened his mouth to say something, but that was when the big doors to the courtroom swung open. Lee Salter exited, wearing a blue suit and dark red tie. He seemed surprised to see the two of them and stood in place for an awkward moment. Then he gave a small wave and walked over.

"Hey, Lonnie," he said, holding out his hand.

Lonnie shook it. "How's it going?"

Lee spread his hands. "I guess we'll see."

Lonnie didn't know what to say to that.

Lee let him off the hook by turning to the woman next to him. "Hi, Melody. How are you?"

"Good," she said. "You?"

"I'm fine. Your kids doing all right? Isaac, and...?"

"Hattie. Yeah, they're good."

"And your husband? Is he flying the friendly skies?"

"Not today. He's home with the kids."

"Oh. Good. That's good."

There was a brief silence. Then Melody said, "How about you? How are you doing with all..." she motioned around the courthouse corridor. "All this."

"I'll be okay," Lee said. "The truth is the truth."

Melody nodded slowly. "It is," she whispered.

Another short silence ensued. Lee broke it first. "Well, I should..." He jerked his head down the hallway.

"Yeah, of course." She held out her hand. "Good to see you."

Lee took it. "You, too."

The door opened behind Lonnie. He turned to see Allen Wesley, trailing behind the more senior, and more confident assistant prosecutor, Morris Tremaine.

"Whoa, what's this?" Tremaine said, looking back and forth between the three of them. He turned to Wesley. "What's this, Allen? Your idea of witness management?"

Wesley appeared flustered. "I set up the schedule so that—"

Tremaine waved him into silence. He turned back to Lee.

"And you? You should know better. *Jesus*, Officer."

"We were just—" Lee began.

"Don't say another word to each other," he ordered brusquely. He pointed at Lee. "*You* go back inside."

Lee scowled at the command. "I've gotta hit the head."

"Fine, but straight back. And talk to *no one*."

Lee glanced at Lonnie, and then Melody. He nodded to them both, then turned and strode away.

Lonnie was confused. When he glanced over at Weaver, she had a similar dumbfounded expression.

"What'd we do wrong?" Lonnie asked Tremaine.

"You *talked*," the lawyer said.

"People talk," Lonnie said. "It's just polite."

"People talk," Tremaine agreed. "Not witnesses. It creates contamination. You need me to explain?"

Lonnie narrowed his eyes. The reply that sprang to his lips almost escaped, but he caught it at the last second. Part of the restraint was because Melody was present. The rest was him not wanting to let this arrogant asshole get his goat.

Tremaine was already moving on. He turned to Wesley. "Go and tell Art that we've got to shuffle witnesses. Weaver is next. If he asks, tell him why. And for God's sake, Allen, whisper it to him, okay? This isn't for the court."

Wesley swallowed nervously. "Is that... I mean, is that ethical?"

Tremaine glowered at him. "Did your mother have any children who lived? Get out of here. And learn the rules of grand jury evidence on your way."

Wesley turned and hurried away, disappearing into the court.

Tremaine turned back to the two of them. "I'm sorry," he told Lonnie, "but I've got to bump Ms. Weaver up the rotation. You'll be next after her."

"All right. Why?"

Tremaine lifted his glasses and rubbed his eyes. "I told you. Witness contamination. If the defense gets wind of this and

objects, I can afford to lose your testimony. I can't lose hers."
He lowered his glasses and met his gaze. "Sorry. But you seem like a person who can deal with the truth."

"I am."

"Good," Tremaine glanced down the hallway. "Feel free to go grab a sandwich or a coffee. Be back in an hour, though."

"All right." Lonnie stood to go. Then he turned toward Melody and held out his hand. "Nice to meet you."

"Oh, man," Tremaine said, looking around to see who was watching. His voice had a trace of a whine, which Lonnie found strangely satisfying. "Don't do that."

Melody took his hand anyway. He was careful to squeeze a little but not too hard. They shook.

"Nice to meet you, too," she said.

"Okay, great. Now let's go, Mrs. Weaver." Tremaine urged her toward the courtroom doors, then waved Lonnie away as if shooing a child.

Lonnie decided he wasn't going to be dismissed by this man. He stood and waited while the pair moved toward the large wooden doors. As Tremaine reached for the handle, Lonnie said, "Hey."

Both of them turned to face him, but he ignored Tremaine and looked directly at Melody.

"Good luck," he said.

Melody held his gaze for a moment. Then she nodded her thanks.

Lonnie watched as she turned and walked through the outer doors that Tremaine held open for her. He wondered what she would say in a few moments when she took the witness stand. What the jury would hear in her words. What their decision would do to the community—his community—no matter what they decided. He found himself wishing for the millionth time that people might actually listen a little more and hate a little less.

The big wooden doors swung shut behind Melody and the lawyers, leaving him alone in the courtroom hallway.

"Good luck," he said again, and not just to her.

Afterword and Acknowledgments

Some readers may find the ending to this book to be abrupt and unresolved. And those readers have a point. We don't show Melody Weaver's testimony, nor do we hang around long enough to see the grand jury's verdict.

Why not?

The answer is simple. It's because that wasn't the important part of the story. While the timing of *The End* may seem sudden, we deliberately chose to end this story at those courtroom doors. After Lonnie Martin utters, "Good luck" (to all of us, no less), we've completed the purpose of this book.

What is the purpose? It is two-fold.

First, this book has the same purpose as any of the short stories, novellas, and novels we have written throughout our respective careers—to tell a compelling story. To capture a moment in time and share that moment with the reader. We think we've done that.

But this book has a second, deeper objective. No doubt, it is obvious either immediately or upon reflection. The purpose was to encourage all of us to *listen to each other*.

Both Lee and Mel lament how little true, open discourse is happening in our country today. They focus on the issues surrounding policing when they make this observation, but the truth is we could apply the same observation to almost any topic and it would be true. People are polarized. They are entrenched. Conversations like the ones Lee and Mel have throughout this book don't often happen. The reason they don't is because people won't listen long enough to get past exchanging a few sound bites or a well-placed barb.

But the two characters in this book *do* get beyond their differences. They have hard but real conversations. Both make their points. Both are moved by points the other makes. There is the promise of progress, at least between the two of them.

In presenting the differing viewpoints of Lee Salter and Melody Weaver throughout the novel, our intention was to be as balanced as possible. The purpose wasn't to set one character or the other up as a straw person to get battered by whoever we saw as "right." It was to show the different perspectives, and to explore the reasons those perspectives exist. To be honest about those points of view.

As such, it is our hope that regardless of where a reader exists on the political spectrum, s/he will have moments of "Yes, I'm glad that point got made!" as well as other moments of disagreeing with what a character said, and hopefully, some moments of, "Huh. I didn't know that" or "I never thought about it that way."

That is why we worked so hard for the balance between these two characters. Perhaps we didn't achieve it perfectly, and things aren't fifty/fifty. But we made a supreme effort to get as close as possible while recognizing we are hampered by our own biases, implicit or otherwise.

If we definitively ended the book by sharing Melody's testimony and the grand jury verdict then we would lose the hard-fought balance we spent an entire book working toward. A resolution would have meant taking a side. That isn't what we wanted a reader to ultimately focus upon. The discussion, the questions, the perspectives, the viewpoints, the issues...that is the greater point. In *The Ride-Along*, this is what matters.

If we showed what happened on those stairs, then we would have given Lee's truth. And if the different viewpoints presented in The Aftermath didn't drive the point home loudly enough—everyone's truth is biased.

Some readers may not accept this, and that's okay. It's not the kind of ending either of us writes very often in any form.

Other readers will get it and not like it. Also okay.

But some will embrace it, and for that, we're grateful. The ideas in this book have their place in the world we all inhabit. We hope to be even a small part of this conversation.

There are a number of people to thank when it comes to the finished product you are reading. That authors would like to extend gratitude to:

Wendy Weber, for sitting around an unlit campfire one August morning at Three Creeks, listening and commenting on what started life as a short story idea.

Beta readers whose feedback tightened and improved upon a difficult story to tell:

Susan Bryson, Jiver Freecloud, Jill Maser, John Emery, Dave Mather, Silver Chan, Ron Sarich, Jake Thompson, and Cathy Geha, for their ideas, thoughts, and many, many catches.

Melanie Donaldson (and her husband, Nate) for their particular insights.

Brad Hallock, for his technical expertise, and for inspiring one of the calls Lee and Mel go on.

Kristi Scalise, for being at that unlit campfire, and every step of the way thereafter, and for helping to give Mel's career background its authenticity.

Lastly, to you, the reader—thank you for taking the challenging journey with us. We know it wasn't necessarily an easy ride.

Frank Zafiro
Colin Conway
March 2022

About the Authors

Frank Zafiro was a police officer in Spokane, Washington, from 1993 to 2013, retiring as a captain. Frank is the author of over thirty novels, most of them gritty crime fiction from both sides of the badge. These include the River City series, SpoCompton series, and Stefan Kopriva mysteries. He also co-authored the Charlie-316 series with Colin Conway and the Bricks & Cam Jobs with Eric Beetner. In addition to writing, Frank hosts the crime fiction podcast Wrong Place, Write Crime. He is an avid hockey fan and a tortured guitarist. He currently lives in Redmond, Oregon. You can keep up with him at frankzafiro.com.

Colin Conway is the creator of the 509 Crime Stories, the Cozy Up series, and the co-creator of the Charlie-316 series (written with Frank Zafiro). He served in the U.S. Army and later was an officer for the Spokane Police Department. He lives in Eastern Washington with his girlfriend and a codependent Vizsla that rules their world. Follow his journey at colinconway.com.

Made in the USA
Columbia, SC
07 September 2022